D0459685

Two Roads Home

Other books by Deborah Raney

The Chicory Inn Novels
Home to Chicory Lane
Two Roads Home
Another Way Home

Because of the Rain
A January Bride
Silver Bells
The Face of the Earth

The Hanover Falls Novels
Almost Forever
Forever After
After All

The Clayburn Novels
Remember to Forget
Leaving November
Yesterday's Embers

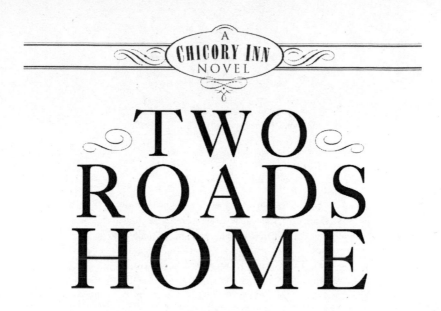

A CHICORY INN NOVEL

TWO ROADS HOME

Deborah Raney

Abingdon fiction
a novel approach to faith

Nashville

Two Roads Home

ISBN-13: 978-1-4267-7041-8

Published by Abingdon Press, 2222 Rosa L. Parks Blvd,
P.O. Box 280988, Nashville, TN 37228-0988.

www.abingdonpress.com

Macro Editor: Jamie Chavez

Published in association with the Steve Laube Literary Agency

Library of Congress Cataloging-in-Publication Data

Raney, Deborah.
Two roads home : a Chicory Inn novel / Deborah Raney.
    pages ; cm. — (A Chicory Inn Novel ; #2)
ISBN 978-1-4267-7041-8 (binding: soft back : alk. paper)
I. Title.
PS3568.A562T96 2015
813'.54—dc23
ISBN 978-1-63088-933-3   2014043568

Printed in the United States of America

1 2 3 4 5 6 7 8 9 10 / 20 19 18 17 16 15

For Jaxon Parker Raney,
our first grandson to carry our name.

Acknowledgments

As I begin another new series, I'm all the more aware that no book ever comes into being by one person's efforts. It would take an entire volume to thank all those who ultimately made this new story possible, but let me name just a few to whom I'm especially beholden for this novel:

Ken Raney, my favorite person in the whole wide world, with whom I've enjoyed the last four decades of life—each year more than the one before. I love you, babe! Let's see if we can do like your grandparents and spend eighty-two years together! We're almost halfway there!

Courtney Walsh, creative and amazing friend, whose casual comment, "You have so many neat family stories. You should write a book about a big extended family!" got these characters swirling in my imagination. It never would have happened without our fun conversation that night, Courtney!

Tamera Alexander, critique partner of more than a decade now (we're gettin' old, friend!) but so much more than a business friend. Thank you for your constant encouragement and for walking this mostly fun but often frustrating path beside me.

Terry Stucky, dear friend, thank you for all the good catches and great ideas and, most of all, for giving us a great excuse to grab a cup of coffee together.

ACKNOWLEDGMENTS

Steve Laube, agent extraordinaire, thank you for a dozen years now of wisdom, guidance, psychological insight (aka talking me down from the ledge when necessary), and always that great wit that makes hard times easier and good times "gooder."

Ramona Richards, Jamie Chavez, Susan Cornell, and the rest of the crew at Abingdon Fiction, thank you for your expertise and insight in seeing the diamond in the rough this book was before you got your talented hands on it.

To my parents and kids, grandkids, in-laws, outlaws, dear friends, and kind acquaintances: you each enrich my days more than you will ever know. Thank you for everything you pour into me and squeeze out of me. I am rich in so many ways because you are in my life.

We are God's accomplishment, created in Christ Jesus to do good things. God planned for these good things to be the way that we live our lives.

Ephesians 2:10

1

Mom, can you get the door behind me?" Corinne Pennington hiked her oversized purse—the one that doubled as a diaper bag—on her shoulder and stooped to pick up Simone. The toddler popped a thumb in her mouth and clung to Corinne like Velcro.

"Listen, baby girl, you should be over the Terrible Twos by now, so sweeten up, okay?"

Simone popped her thumb right back out of her mouth and answered with an ear-piercing wail.

"Sadie?" Corinne called to her dawdling four-year-old. "Come on . . . Hurry up."

"Wait, Mama. I gotta go tell Huckleberry g'bye."

"No, sweetie." Corinne's mother came to the rescue, taking Sadie firmly by the shoulders and turning her toward the door. "You already told Huck good-bye. You do what your mama says now."

"Get in the car, Sadie, we're going to be late picking up your sister." Corinne gave her mother a grateful look and waved a free elbow. "I'll see you Sunday."

"Okay. And you'll let Landyn and Chase know about Sunday dinner?"

"I will. Tell Dad I'm sorry I missed him."

"Will do. And you tell Jesse hello when you talk to him."

11

"Sure. Come on, Sadie, hustle up!" Corinne herded her entourage down the wide steps of the house she'd grown up in.

"How's come Sari got to go to skating and I didn't?"

"Because it was her friend's birthday party, and you weren't invited."

Wrong thing to say. Sadie pasted on a pout and stomped her Croc-clad foot.

"You'll get to go another time."

Corinne's mom stood waving at the door, looking just a little too happy to see them go.

Well, who could blame her? The girls had been brats all morning—all week really. Ever since Jesse had left for his second consecutive week in Chicago. Her husband worked hard as a sales manager at Preston-Brilon Manufacturing just outside Cape Girardeau. The company made high-end industrial vacuum sweepers, and despite the inevitable jokes about him being a vacuum cleaner salesman, Jesse made good money. She was lucky—blessed—that she got to stay home with the kids. But she wasn't sure how many more of these business trips she could survive. It was hard being a single parent, even if it was just for a week or two.

She buckled the girls into their car seats, closed the door of the SUV, then turned and promptly tripped over Huckleberry.

"Huck! Get! Get out of the way." *Stupid dog.*

The chocolate Lab panted up at her like she'd just offered him a T-bone.

"Get back on the porch, boy."

Huck pranced backward, then looked up at her, testing to see if she really meant it.

"Go, Huck. Now."

Huckleberry trotted back to the wide front porch and plopped down beside an urn of freshly potted red geraniums, watching her with mopey eyes. It made an idyllic picture. The Chicory Inn, her parents' empty nest project, looked beautiful in the waning May sunshine. Mom and Dad had done wonders with the remodel of the house her grandparents had built almost one hundred years ago.

This was the only home she'd known for the first eighteen years of her life. But sometimes she missed the place she remembered—the spacious, creaky house where the cupboards wore chipped paint, the heavy doors sometimes stuck, and the floors boasted shag carpet in garish shades of orange and blue.

But it had been almost a decade since she'd lived here—not counting summers after she'd left for college—and she couldn't begrudge her parents' right to bring the house into modern times, and even to make a business of it by opening the Chicory Inn.

And she had to admit they'd done the house proud. New cream-painted woodwork and wainscoting, refinished original hardwood floors, and bright contemporary rugs, curtains, and paintings gave the century-old house an elegant, yet still cozy vibe. At first, she'd had trouble making the rather trendy style fit her very traditional mother. But seeing Mom in her element, entertaining guests and cooking in the new state-of-the-art kitchen, she couldn't help but be happy for her.

And maybe a wee bit jealous. Not that she had any reason to be. Three years ago, she and Jesse had built a beautiful new home in Cape Girardeau just a few miles up the road. And as much as she loved the charm and history of an older home in the country, she appreciated living near every convenience, in a house where everything was brand new, where she'd had a say in every inch of the design, and where nothing would need repairing for many years to come.

Corinne climbed into the SUV and sighed. She didn't know why she was worrying about houses, since it seemed as if she spent half her life in this vehicle. Checking on her daughters in the rearview mirror, she started down the long driveway that led out to Chicory Lane, the country road that was the inn's namesake.

She flipped on the AC and adjusted the vents. The interior was like a sauna. She checked the dashboard. Why was it taking so long for the seat coolers to kick in?

Her mother had been a little short-tempered with the girls today—and with her. Yes, there was a full slate of guests scheduled at the inn this weekend, but Audrey Whitman had always claimed the inn would never come before her kids or grandkids. Lately, it seemed like that was exactly what was happening.

Oh, the girls thought their Gram hung the moon. And Corinne knew Mom adored her daughters—she'd practically bought out the Baby Boutique in Cape Girardeau when Sari was born— and she doted on all three of them. Though now that Chase and Landyn's twins had arrived, they seemed to get the lion's share of both Gram's and Poppa's attention. But then her sister had always been the spoiled baby of the family. Nothing had changed there. Corinne was used to that and prided herself on being more independent as the oldest. Still—

Oh, waah waah waah, Pennington. Grow up. She was being over-sensitive. Still, it would be nice if once in a while—

Her cell phone trilled from her purse. Keeping her eyes on the road, she snuck a glance at the Bluetooth screen on the dashboard. She didn't recognize the number, but with Jesse out of town, she hated to ignore it.

She clicked Accept Call. "Hello?"

"Hey, Mrs. Pennington, this is Michaela Creeve. I work with Jesse."

For the space of a heartbeat she stopped breathing. Had something happened to him?

"Jesse wanted me to let you know that our flight has been delayed."

"Oh—okay . . ."

"We're not sure by how much, but we'll let you know as soon as they announce anything."

"Um . . . okay. Thank you."

What? She stared at the display on the dashboard. Jesse couldn't call her himself? Now he was communicating with her through his *staff?* She'd never met Michaela, but she instantly disliked the perkiness in the woman's voice.

"Could you put Jesse on for a minute, please?"

"Well, he's . . . Just a minute. I'll see if he can come to the phone."

A flash of heat went through her and she gripped the steering wheel harder. How dare she screen Jesse's calls! Corinne bit the inside of her cheek, knowing she'd be sorry if she said what she was thinking.

She heard the feminine voice in the background, and then Jesse's familiar deep timbre. But it was Michaela who came back on the line. "Mrs. Pennington, Jesse's on the phone with a client right now."

"Oh . . ." So *he* was "Jesse" but *she* was "Mrs. Pennington"? She felt her arteries hardening by the minute. "Well, I guess—"

"Oh . . . Hang on. They just announced our flight." A pregnant pause. "It looks like it gets in around ten. Into St. Louis, not Cape. Jesse says we'll rent a car from there, but it'll probably be after midnight by the time we get home."

Corinne wracked her brain to remember who else had made the trip with Jesse this time. Usually Wayne from the Cape office went, but she didn't remember Jesse mentioning him. Probably too busy flirting with Miss Perky—

"Mama?"

"Shh . . . I'm on the phone, Sadie."

"Why are we goin' so slow? I thought we were in a hurry."

She glanced at the speedometer and pressed the accelerator. She shushed her daughter again, then saw that Simone had fallen asleep in the car seat. Great. There went the afternoon nap . . . her only time to get a break.

"Oh—I've got to run, Mrs. Pennington, but just wanted to get that message to you."

"Yes. Thank you, Michaela—" But the girl had hung up.

* * *

Audrey pulled a ginger pear torte from the oven and set it on the counter to cool. The spicy fragrance filled the house, mingling pleasantly with the Mozart concerto wafting from the CD player. She smiled, imagining what their current guest's reaction would be. It was a bit intimidating to have a professional chef as a guest, but she was pretty sure she'd hit a home run with this new recipe—thanks to the gift of some perfect Harry & David pears from a guest who'd stayed with them for a full two weeks last month.

"Something smells good." Grant came in from the side porch, brushing his hands together.

"Grant! Honey, I *just* swept that floor." She rolled her eyes and tossed him a damp rag.

"What? My hands are clean."

"Then why were you brushing them off, and why did I see dust falling from them? And debris."

He chuckled. "A little dust maybe, but I assure you there was no debris." But he knelt and gave a half-hearted swipe of the rag over the smooth, wide planks.

She let it go. "Corinne said to tell you hi."

"Oh. Sorry I missed her. I think it's been two weeks since I've talked to her more than waving as she pulls out of the drive. How's everything going in their neck of the woods?"

"Okay . . . I guess."

He studied her, a frown creasing his brow. "What's going on?"

She reached to turn down the CD player, then opened the cupboard and retrieved the powdered sugar. "Probably nothing. I just—" She sifted sugar liberally over the still-warm torte, trying to decide how much to say to Grant. She didn't want to get him worried over nothing. "I just think Corinne is getting tired of Jesse's traveling, that's all."

"Why? Did she say something?"

"It's more what she doesn't say."

"And what doesn't she say?"

Grant hated her putting words in people's mouths. She quickly edited herself. "Maybe it's more just her attitude. She just seems— tired. And maybe a little depressed."

He frowned. "That's not like our girl."

"I know. That's what worries me."

"Well, hopefully Jesse won't be traveling forever. But Corinne can't complain about his income."

She sighed. "She does like the finer things in life. Always has."

"As does her mother." He reached for a pear slice at the edge of the springform pan.

Audrey slapped his hand away. "Huh-uh. Don't you dare ruin my presentation."

"I thought you *were* presenting it—to the man you supposedly love." He batted sad puppy-dog eyes at her.

She laughed. "I'm presenting it to the chef who is currently our guest. Once he's seen and tasted it, you can have at it—my love." She planted a kiss on his cheek.

Frowning, Grant glanced toward the staircase that led to the guest rooms on the second floor. "Where is His Royal Highness?"

She shushed him, even though she knew Chef Jared Filmore hadn't returned for the day from the conference in Cape, where he was presenting. "He promised he'd be back around seven."

"I say don't ever trust a skinny chef." Grant reached for the slice of pear again with the same result. "Ouch."

"Sorry, but you knew better."

He rubbed his hand. "Fine, then. What's for supper."

She thought fast. "Tell you what . . . If you'll eat that leftover pizza, I'll do a pre-sliced presentation of the torte and you can have a piece now."

"Deal!" His delighted grin made him look ten years younger than his almost sixty. Even after thirty-five years, she loved this man so much it hurt.

But his offhand remark about her liking the finer things in life—and the tone he'd used—stung a little. She tucked it away to examine later. Right now, she had a world-class chef to impress.

2

How'd you talk Chase into letting you come?" Corinne stirred her decaf and leaned back in her chair, pushing down her guilt over leaving the girls with a sitter on a Thursday night while she had dessert and coffee with her sisters.

"Corinne. *Please*." Landyn hung her head dramatically. "Chase doesn't *let* me do anything."

Corinne laughed. "Let me rephrase that. How did you talk Chase into babysitting."

"Really? You call it *babysitting* when the father of your children takes care of them?"

"Oh, good grief, Landyn. Get off your high horse." Danae rolled her eyes and gave a short laugh.

But Corinne thought her words held a bite. "Babysitting? Hmm . . ." She tried to diffuse the tension. "Actually, I don't have a clue what I call it because it never happens." She immediately felt guilty. Jesse worked hard so she could stay home with their kids. That had been her dream for as long as she could remember.

"How long has he been gone this time?" She could read Danae's expression even in the dimly lit restaurant. And she didn't like the judgment she saw there.

She picked up her empty coffee cup and bought some time pretending to take a sip. "Only four days this week. But he was gone a full week earlier this month. It's getting old."

"Does he have a choice?" Landyn asked. "Couldn't he just tell them he'll only travel once a month? They surely understand that he has a family. I know Chase would never be gone from the babies for more than a night or two."

Danae looked away and Corinne could almost see the longing in her eyes. She and Dallas had been trying for a baby for at least two years—maybe longer. Corinne cleared her throat and tried to give her youngest sister a warning look. Landyn could be so clueless sometimes. She and Chase both worked freelance and made their own hours. Corinne envied them a little. Though not the part where they were up at three in the morning feeding twins. But the Spencers had lived and worked in New York as newlyweds, and now they'd fixed up a cute little loft apartment where Chase had an art studio. Landyn had taken on several marketing projects before the babies came, but now she was pretty much a stay-at-home mom, too, though Corinne couldn't see her staying home full-time for long.

"So who has your kids tonight, Corinne?" Danae licked her finger and retrieved the last crumbs from her dessert plate.

"A girl from our church. She's only thirteen, but I'm telling you, if you don't get them before they're old enough to date, you'd never get a sitter."

"Tell me about it," Landyn said. "What's your girl's name?"

"Huh-uh," Corinne said, laughing. "Don't think I'm going to let you steal her when I just got her broken in."

Landyn affected a pout. "Some sister you are."

Danae pushed her plate to the center of the table, looking bored with the conversation, but Corinne knew it was more than that. Her poor sister. Danae had confided with her a few weeks ago that she was beginning to worry she might never be able to become pregnant. It hadn't helped when Landyn popped out twins barely a year after she got married. Unplanned—and at first, unwanted—twins.

Corinne cast about the room, looking for something to change the subject. Jesse's ringtone pealed before she could think of a new topic. She held up a hand and slid her chair back. "It's Jesse. I'm going to take this outside. Don't let them take my coffee."

She pressed Answer as she made her way to the front entrance. "Hang on, babe." She didn't want to lie, but neither did she want to admit to her husband that she'd left the kids with a sitter. Not that he would care about her getting away with her sisters, but he wouldn't be too happy about her spending the extra money he was making on what he viewed as a luxury. Well, it was cheaper than psychiatric help, which was what she'd need if she didn't get out without the girls once in a while.

"Hey, you there?" Jesse sounded impatient.

She stepped outside and moved to the side of the door, turning away from the chill breeze that came off the Mississippi just two blocks behind the restaurant. "I'm here. How are you?"

A fishy odor laced with whiffs of diesel fuel wafted up from the river, and a low horn from a barge threatened to give away her location.

But Jesse seemed not to notice. "I'm okay. Where are you?"

"Please don't tell me your flight got cancelled again."

"Not cancelled, but delayed."

"Jesse—"

"Only by an hour. I'll be home by one a.m. And I'm taking tomorrow off."

"Well, that's big of them to let you have a day with your family." She hadn't meant it to come out so snarky.

"I'm sorry, babe. There wasn't anything we could do about it outside of booking a new flight out of *our* pocket, and that would have defeated the purpose of all these extra hours I've been putting in."

"I know. I'm sorry. I just—I miss you, that's all."

"I know. Me too. Are the girls still up?"

So much for dodging that question. "I'm betting they are. Emily from church is babysitting."

"Oh? Where are you?"

"Having coffee with my sisters. And dessert. We're at Bella Italia."

"I thought I heard boats—oh, hey, I've got to run."

She heard a feminine voice in the background, and she could tell Jesse was distracted.

"Okay," she said. "I'll see you in a few hours?"

"Yeah. Sure." And he hung up.

She knew when she'd been upstaged. She hated the way that made her feel. Like a jealous high school girl who wasn't sure her boyfriend liked her anymore.

She was being irrational. She'd talked to Jesse last night and there hadn't been anything in his voice that made her suspicious. Still, she had to wonder what he'd been thinking, having that girl—Michaela—call her earlier instead of calling himself.

She went back inside and wove her way through the maze of tables.

"We were beginning to think you weren't coming back."

"Jesse's flight is finally leaving. And hey—listen, guys, I feel bad . . . what I said earlier about Jesse. He's working his tail off so I can stay home with the kids, and I really am grateful. I feel guilty I said that."

"Yeah." Danae nodded. "There's a lot of that going around."

"What's going around?" Landyn looked confused.

Danae wrinkled her nose and gave a contrite smile. "Guilt. I'm sorry I snapped at you."

Landyn waved her off. "I'm used to it."

Corinne laughed, but Landyn had a point. Danae had been super sensitive ever since Chase and Landyn's twins came along. Sometimes it felt like walking on eggshells when they were together.

Danae pushed her chair back and wriggled into her jacket. "I need to get home."

"Yeah, me too. I feel my babies calling me." Landyn pressed her forearms over her breasts.

It was a gesture Corinne remembered so well. Even though it'd been almost a year since she'd last nursed Simone, she could still almost feel that unmistakable tingle and the sense of urgency to get back to a hungry nursing baby. Such a precious and mysterious connection between mother and child. She and Jesse had agreed that three were enough, but for a brief moment it made her wonder if she was really ready to be done with having babies.

But twins? The mere thought of all that Landyn and Chase had ahead of them raising two babies at once was enough to convince her. Especially with Danae's struggle to get pregnant. It would add insult to injury for Danae if anyone else in the family were to get pregnant now—and she sure didn't want to wait until Simone was in school and then start all over.

No. Though it made her a little sad, she knew she was done. They were done.

Landyn grabbed the check from the tabletop. "I've got it."

"Don't be silly, Landyn," Danae said. "You're the last one who should be picking up the tab."

Landyn gave her a look. "What's that supposed to mean?"

"I don't mean anything by it. But you guys are trying to get new businesses off the ground, and you've got the babies."

"We're doing fine, thank you."

"Let me at least leave the tip then," Danae said, pushing her chair in.

"I've got it. Can you two just let me do something nice once in a while? I might be your baby sister, but I'm not a baby anymore," Landyn huffed.

"Fine." Danae turned and headed toward the door. She stopped to throw a "thank you" over her shoulder, but it didn't sound very genuine.

Corrine hung back and waited while Landyn paid at the counter.

"What's up with her?" Landyn whispered while she waited for the cashier.

"Shh," Corinne said. "I'll tell you later." Through the front window she saw Danae waiting outside, her back to them.

"What's the deal?"

"I think it's bothering her that we both have babies."

"Oh." Landyn looked genuinely surprised. "I knew she and Dallas wanted kids, but I didn't know it was that big of a deal. Did I say something . . . wrong?"

"No. You just might be aware that she's super sensitive about that. You missed some of the situation with Danae and Dallas while you were living in New York. She wants to try some expensive fertility treatments, but I don't think Dallas is too hot on the idea."

"Wow. Fertility? I'd probably end up with quintuplets if I tried that."

Corinne winced. "Don't say that to Danae. Please."

"I'm not stupid. But I'm not going to pretend my babies don't exist either."

"I'm not saying that. Just—never mind."

Landyn shook her head and opened the door.

Her sister could be a little obtuse sometimes, but then Danae wasn't exactly being easy to deal with either. As much as Corinne understood her sister's concern, she wanted to tell her to just enjoy her days of not having toddlers underfoot. And yet, Corinne understood that it had been especially hard for Danae when Landyn—who'd apparently gotten pregnant on her honeymoon—popped out twins like it was the easiest thing in the world.

Fortunately, when they got outside, Danae seemed to have cooled off.

Corinne told her sisters good-bye and drove through Starbucks for a decaf latte on the way home. She was going to pay for this Starbucks habit she'd let herself get into since Jesse started traveling. Not just the fact that four-fifty a pop added up, but five hundred calories a pop was adding up on her hips too.

She took a sip of the sweet, warm liquid. But it didn't soothe her like it usually did. Between the whole thing with Jesse and now the tension with her sisters, a feeling of melancholy attached itself to her and wouldn't let go. She couldn't quit thinking about the way Michaela— Corinne realized she didn't remember the woman's last name. But there'd been something awfully . . . *possessive* in her tone.

Something wasn't quite right, and Corinne wasn't sure she was ready to analyze just what it was.

3

Jesse reclined his seat and bent his head to stare out the window of the 747. The lights of Chicago's skyline receded below, and he caught a glimpse of the moon reflected in Lake Michigan before everything disappeared in a bank of heavy clouds.

He couldn't wait to be home with Corinne and the girls, yet he hoped they'd let him sleep till noon tomorrow. These all-day-in-the-airport stints were killers.

He felt a light pressure on his arm and turned to see Michaela watching him.

"You look exhausted," she whispered.

"I'm pretty wiped. We all are."

"When do you have to travel again? Do you know yet?"

"I'm home two weeks, then out again."

"Poor baby." She patted his knee.

He pulled his leg away as if her touch were a flame. She put her hand back in her lap, apparently oblivious to his reaction. He and Michaela had both been on the same travel schedule before, but they'd worked together more closely this time, and he didn't like the direction her "friendliness" had taken.

He quickly edited his thought. Who was he kidding? Of course he liked it—at least a part of him did. What red-blooded male wouldn't want to have a young, attractive woman flirting with him, paying him special attention? But it did make him uncomfortable.

He felt certain he hadn't given Michaela any indication that he was receptive to her . . . advances. Quite the opposite.

He closed his eyes and turned his head away from her, pretending to be asleep, hoping he could avoid having to say something to her. He worked to turn off the images that crowded in—images he had no business entertaining—and instead tried to fill his mind with thoughts of Corinne and their daughters.

It was more of a struggle than he wanted to admit, yet he must have drifted off because when he opened his eyes again, it was to feel the plane touching down on the tarmac, and the lights of Lambert-St. Louis Airport flickering above the runway.

As he stretched, unfolded himself from the cramped seat, and gathered his briefcase from the overhead compartment, he did his best to ignore Michaela. But she wasn't an easy woman to ignore, and they still had a two-hour ride ahead of them, back to Cape Girardeau's small regional airport where they'd flown out of on Monday. He hated that their schedule, thanks to the flight delays, had worked out this way. Usually he did his best to avoid traveling alone with a female coworker. But when this had happened before, he and Corinne had discussed it and agreed that it would be foolish for him and Michaela to rent separate cars when they were going to the same place.

"I trust you, babe," Corinne had said. And he knew she meant it. But she might not be so confident if she ever met Michaela. He would do his best to prevent that from ever happening.

While he waited for their bags at the luggage carousel, Michaela went to the Hertz counter.

Their bags still hadn't showed up when she appeared, flashing the rental car keys. "We're all set."

"Okay. I'd offer to go get the car, but I don't want to leave you to wrestle with both our bags."

"It's okay." She shifted her overstuffed laptop case to the opposite hip and moved closer to him. "I don't mind waiting with you."

He ignored that and focused on the slow-moving carousel. Finally their luggage showed up, her bag leaning against his.

"Well! There you go!" she said, grinning.

He tried not to read anything into it, but it didn't take a genius to catch her innuendo.

In the car, he turned the radio up loud enough to discourage conversation. But every song that came on the pre-set pop station seemed inappropriate at best, downright suggestive at worst.

Thankfully, Michaela was quiet on the drive back to Cape Girardeau, even dozing briefly at one point. But Jesse had to hold back a sigh of relief when they finally reached the company parking lot. "Do you remember where you're parked?"

"Barely," she said. "It feels like we've been out of town forever." But she directed him to the spot, and he parked the car and got out to help her with her luggage.

When he straightened from closing the trunk of her car, she reached and wrapped him in a hug. "Thanks, Jess." She shortened his name in an overly familiar way. "It was a good trip. I'm going to miss spending time with you."

He gave her an awkward pat on the shoulder and took a wide step backward. Feeling his face heat, he was glad for the dim lights of the parking lot. "Well . . . I guess you have everything. Drive safe."

"Oh, don't worry about me. I don't have far to go."

He hadn't intended his comment to convey worry. But he knew protesting would only dig him a deeper hole. He lifted a hand in a half wave and got back into the rental car.

Feeling flustered by more than early morning brain fog, he exited the parking lot. Had he sent the wrong signals somehow where Michaela was concerned? He truly didn't think so, but Corinne had told him on more than one occasion that he sometimes came off as a flirt when that was never his intention. Certainly not with Michaela.

He punched the accelerator and merged onto the Interstate. Traffic was light at two a.m. and he'd be home within twenty minutes. He'd missed Corinne and the girls, and was eager to see them, but at the same time he felt unsettled.

His time in Chicago had brought unsettling feelings to the surface. A sense of discontentment he hadn't examined in a while. It wasn't Michaela, and it wasn't any "deficiency" in Corinne—at least he didn't think so. But he'd been wrestling with this feeling more and more.

It had grown stronger since his dad had died three weeks after Christmas. Dad was only sixty-four, the same age his grandfather had been when he passed away. Life was a breath. And then you died. And he was halfway there.

He labored for air. An all-too-familiar feeling of heaviness settled on him. It wasn't a physical thing. He knew that somehow. But it was there. Shadowing him. Stalking him.

And the only label he could put on it was . . . *trapped*.

⸺✦⸺

"Does your mommy let you do that?" Audrey held the remote high enough that her granddaughter couldn't reach it.

Sadie propped her hands on her hips and jutted her chin. "She does if I'm at Poppa's house."

Grant stifled a laugh.

Audrey shot him a stern look. "Gram and Poppa make the rules at Poppa's house." But she had to turn away to hide a smile herself.

At four, Sadie was learning to test the limits of just about any authority. It was a good thing she was so adorable. But Audrey knew Sadie's belligerence was wearing on Corinne, especially with Jesse gone so much. His absence had no doubt escalated the child's attitude. But Corinne and Jesse were good parents. Audrey had no doubt they'd get Sadie back on track once things slowed down with his work. She just hoped it *did* slow down.

Grant kissed Sadie's forehead. "You run and play with your sisters. Maybe we can watch a movie after naps."

She stuck out her bottom lip, but didn't argue and ran from the room, calling for Sari.

Grant shook his head, chuckling. "That little pistol."

"She needs her daddy's firm hand."

"Jesse's back now, isn't he?"

"Late last night. Or I should say early this morning. That's why we have the girls—so Jesse can sleep. And then they can have a date night."

"Ah. Good call."

"Yes, but the girls need their dad too." Audrey frowned. "It's a shame that a family can scarcely make it on one income these days."

"It wasn't exactly a piece of cake when we were their age," Grant reminded her. "Of course, we didn't expect to have everything all at once. I'd guess Jesse doesn't have much choice but to work the hours he does."

Audrey opened her mouth to defend Corinne, but Grant had a point. Jesse and Corinne lived well. They'd built a new home before Simone was born. Corinne had done a beautiful job decorating and furnishing it, but five bedrooms? It seemed excessive. And yes, a home was a good investment, and Audrey thought her daughter appreciated how hard Jesse worked so they could live as comfortably as they did. She just hoped they weren't making a trade-off of nice furniture for an absentee daddy.

Grant folded his newspaper and headed toward the kitchen. He stopped to kiss the back of Audrey's neck. "What do you say we let our kids work out their own problems?"

"I wasn't trying to fix any problems. I was just . . . thinking."

"And haven't we established that thinking usually gets you in trouble?"

"Very funny." But she reached behind her and pulled him close. "You'd better go see what rule Sadie has found to bend.

And while you're at it, would you check on Simone? She ought to be waking up from her nap any minute now."

She'd managed to change the subject, but Grant was right— they'd made it their policy to stay out of their kids' business as much as possible, especially when it came to marital issues. Still, the whole situation with Corinne weighed heavy on her mind.

4

Corinne looked across the table at her husband. In the candle-light of the dimly lit restaurant Jesse's tanned skin and chiseled features were more pronounced. He wore his fresh-this-morning haircut well, and it made his perpetual five-o'clock shadow look intentional and GQ.

When had she quit noticing how handsome Jesse was? The man had practically made her swoon when they were dating, and even when Sari was a baby, she remembered how the mere sight of Jesse holding the baby had the power to move her to tears. But she'd stopped noticing. Except tonight she'd noticed, only because their server—a twenty-something blonde who'd introduced herself as Tiffany—was flirting with Jesse. As usual, he seemed oblivious. The girl came to their table and, ignoring Corinne, asked Jesse if she could take his salad plate.

"Yes, thank you. I'm finished."

He was being his polite and friendly self, and Corinne couldn't accuse him of flirting back the way he sometimes did. Never intentionally, but in a way that did encourage some women.

This one didn't seem to need any encouragement. "Be sure you leave some room for dessert," Tiffany purred.

"Are you going to want dessert, babe?" He looked Corinne's way without meeting her eyes, which told her he was probably beginning to pick up on the girl's vibes.

The server gave Corinne an apathetic glance before turning back to Jesse. "Our Chocolate Avalanche is to die for. A dark cookie layer with vanilla cream filling and silky chocolate sauce topped with real whipped cream. I've never had a disappointed customer yet."

The girl sounded like she was describing something other than a dessert. Corinne resisted the urge to roll her eyes. "Do you want to split that?"

"Sure. Sounds good." He turned his million-watt smile on the server. "We'll take one of those. Two spoons, please."

"You can have all the whipped cream," he said when the server left.

"And you can have all the calories."

"Oh, no you don't." He patted his belly. "I've got enough problems with all the junk we've been eating on the road."

"Cut it out. You could eat your way across America and never gain a pound." It was true, and it was a bone of contention between them, whether Jesse knew it or not. She wasn't a blob or anything, but neither was she the one-hundred-and-twenty-pound waif Jesse had married. Three pregnancies had taken a toll on her figure, and though Jesse never said anything, she knew he'd be happy if she shed a few pounds.

"Maybe that used to be true," he said. "Not any more. I'm getting to be an old man."

She smirked and ran a hand through her hair—mousy brown hair that she never had time to do more with than pull up into a messy ponytail. She was frumpy and boring, and who could blame her husband if he enjoyed the attention this perky waitress heaped on him.

"Hey, you in there?"

She looked up and realized Jesse had been talking to her. "Sorry . . . What'd you say?"

"I said, I might be getting old but I still love you."

She loved the words, but somehow they seemed forced and not altogether genuine. "I love you too."

The sizzle had gone out of their marriage. She was pretty sure that was what the expression on Jesse's face said. But he didn't understand how hard it was when he left her alone with the kids for days on end while he jetted all over the country being wined and dined, not to mention having someone taller than two feet to have an intelligent conversation with.

He'd seemed distracted lately, and despite Corinne's utter trust in him, she wouldn't blame him if he found the intelligent, attractive women he worked and traveled with to be more interesting than she was. She blew a wisp of hair off her forehead and risked a glance across the table.

Jesse started to say something, but just then the waitress appeared with their dessert and he turned his attention to Tiffany, as if she'd baked the thing herself.

In the car on the way home, Jesse took her hand and made overtures she knew all too well. She shifted in her seat, scooting closer to the passenger door. She felt guilty for rebuffing him, but how could he think she would be in the mood when they'd drifted so far apart. And when he seemed to have more to say to the lovely Tiffany than to his own wife?

"Everything okay, babe?" Jesse rubbed her shoulder in the first steps of a dance that was almost as old as their marriage.

"I don't know. Is it?"

"What do you mean? Did I do something wrong?"

She released a sigh she'd been holding all night. "Jesse . . . It's not that you did anything wrong. It's that you don't—"

"—do anything right? Like I haven't heard that before." He moved his hand back to the steering wheel.

She knew she'd successfully fended off any romantic ideas he might have had, and an odd mixture of relief and disappointment battled with her emotions. "That's not what I said."

"It's what you meant though. I can see it in your face, Corinne."

"Jesse, I don't want to fight. Not when you just got back. Can't we just forget it?"

"I don't think you can."

"What's that supposed to mean?"

"It means when you get like this, you're going to fight to the bitter end." He gritted his teeth and looked straight ahead.

She could tell he'd gone beyond a point of no return. They were going to have a fight, and it was going to be a big one. She'd seen the pattern before. "No. I'm not going to fight at all."

He mumbled something she couldn't understand, but she had a pretty good guess what he'd said.

She didn't ask him to repeat himself, and they drove without speaking the rest of the way home. They unloaded the car in more silence, and she could almost feel Jesse's disappointment at "wasting" a night without kids.

She took a quick shower, knowing he was hoping she'd have a change of heart by the time she got out. But she put on her night-gown—the shapeless one she knew he didn't like, and by the time he crawled into bed, she was too tired for either finishing their fight or making up.

He slept as close to the edge of the bed as he could have without rolling off. She lay on her side, watching the ceiling fan spin high above them, wondering if she'd have been better off just faking it. Except Jesse could always tell. And that was a surefire way to alienate a husband. Especially a handsome husband who had the attentions of a perky young coworker and a waitress named Tiffany.

❦

Jesse rolled over and squinted through the early morning darkness. Corinne's side of the bed was empty, the blankets pulled up over the pillows like she didn't intend to crawl back into the bed any time soon. He listened for a minute and heard the sound of dishes rattling in the sink.

He'd ended up on the far edge of the bed the entire night. Any normal husband would have gone to the guest room or slept on the couch, but early in their marriage, after the first time he'd exiled himself to the sofa after a fight, he and Corinne had agreed they would never sleep apart if they could help it—even if they were fighting. *Especially* if they were fighting.

But this morning it felt like he might as well be down on the sofa . . . or six hundred miles away in some nameless hotel.

He eased his long legs over the side of the bed and steeled himself to go down and try to make amends with his wife. He hoped she'd have realized by now how petty she was being. But it seemed like Corinne held a grudge longer than usual lately. Still, he was determined to take the high road.

He found her in front of the sink loading dishes into the dishwasher. Her hair escaped the ponytail holder, creating a wispy halo around her face. He went to her and put his arms around her from behind. "You sleep okay?"

She shrugged beneath his embrace and scrubbed the bottom of a skillet—a little harder than necessary, he thought. "I got a few hours. You?"

"My edge of the bed isn't as soft as the middle."

She laughed in a way that let him venture a quick reconciliation. "Are we okay?" he whispered nuzzling the top of her head with his chin.

She shrugged again, but quit scrubbing. "I think we will be . . . Eventually." He recognized the hint of teasing in her voice.

"I was coming down to do the dishes for you . . . thought I could earn a few brownie points. But you beat me to it."

"Don't worry." She poked her left hand under the faucet, then flicked her fingers behind her, spraying him. "There's still laundry to do."

He gave her ponytail a tug. "I'm not *that* intent on making up."

She jabbed a playful elbow at his belly. "Careful buster. You're skating on thin ice already."

He wrapped her tighter and planted a kiss at the nape of her neck.

Without bothering to dry her hands, she turned from the sink and wrapped her arms around him, nestling her head against his chest. "I'm sorry I picked a fight."

"It's okay. I'm sorry, too." He decided against naming his offense since he wasn't sure he'd get it right. He kissed her forehead, yearning to be back in her good graces, homesick for her in a way that didn't fit with the fact that he was holding her in his arms.

"I'm really sorry I wasted a perfectly good night with a sitter."

"We've probably got a few years to make up for it."

"A few years, my eye." She glanced over his shoulder in the direction of the clock. "We've still got an hour before we have to pick the kids up from my folks'."

He pulled back, studying her face to be sure she was serious and loving what he saw in her eyes.

She ran her hands down his arms and entwined her fingers with his. Tugging him toward the staircase, she wriggled her eyebrows comically.

He laughed and followed her, feeling the weight of the past weeks roll off of him. Making love with his wife had always been a potent elixir for what ailed him. What ailed them.

But he sensed this time it would only be a temporary fix. That it wouldn't really settle things for Corinne.

And it wasn't just her. *He* was unsettled. Something inside him—deep inside—was uneasy. He was just beginning to understand the roiling disturbance within him. And he knew now that until he dealt with it, he and Corinne would find themselves on opposite edges of the bed so often that they might not be able to meet in the middle again.

He had a hard choice to make: either he needed to decide he could accept his life the way it was, or he needed to make some changes. Changes that would rock the worlds of all the people he loved most.

He wasn't even sure it was possible to accomplish what he found himself contemplating—obsessing about—lately, without making a few people as miserable as he was in the process. Would it even be worth it in the end?

5

Your dad has to come in to town anyway. He can bring the girls home after lunch."

Corinne wedged the phone between her shoulder and ear and attacked a skillet with a bedraggled steel wool pad. "Are you sure, Mom?" But relief rushed through her at the offer.

"I'm sure. The girls are heavy into a project with Poppa right now anyway."

Corinne smiled into the phone. "You just made my day." She hung up and breathed a contented sigh. She so rarely got a few hours without the kids underfoot.

"What was that about?" Jesse, still in pajama bottoms and T-shirt and looking sexy as all get out, looked up at her from the morning paper.

"We don't have to go pick up the girls after all. Dad's going to bring them home after lunch."

"Really?" He looked disappointed. "Well . . . I guess I can spend time with them later."

"Oh." She frowned. "I guess I should have asked if you were okay with that. I can still go get them if you'd rather . . ."

"No, it's fine. I'm home all next week so I'll make it up to them."

"You sure?"

He nodded. "And remember we have Monday off for Memorial Day."

"Oh, that's right. Good."

Jesse went back to his paper without comment.

Corrine poured a second cup of coffee, but she felt guilty about depriving him of the time with their daughters. And even guiltier that she was so happy about having a few hours without them.

Her mom was practically pushing sixty. Why did she have more energy than Corinne did? And despite how much she'd mourned the empty nest, her mother seemed happier and more fulfilled than Corinne was in this supposed prime of her life. Something was wrong with this picture. She was living her dream. She had a beautiful home, three precious, healthy daughters, a handsome husband who made enough money that she could stay home with the girls as she'd always desired. Why wasn't she counting her blessings?

Feeling exhausted was to be expected when you were chasing after three children—and pulling double duty because your husband was on the road. But there was something else. Something she couldn't quite put her finger on. She wasn't in a depression. At least she didn't think so. But she felt a burden on her shoulders that hadn't always been there.

They'd struggled a little financially since buying the house—house poor, as Jesse always put it. He'd wanted something a little more modest, but she'd fought for this house, and it was worth it to her, especially since this was where she spent most of her time.

Yes, they'd sunk most of their savings into the mortgage, but they'd only financed half the home's price, so they'd kept their payments relatively low and built some nice equity. The new Nissan Pathfinder had pinched their budget further, but it was a necessity to safely transport the kids. And the sprinkler system they'd put in last fall had set them back several thousand dollars. Still, it wasn't like they were on the verge of being homeless or anything. The truth was, they lived far better than most of their friends. All of them, actually. She sometimes found herself apologizing for the material things they had. Especially when she'd been able to stay home with the kids.

Simone had grown up so quickly. Corinne could barely remember her youngest as an infant. And with Sari in school and Sadie soon to be, she sometimes wondered if they should have another one. But with one still in diapers, it was hard to think about having a tiny one again. Still, it went by so fast . . . And she did love being a mom.

Yet, as much as Jesse adored his daughters, Corinne knew he'd like to have a son. Still, whenever they'd talked about it recently, they agreed three was probably enough. Just putting the trio they had through college was going to take a major financial miracle.

Her friend Beth had confessed more than once that she still got baby fever once in a while—and the Hodges had five kids. All boys. "Especially if you could guarantee me a girl," Beth said. "I'm not sure what it takes to get over that amazing feeling of holding a brand-new baby in your arms."

She smiled, remembering her mother's reaction when she'd repeated Beth's comment. "Turning forty did the trick for me," Mom had said with a wry smile.

Corinne had a ways to go before she hit forty—

"So what are you going to do with the rest of your morning?" Jesse's voice broke into her thoughts.

"Try to catch up with the laundry, for one thing. And maybe get a couple of Crock-Pot meals made ahead."

"Why don't you do something fun? Something just for you."

She sighed. "Because the laundry and hungry tummies will still be waiting when I'm done with 'something fun.' I'd rather get caught up."

"Anything I can help with?"

He didn't meet her eyes. She laughed, knowing he was only offering to be nice and was silently begging her not to actually give him a to-do list.

"What's so funny?"

"Never mind. It's sweet of you to ask, but you've been gone all week . . . working. I'm sure you have things you'd like to catch up on too."

"Well, I do need to check the oil in your car and gas it up."

"Right. Thank you." She went to stand behind him and massaged his neck while he perused the sports section.

"Mmmm . . . Feels good."

"I'm glad you're home."

"Yeah, me too." But he was already deep into page three.

She gave his neck one last squeeze and headed to gather the dirty laundry from the girls' rooms. But she couldn't shake this . . . heaviness. Their house had been designed—and situated on the lot—to capture maximum light. Why, then did everything feel so dark inside these walls?

○━━✦━━○

"Is there room in the fridge for this salad, Mom?" Corinne lifted up the fancy bowl that held a fruit salad—a new recipe she'd been wanting to try.

Her mother paused and looked up from the pork tenderloin she was slicing. "Your sisters beat you to the fridge space. You'll probably have to take yours out to the fridge in the garage."

Corinne rearranged a couple of shelves in vain, and finally heeded her mom's suggestion and took her salad to the garage. These Tuesday night family dinners her dad had instituted were blessing or bane, depending on what she and Jesse had going on. But since opening the B&B, Dad insisted the whole family get together every week for dinner and games.

He and Mom did the bulk of the cooking, and she and her sisters took turns providing salads and desserts. Unless CeeCee came. Dad's mother, at eighty-four, fancied herself a mother hen to them all. And CeeCee had dibs on dessert duty—unless her bridge club got changed to Tuesday night. Then all bets were off.

The dinners were a nice idea, and Corinne appreciated that not every family was blessed to live close enough to each other that they could do this—or *liked* each other enough that they'd want to. But she wondered how long it could continue. Already she and Jesse had needed to bow out of some church activities and rearrange Sari's dance lessons to clear their Tuesdays. Things would only get crazier as the girls got older.

But at least Jesse was amenable to the idea—probably mostly because Mom was a much better cook than she was. And CeeCee's dessert offerings got more elaborate every week, making Jesse's sweet tooth very happy. He'd dubbed CeeCee the Dessert Diva. Oddly enough, Jesse's favorite part of Tuesday nights—next to CeeCee—was that the men did the dishes. Not that he was crazy about kitchen cleanup, but he was crazy about her dad and her brother Link, and Danae and Landyn's husbands, too. That affection had only grown stronger since Jesse's father had died. With his mom staying indefinitely at his sister's out in California, the Whitmans were the only family Jesse had in the state.

It warmed Corinne's heart to see the way he fit in with her family. Especially when she knew some of her friends' husbands couldn't stand their in-laws and made elaborate excuses to get out of spending time with them.

She loved spending time with family too. But being together with her family, even just being on Chicory Lane where she'd grown up, also brought back memories of Tim. Things would never seem quite right at a Whitman gathering without her youngest brother. Tim's wife—widow—would be here, and they loved Bree like a sister. And yet her presence also emphasized the empty place at the table.

If only Tim hadn't gone to Afghanistan . . . Corinne was proud of the sacrifice her marine brother had made for his country. And in many ways, his death had brought their family even closer. Still, where Tim was concerned, even after four years, she was still smothered in *if onlys.*

She brushed off the thoughts and pushed up her sleeves. "What can I do, Mom?" Turning on the faucet in the deep kitchen sink, she let the water run until it was warm, then washed and dried her hands.

"You can cut up some celery and green peppers for a relish tray. I think Dad invited our guests to supper tonight. We might need to stretch things a bit." She looked toward the staircase that led to the upstairs guest rooms and made a face that said she wasn't crazy about the prospect.

Corinne lowered her voice. "Is it someone you know?"

"No. Complete strangers from Ohio. And they've got their kids with them. Good kids though," she added quickly. She looked across the kitchen through the window to the backyard. "Looks like Jesse already has something organized out there with them."

Jesse had shed his hoodie and was directing some sort of game that involved a giant bouncy ball from Walmart and a whiffle ball bat. No doubt some crazy game he and Link had invented on the spot. Sari and Sadie were playing with the two boys from Ohio as if they were favorite cousins.

Corinne rolled her eyes, grinning. "I married the Pied Piper of Chicory Lane."

"You married well," Mom said, shaking a finger at her. "He's so good with the kids. Not only yours, I mean, but he just has a way with children."

"He does." Pride swelled her heart as she watched him out the window. "I hope they don't get too dirty before—"

"Are we the last ones here?" Danae and Dallas appeared in the kitchen door, each bearing a covered bowl. Danae went immediately to the refrigerator and within seconds had deposited her bowls and shut the door.

"Hey! How did you do that? I couldn't get my dish in there with a shoehorn."

Danae shrugged, smiling. "Just talented, I guess."

"The guys are in the backyard, Dallas," Mom said. Again, she glanced upstairs and lowered her voice. "Just to warn you, we have extra guests tonight. Your dad hit it off with some people who had reservations for graduation this past weekend. Apparently he invited them to join us for dinner."

Danae shot Corinne a look that said she felt the same as Mom about the *outsiders.* "Is that who the little boys running around outside belong to?"

Mom nodded.

"I wondered."

Dallas winked at Corinne. "I thought maybe you were trying to arrange marriages for your girls."

"Please! According to Jesse they aren't even allowed to *date* till they're thirty-five, so don't let him hear you say that."

Her brother-in-law made a motion of zipping his lip before he headed out to the backyard to join the others.

Landyn and Chase arrived with the twins and enough paraphernalia in tow to open a Babies"R"Us franchise.

"Dibs!" Corinne called, quickly drying her hands and racing to relieve Chase of the infant he was holding. "Come here, sweetie. I can't believe how much you've grown already." She cooed at the tiny girl. "This is Emma, right? Or wait . . . is it Grace?"

The twins weren't identical, but at one month old and both with heads as slick as cue balls, it was hard to tell them apart.

"That's Grace. You can tell by the G on her shirt." Chase gave her a sarcastic thumbs up. "Emma's got an E. Oh and"—he tapped his daughter on the top of the head—"this end goes up."

"Okay, smart aleck." She rolled her eyes at her brother-in-law. "I think I can figure it out from here."

Landyn helped her settle in the living room with the twins, and twenty minutes later Corinne had worked her magic, and the babies were sleeping side by side on a pallet of quilts behind the sofa.

Mom came to the doorway. "Everything's ready. Can you girls come and eat?"

Huckleberry came over to sniff at the quilt. "No, Huck," Corinne said gruffly, pushing the Lab's head away from the makeshift bed. "Don't you dare wake those babies up."

"Come on, boy." Mom lured the dog away with the promise of scraps.

When everyone had straggled in from the backyard and gathered in the great room, Dad made introductions to the inn's guests he'd invited.

The Pattersons seemed like a nice family, but it struck Corinne that her dad might've had an ulterior motive in inviting them to stay for family dinner. The man loved to show off his family. She curbed a grin and thought Dad might literally burst his buttons with pride.

She only hoped her girls behaved during dinner. Simone had been a bit of a brat these last couple of weeks while Jesse was gone. She shouldered the blame for a lot of it. She hadn't kept the girls on their regular bedtime schedule, and she'd let them watch way too much TV. She might pay for it now. She shot up a quick prayer that they'd make their Poppa proud tonight.

After she'd fixed the girls' plates and gotten them settled at the kids' table with the Patterson boys, she slipped in line at the buffet beside Jesse. She was filling her own plate when his cell phone chirped the tone he'd assigned to his office.

She gave him a questioning look. "Please tell me they're not going to ask you to come in to work." It was getting ridiculous how many hours they expected him to put in.

Jesse shook his head. "I don't think so, but I'd better take this. Save me a place. I'll be right back." He put the phone to his ear and headed out to the front hall, swinging his still empty plate at his side.

Mom slipped in line behind her, eyeing the hall. "Everything okay?"

"It is unless they make Jesse come in and work tonight. They seem to think he has to do the marketing guys' jobs too."

Thankfully, he was back a minute later. He loaded his plate and took the seat Corinne had reserved for him. "Do you have to go in?"

He shook his head, not meeting her gaze and instead, stuffed his mouth. "Somebody just had a question," he said over a forkful of barbecue.

"Thank goodness." She was relieved, yet something seemed odd about Jesse's refusal to look her in the eye. She hoped he wasn't just telling her what she wanted to hear for now.

After the guys finished the dishes and it was beginning to get dark, Corinne found Jesse in the front yard pointing out the constellations to the girls—and to the Patterson boys, who apparently lived in LA and had never seen a starry night sky. Jesse had a rapt audience, and Corinne was grateful he hadn't had to go in to work.

No sooner had the thought entered her mind than his phone rang again. This time, from the pocket of his jacket that he'd left flopped over the porch railing.

She was tempted to let it go to voice mail, but this one wasn't his office phone. It might be important. "Hey, Jesse. Your phone. Do you want me to get it?"

He didn't hear her, so she fished it out of his pocket. Michaela Creeve's name was in the Caller ID, and a photo of her that looked like some attention-starved teenager's Facebook profile pic. What was she doing calling Jesse after work hours?

She debated whether or not to answer, not wanting to pull Jesse away from the kids. But curiosity ultimately got the best of her and she clicked Answer. "Hello?"

The line instantly went dead. Interesting. Was it just a coincidence that Michaela had given up on Jesse answering just as Corinne picked up? Or did the woman just not want to talk to her?

In the car on the short trip home, she tried to broach the subject casually with Jesse. "You missed a call when you were outside with the kids. After dinner."

47

"Oh?" Jesse seemed intent on the gravel road, familiar though it was. "Who was it?"

"Michaela Creeve."

That earned her a glance. "What did she want?"

"I don't know. She hung up as soon as I answered." She looked out her window, waiting for some kind of response. It didn't comfort her that her husband didn't reply.

6

Jesse put the car in Park and slowly opened his door. He'd never dreaded going in to work before, but he had an onerous task before him today. He'd wrestled with this decision ever since returning from Chicago, but last night had been the last straw. He couldn't just ignore it any longer.

Michaela's car wasn't in the Preston-Brilon parking lot. He wished she wasn't always late getting in to work. He would rather have had the dreaded conversation away from prying eyes at work, but that would have made him a complete hypocrite about the very things he needed to discuss with her.

He went down to the break room for a cup of coffee. When he came back upstairs, he was surprised to see her at her desk.

"Good morning, Jesse." She was all smiles as if they shared some secret.

"Morning. Uh . . . do you have a minute?"

"Sure. What's up?"

He looked around the sales room. Larry and Wayne were on the phone and Delia looked engrossed in whatever was on her computer screen, but this conversation had the potential to get uncomfortable quickly. "Would you mind if we went into the conference room?"

She raised a penciled eyebrow. "Sure." She grabbed a lip gloss from her top desk drawer and coated her lips quickly before rising and following him down the hallway.

Before he got to the conference room, he could hear that someone had beaten them to it. He turned on his heel and almost ran headlong into Michaela. He sidestepped and pointed the other way back toward his office. "It's taken already. I guess we can use my office if you don't mind."

"Of course." The mild curiosity that had coated her voice earlier edged up a notch. "Am I in trouble?" But her playful laughter said it had never crossed her mind that she might actually be in trouble.

He ignored her question and quickened his step. Once in his office, he cleared off the chair in front of his desk and motioned for her to take it, then went behind his desk and sat down.

She looked behind her at the door. "You look pretty serious. Do I need to close the door?"

"No." *Absolutely not.* "I just wanted to talk with you about—" He'd rehearsed fifteen different speeches on the drive to work, but now they all sounded accusatory and a little ridiculous. "Corinne said you called last night. Was there something work related that—"

"Oh, Jesse!" She clapped a hand over her mouth. "Did I get you in trouble? I'm so sorry."

"Get me in trouble?"

"With your wife. I wasn't expecting her to answer and I guess I might have hung up on her. I just—"

"I'm not sure what you mean by getting me in trouble, but no. I just wondered what you wanted."

She glanced toward the hallway again and her voice went sultry. "You needed privacy to ask me that?"

"Was there something . . ." He cleared his throat and started again, making an effort to sound fully business-like. "Did you have a question about work?"

"Last night you mean?"

"Yes."

"Not really. I just wanted to . . . talk. I was thinking about our conversation in Chicago, and I just had a few other thoughts."

"Our conversation?" They'd talked about a lot of things during the trip—most of them at dinner with other sales associates and clients.

She gave him a coy look, as if he should remember the conversation.

Not wanting to encourage her attitude, he cut to the chase. "Michaela, I'd prefer you not call me at home—or outside of work."

She crossed and uncrossed her legs, watching him intently as she did so. "That's not the vibe I was getting last week."

"Wha—?" He drew back as if she'd slapped him. "I'm not sure what you're referring to, but if I somehow gave the wrong—*impression*, I sincerely apologize."

"Oh, you gave an impression all right. But hey"—she held up a hand—"if Mrs. Pennington got a whiff of what was going on and I got you in trouble, then I apologize."

"Of what was . . . going on? Listen, I don't know what you're implying, but there was nothing going on." He motioned between them. "Nothing between us, I mean." He pushed back his chair and rose, eager to have her out of his office.

He came around from behind his desk, but she didn't budge. "So what exactly was this meeting about?"

He took two steps backward and reached to steady himself with a hand on his desk. "I simply wanted to ask that you not call me outside of work hours—unless it's an emergency, of course."

Her chin went up. "I resent what you are implying, Mr. Pennington." She'd never called him that. He'd been simply *Jesse* to her from the first time they'd been introduced the day she started work at Preston-Brilon. And recently, the too-familiar Jess.

"I am not implying anything. Truly. I'm just . . . requesting. That's all."

"We'll see about that."

"What?" *What, indeed.* What had he gotten himself into?

Michaela jumped up and huffed. "Don't worry. And you can tell your wife she has nothing to worry about."

"This has *nothing* to do with my wife."

"Yeah, right." She rolled her eyes, looking more like a sixteen-year-old than the twenty-six she'd claimed to be.

He balled his fingers into fists and counted slowly to himself, knowing he could not afford to let her get to him. Stepping around her, he gripped the door to his office, eager to close it behind her. When she didn't budge, he said, "That's all."

The look she gave him sent a shard of something close to fear racing through him.

"Oh, you'll wish that was all," she said between clenched teeth. She rose, swept past him, and stormed down the hall.

⚓

"Aren't you hungry?" Corinne put the bowl of scalloped potatoes in front of Jesse. "Did I get them too salty?"

"No, they're fine. I'm just full."

"How can you be full? You barely touched your food and we're eating later than usual tonight." An hour later than they normally had supper. Simone was already in bed for the night and it would soon be the older girls' bedtime. "Do you want me to make you a sandwich?"

"No, I'm fine." He pushed his plate away, then, as if an afterthought, patted her hand. "It was great. Really. I'm just not hungry."

"Okay. Suit yourself." She turned to the girls. "Sadie, eat your beans."

"I did, Mama. See?" The four-year-old tipped her mostly untouched plate up for inspection.

"You need to eat a few more. I can't even tell you made a dent."

"Can I eat two and be done?"

"Eat the two biggest beans and you can be done, or eat the five biggest ones and get dessert."

"Mo-om!" The whining started in earnest. "I don't want to eat *five.*"

"Fine, you don't have to. You only have to eat two. I'm just saying if you want dessert, you need to eat five."

"But I don't—"

"Sadie!" Jesse banged a fist on the table. "Do as your mother says."

That put a stop to the whining, but Sadie slumped in her chair and sat with her lower lip pushed out as far as it would go.

Something was eating at Jesse, and his foul mood was rubbing off on the whole family.

"Mom brought over some leftover cobbler from the inn. Do you want some? There's ice cream." That was usually the ticket out of his moods.

But Jesse pushed away from the table. "Maybe later." He carried his plate and glass to the sink and scraped his food into the disposal.

"Finish up, girls . . . Come on now. It's time for baths." Corinne rose and cleared her own plate, then followed Jesse into the living room. She studied him for a minute. "Is everything okay?"

"I'm fine. Why?" He wouldn't meet her eyes.

"You just seem . . . I don't know . . . *preoccupied.*"

"Just work stuff. It's nothing."

"It doesn't seem like nothing. Do you want to talk about it?"

"No. It's no big deal." He turned and grabbed the newspaper off the end table. "I'm going down to watch the news and read the paper."

"Okay. If you want some cobbler later, I'll bring some down. I'm going to get the girls in bed."

"You need help?"

"No, it's okay. I'll do it tonight."

She was short with the girls, and bedtime was chaos, but when she finally got them tucked in, she went down to the family room.

Jesse was stretched out in the recliner with the newspaper over his face.

She nudged him. "Hey, babe. Why don't you just go to bed."

He slid the paper down and peered at her. "I'm not asleep."

She eased down on the arm of the recliner. "What's going on? I can tell something's bothering you."

"It's nothing that won't work itself out."

"You're sure it's only work? You're not upset with me about anything?"

"No. Of course not. It's just work. Don't worry your pretty little head about it."

That would ordinarily get a rise out of her. But she merely rolled her eyes at him and went to get a load of laundry started. That seemed like a never-ending chore around here.

She was pouring detergent into the washing machine when she felt Jesse's breath on the back of her neck.

"I think I am going to go to bed." He sounded defeated. "You need help with anything first?"

"No. I just wanted to get the laundry going first." She closed the lid on the washer and turned to look at him. In the yellow light of the laundry room, he looked pasty and drawn. "Do you feel okay? You don't look so great."

"I'm just tired." He embraced her and gave her a perfunctory goodnight kiss. "I'll see you in the morning. Love you."

"Love you too, baby."

She straightened up the house and read a couple of chapters in the novel she'd started last week when Jesse was gone. But the living room felt empty without him, and she couldn't shake the disappointment that while her husband wasn't traveling, it didn't quite feel like he'd come home either.

7

Oh, my! Something certainly smells delicious!" Mr. Hager stuck his nose in the air and inhaled deeply.

Audrey knew a hint when she heard one, but she wasn't biting. "Yes, as I hope my husband mentioned when you booked your room, we aren't ordinarily open on Tuesday nights. It's our family night—there are sixteen of us when we're all here, so we pretty much pack out the great room, unless we can be outside. I hope we don't disturb you." They'd had outsiders at their last Tuesday night with the kids, and while it had gone fine, it simply wasn't the same as when it was just their family.

"Oh, you won't bother me," Mr. Hager said. "I'll just take out my hearing aids and be none the wiser."

She didn't tell him that their wild games of Slap Jack sometimes literally shook the house. But at least he'd taken the hint.

Running the inn had taken far more of her time than she'd bargained for. She wasn't about to start sharing her Tuesday nights, too. She'd have to talk to Grant—again—about his scheduling. Tuesdays were the one night of the week they rarely had guests. It was why they'd chosen that day of the week for family dinners. She should be glad business had picked up to fill the empty night, but now she wondered if they should make it a hard and fast rule that they were closed on Tuesdays.

"I suppose I'll go into town to eat," the elderly man said. "If the cafe in Langhorne is open for dinner."

Maybe he hadn't taken the hint after all. But she played dumb. "If you get there early. They don't serve after eight."

"Well, then I best be getting ready." The man started up the stairs. "Do I need a key to get back in to the inn tonight?"

"We won't lock the doors until you're in for the night."

"I appreciate that."

"I hope you'll be staying for breakfast with us in the morning?"

"Oh, yes. I'll count on it."

A twinge of regret nipped at her conscience. He seemed like a nice man, and he'd told her earlier that he'd lost his wife about this time last year. Though he hadn't said it in so many words, Audrey gathered that this trip was part of his grieving process, retracing trips they'd taken during their forty-year marriage.

She and Grant would celebrate their fortieth anniversary not that many years from now, and she could hardly let herself imagine what life might be like without him.

She shook off the guilt. She couldn't be responsible for the emotional state of every guest that darkened their doors. She had not signed up to run a counseling center—or a restaurant for that matter. It was already more frazzling than she'd counted on just getting breakfast for guests who wanted their coffee and rolls served anywhere from five a.m. to nearly lunch time.

She turned back to the fragrant pot roast and potatoes simmering in the roaster and hoped Link remembered that he'd promised to pick up some rolls to go with their feast.

Grant came in from the backyard with Huckleberry at his heels. They started across the wood floors, mud flying from one of them. Audrey flew from behind the counter and put up a hand.

"Grant, stop! Look at your shoes! You're tracking mud everywhere."

"Must be Huck. I don't have any mud—" He lifted one foot and looked over his shoulder. "Oops. I guess it is me. Sorry about that."

"Stay right there." She sighed. "I'll get a rag. Huck, sit. Stay. Do you have mud on your feet, too?"

The dog did as he was told, and Grant took off one shoe and balanced on one stockinged foot while Audrey went to round up an old putty knife and some rags.

Grant leaned on her shoulder and slipped out of his shoes. She followed him to the back deck and helped him scrape off the worst of the mud.

"You would wear your shoes with the deepest tread," she scolded.

"Hey, did you invite Mr. Hager to have dinner with us tonight?"

She stopped and looked hard at her husband. "No, I did not. Despite his broad hints. You didn't, did you?" She went back to scraping the clay-like mud from the crevices of his soles.

"We'd have enough for one more, wouldn't we?"

"That's not the point, Grant. It's family night. It changes the whole flavor of the evening when we have outside guests."

He didn't say anything and she seized the opening to further make her case. "I really wish you wouldn't even schedule guests on Tuesday nights. It's all I can do just to get dinner ready for the kids."

"I thought the girls all brought food. Link, too. The idea was that it would be pot luck, right?"

"It is. And they've been great to help, but I'm making the main dish and trying to get the house clean and the tables ready and—"

"Audrey . . ." Grant chuckled and wagged his head. "It doesn't even make sense to clean the house before that crew comes."

"Well, maybe clean isn't the word, but still . . . And by the way, I thought we had a no kids policy at the Chicory Inn."

He stopped scrubbing and turned off the water. "What are you talking about. You want to ban the grandkids now?"

"No, silly. I'm talking about last week's Tuesday guests. The couple with the kids. Did you know they were coming?"

"He promised me the kids were well behaved. And they were."

57

"This time. But our guests tell their friends about us, and we can't say yes to some families with kids and no to others. Besides, what parents are going to tell you their kids are brats? You just lucked out that time."

"Audrey, what is going on?" Grant studied her. "Have you been saving up this hit list for the past month?"

"No, but I do think we need to discuss this. If you want to have these weekly family dinners, I think you need to not schedule guests on Tuesdays."

"Listen, you're the one who's always saying we have bills to pay. We're lucky to book guests during the week at all."

At Grant's strident voice, Huck lifted his chocolate head and looked back and forth between them.

"It's okay, boy." Grant stooped to scratch behind the dogs ears, and Huck lay back down. "Audrey, I'm just trying to pay the bills."

She opened her mouth out of habit, but she couldn't very well argue with that.

⚓

It was almost four when Jesse pulled into the parking lot of Preston-Brilon. He'd spent the day in St. Louis visiting the firm's various clients there, but he was still trying to catch up on the work that had piled up on his desk since Chicago.

He was starving despite lunch with one of the clients. Oh, but it was Tuesday. That meant a big meal—a great meal—at Corinne's parents'. Corinne was a decent cook, but it was hard to beat these Tuesday family potlucks. Maybe if he stayed till six and just met Corinne and the girls out at the inn, he could get caught up.

He entered the building and checked in with the department secretary. "Any messages for me, Sharon?"

"Hi, Jesse. I left a couple of things on your desk, and I'm guessing Ferreman got hold of you? They said they'd call your cell."

"Oh, they did. Right in the middle of lunch." The distributor was notorious for bad timing.

Sharon looked sheepish. "Sorry."

"Hey, not your fault. Okay, guess I'd better go see if I can find the top of my desk." He turned and started out of the reception area.

"Oh, I almost forgot . . . Frank wants to see you in his office."

Jesse braced an arm on the door jamb. "Now?"

She shrugged. "He just said when you get back. It didn't sound urgent."

"Okay. Thanks." He went to his desk, but his curiosity wouldn't let him sit down. It was unusual for Frank Preston to summon any employee into his office. He was far more likely to come to his employee's desk, perch on the corner, and have a chat. Something must be up. May as well see what that was about before he dug into his paperwork.

He went down the hall and knocked on the open door.

Frank looked up from his desk, smiling. "Jesse, come in."

Jesse's mood lightened. Maybe this was about that raise he'd been promised. Wouldn't that be fun news to deliver to Corinne?

"Close that door behind you, would you?"

"Sure." Definitely about the raise. Couldn't risk one of the other sales managers overhearing and demanding the same. Of course, Jesse often suspected he was on the bottom of the managers salary totem pole already. Not that he could complain. He made good money.

Frank pulled a stapled sheaf of papers out of his top drawer and came around to sit on the corner of his desk, one ankle propped on the opposite knee.

"I hate to even have to bring this up, Jesse, but"—he held out the stapled pages and gave a sigh that punctured Jesse's ballooning hope—"Michaela Creeve brought this in to my office this morning."

"What is this?" Jesse scanned the title and the seal of the State of Missouri. The Commission on Human Rights? While its significance was still registering in his brain, he flipped through the pages to see Michaela's feminine, scrolling signature across the final page. He flipped back two pages and saw his name neatly typed into the form. "Discrimination? On what basis."

"She claims that you—" Frank cleared his throat. His gaze dropped to the carpeting. "Well, bottom line . . . She's threatening to file for sexual harassment."

Jesse drew back in the chair. "What?"

"She claims you . . . made improper advances."

"That's ridiculous. Completely ridiculous. Come on, Frank, you know me better than that."

"She says it happened while you were in Chicago together."

Jesse shot to his feet. "Frank, I swear to you, I did nothing in the least improper, but if you must know, she made . . . I guess you'd call it *advances* toward me."

"Which you rebuffed?"

"Yes. In no uncertain terms."

"Can you prove that?"

"I don't know how I could prove it. It started on the flight home—at least the blatant, obvious part . . . Corinne says I'm not always the sharpest pencil when it comes to this kind of stuff, but I realized Michaela had kind of been"—he shrugged—"I don't know . . . putting the moves on me the whole time."

"In what way?"

"Stuff like . . . leaning against me. Putting her hand on my knee. Flirting . . ." It was embarrassing to even have to voice these things. *Because why hadn't he stopped it after the first incident?*

As if reading his mind, Frank asked, "And did you reciprocate in any way?"

"No!" He wished it had come out more evenly. He steadied his voice before speaking again. "Absolutely not."

"Michaela claims you hugged her."

He closed his eyes, fighting the wave of nausea that rolled through his gut. "She hugged me . . . when I dropped her off at her car."

"Where?"

"Here. In the parking lot." He gestured in the direction of the company parking lot.

Frank shook his head. "So, on company property?"

"Yes." He was surprised to find his voice trembling. He'd done nothing wrong. It was completely unfair that he was being put on the defensive like this. He took a deep breath before speaking again. "I was . . . taken aback when she did that. Hugged me. But—" He tried to remember. "I suppose I probably hugged back. It would have been awkward not to. But I assure you there was nothing inappropriate whatsoever. Shoot, Frank, you know Corinne. I would never do anything to jeopardize my marriage. Or this company. It—"

"I know, Jesse." Frank held up a hand. "Unfortunately, it's your word against hers at this point."

"So . . . what do we do?"

"Well, she hasn't actually filed with the State Department of Labor yet. This"—he tapped the papers in Jesse's hand—"is just a 'courtesy copy' to inform us of her intentions. And even if she does submit this to the Commission, that in itself doesn't constitute a legal complaint. You can see there at the top of the first page that this is just the preliminary step to making such a claim. Frankly, I doubt she takes this any further, but we do need to handle it with care in-house."

"What does that involve?" Jesse leafed through the papers and saw the phrases "improper advances" and "inappropriate touch" in Michaela's precise, flowing handwriting. The sick feeling returned with a vengeance.

"We'll need to meet with HR and with Michaela. See if we can iron things out. I need you to think this through though. Is there anything else we should know? We don't want her springing something on us unaware."

He blew out a breath and raked a hand through his hair. "I guess you should know that I talked to her on Wednesday. She'd called my cell phone Tuesday night, and I just wanted to establish that I didn't appreciate getting calls after work hours."

"She called you at home? Where did the conversation take place? Wednesday, I mean."

"I tried to meet with her in one of the conference rooms but they were all in use, so we talked in my office."

"Please tell me you left your office door open."

"Of course. But the conversation did not go well. She implied that I'd made advances toward her, and she accused Corinne of being responsible for me ending things with her, which is ridiculous because there was absolutely nothing to end."

"Ah . . . Well, that makes sense. Hell hath no fury and all that."

Like a woman scorned. He'd never once thought that old adage would have any place in his life. Adrenaline pumped through his veins as the realization dawned: he would have to tell Corinne everything. Whether it ever became public or not, he didn't want a secret like that between them.

And he knew how she'd feel when she discovered he hadn't told her anything that led up to this nightmare. Shocked. Betrayed. Suspicious.

The same as he would have felt if the tables were turned.

8

If you can get the girls buckled in, I can get the food." Corinne shut the refrigerator with one hip and stacked the salad bowl precariously atop the Tupperware that cradled her just-frosted Chocolate Heath Cake—Jesse's favorite.

Jesse snapped his fingers. "Come on, girls. Get your jackets and head for the car."

"But, Daddy," Sari whined, "Remember I lost my jacket. At school."

"Then grab a sweater or something."

"It's not even cold. Why do I have to wear a coat?"

"Because it will be colder when we leave Poppa and Gram's tonight."

"I'll just take my blanket."

"No, you won't," Corinne yelled from the kitchen. "Wear that yellow sweater Gram gave you. She'll like seeing you in it."

"It's too itchy."

"Sari!" Jesse snapped. "Go right now! You *do* what your mom says."

Corinne caught Sari's eye and shot her a look that said "you'd better get moving."

She appreciated Jesse backing her up, but he had been short with all of them since he got home from work twenty minutes ago. She knew things were stressful at his job, but she hated it

63

when he took it out on their daughters. Of course, she did the same thing when she was stressed. But it felt harsher somehow, coming from Jesse, who was usually so gentle and easygoing.

She carried the food out to the car, then came back in to help Jesse with the girls. His jaw was tight and he struggled with the zipper on Simone's jacket.

"Here . . . Let me get that." She knelt in front of the toddler.

He stepped aside and she quickly popped the zipper into place, then tied the strings on the little hood. Measuring her words, she looked up at him. "What's up with you?"

"What do you mean 'what's up?' "

She shook her head and looked pointedly at Simone, not wanting to argue in front of the girls.

He took a step toward the garage, but turned on his heel. "Hey."

She turned to face him, expecting an apology.

Instead he frowned. "We need to talk."

"Now?" They were already running late to get to her parents' house.

"Yes. We can talk more when we get home, but you need to know something. Now."

The tremor in his voice made her stop. She finished knotting the strings on Simone's jacket and stood, studying her husband's face. "What's going on?"

"Sari, you and Sadie take Simone out in the yard to play for a few minutes."

That made her breath catch. Something was up. Something serious.

When the girls were safely in the fenced backyard, Jesse pulled out a chair at the kitchen table. "You might want to sit down."

"What in the world is going on?" She sank into the chair, bracing her elbows on the table. The surface was sticky from lunch's peanut butter and honey sandwiches. She jumped up and wrung out a sour-smelling dishrag, wiped her elbow, then the table, before sitting down again.

Had Jesse been laid off from his job? That was the only thing she could think of that would make him so serious—oh, but wait . . . that girl from work. Michaela. *Oh please, God. No.*

She knew Jesse had seemed a little restless recently. But she'd figured work was just stressful. And he'd been traveling a lot. She'd always trusted her husband. Completely. But the phone call from Michaela . . . That had been odd. And what man wouldn't face temptation traveling with female colleagues who were younger and far more fascinating than she was?

Since Simone came along it was all she could do to get through a day getting everyone fed and clothed and laundry done. She'd turned into a frump, taking time to do her hair and makeup only on Sunday—if they even went to church on Sunday. Of course, Jesse always went because he taught a junior-high Sunday school class, but too often, it was just easier for her and the girls to stay home and play catch-up before the next crazy week steamrolled them.

In the space of a blink, her life passed in front of her and she saw her history with Jesse, their sweet romance, picture-perfect wedding, bringing each of the girls home from the hospital . . . Was this the moment her perfect life was going to come crashing down around her? Was it all going to end with something so ugly that she couldn't even bring herself to speak of it?

"Frank called me into his office today. He had some bad news. Strange news."

A trickle of relief wove a path through her. The way her imagination had filled in the blanks made unemployment seem like a picnic. "You got laid off?" she ventured softly, surprised at how much she hoped that was all it was.

"No. No, nothing that bad. But . . . I guess it has the potential to be." He bit his lip, the words apparently harder to say than he'd expected. "Apparently I've been accused of—sexual harassment." It sounded like he almost choked on the phrase.

"What?" Surely she heard him wrong. But this was too close to the nightmare her imagination had been toying with seconds earlier. "By *who*? On what grounds?"

Jesse propped his elbows on the table and rubbed his hands over his face. "I should have told you before, Corinne. I didn't think it was any big deal. I sure didn't think it would come to this."

"Told me what earlier?" A sudden image floated in her mind— that woman on Jesse's phone. The one who called him *Jess* and signed her texts simply M. "*Who* made the accusation, Jesse?" Her breath caught and she waited, hoping his answer could relieve the sick feeling in the pit of her stomach.

"Michaela Creeve."

"When?" She could hardly croak out the words. But she had to know. "When did it happen?"

"When we were in Chicago."

"Wait a minute." She scooted her chair back a few inches. "Something happened in Chicago? Or she accused you in Chicago?" That awful heaviness returned.

"No." He held up a hand. "I'm not being very clear. I just found out about her accusations. But in Chicago Michaela got pretty . . . familiar. A little too friendly for my taste. So when we got back, I—"

Corinne stiffened. "What do you mean, 'too friendly'?"

"Just . . . stupid little things. Like leaning on me. Touching me when she was talking to me and—"

"*Leaning* on you? *Touching* you? Where did she touch you?"

"Just . . . putting her hand on my arm. Or my shoulder. Nothing that I could really make accusations about, but it made me uncomfortable. And when I dropped her off at her car when we got back from the trip—she hugged me."

Her face must have conveyed something because Jesse held up a hand. "Even that was nothing inappropriate exactly. No different than the way your sisters hug me— Well, maybe more than that. I'm sure you would have considered it flirting."

"Yes, and you never see that. You never get when women are flirting with you until it's gone too far."

"I know. I know . . . I thought of how often you've said that. But it truly wasn't anything I could accuse her about. I tried to just ignore it, but then after she called me at your folks' house last week, I figured I'd better nip it in the bud."

"What did she want that night anyway?"

He shrugged. "I don't know. She never mentioned it at work and I didn't ask."

"And she's claiming sexual harassment for that? That's ridiculous!"

"Well, I think it's more than that."

She tilted her head and eyed him. "Like?"

"Wednesday morning I asked to meet with her. Just to politely ask her again not to call my cell phone outside of work hours. I tried to get a conference room—so no one would overhear and misunderstand. But they were all taken, so I called her into my office."

Corinne waited, trying to picture it all unfolding. Outside the window, she could hear their daughters' laughter. *Oh, to be so carefree and innocent again.*

Jesse sighed and gave a lopsided grin. "It didn't go so well. She said I gave her the 'wrong impression'"—he chalked quote marks in the air—"but I swear, Corinne, I have no idea what she's even talking about."

"So she thought you were coming on to her?"

He shrugged. "I guess. I didn't ask what she meant because I didn't want to know."

"Well, maybe you should have." She looked down and saw that her hands were shaking. She wanted to believe Jesse, but the fact that the first thing her mind had gone to—when he'd said he needed to talk to her—was Michaela . . . That had to mean something, didn't it?

"Corinne, I did not do anything remotely inappropriate."

"Then how can she be accusing you? What exactly is she claiming?"

"That I made inappropriate advances . . . of a sexual nature."

"You didn't though?" She held her breath, praying there wasn't more to this.

"Of course not. Corinne." His voice took on an edge, and she saw the hurt in his eyes. "You can't really mean that?"

"I don't know what to believe, Jesse. I must admit I thought it was odd that she was the one who called to tell me your flights were delayed—flying back from Chicago."

"I was on the phone with a client. We were about to board. I didn't want you worrying."

She did believe him . . . Didn't she? "Why didn't you tell me about this?"

"Because there was nothing to tell. Not really."

"Apparently there was." She hadn't intended her voice to sound so hard.

"I did nothing wrong, Corinne. This is all completely trumped up." He looked over her head at the clock on the dining room wall. "We're going to be late."

"I know." She scooted her chair back a few inches. "We'll talk more when we get home. I don't want to keep them waiting."

"I'm sorry, babe."

She tipped her head. "Why are you sorry?" Should she be reading some kind of confession into that?

"I'm sorry to have to drag you through this."

"Wait—is this going to be . . . public? Did she talk to someone else about it?" She hadn't thought about that aspect of it until this moment.

"I don't know. I hope not. But she filled out a form with some State commission."

"What?" Corinne tensed. "You mean she's accusing you . . . legally?"

"Frank says it's not legal yet."

"Yet?"

"She essentially filled out the forms and gave them to Frank . . . as a warning, he says. He doesn't think she'll even turn them in to the State. But he feels like they have to handle it in-house."

"What does that mean? Some kind of slap on the hand for you?"

He shrugged. "I honestly don't know."

"That makes me furious! Why should they take her word over yours?"

"I don't know, Corinne. But let's not worry before we have to."

Easy for him to say. She immediately felt bad for thinking it. This wasn't easy for him. Of course not. But it was no picnic for her either.

He pushed back his chair and stood. "We really need to get going. I'll get the girls. And we'll talk more tonight. I'll tell you anything you want to know. I just didn't want to go to your parents' without telling you—just in case rumors have already gotten around."

"Do you really think people will find out about this? About her accusations?"

"I hope not. But you know Langhorne. It is a small town. I wonder if I need to warn my mom? I'd hate for her to hear this from someone else."

She looked at the ceiling. "Oh, please, God. Don't let that happen."

"Believe me, I've been praying that all day."

All day? How long had he known about this?

But before she could ask him, Jesse came around the table and took her hands in his, pulling her up. He cradled her hands against his chest and leaned forward, touching his forehead to hers. She recognized his prelude to prayer. It comforted her to realize that it was a habit as ingrained in their marriage as their good-night kisses.

"Dear God," Jesse said, sounding strong and confident. "Just please help us get through this. Don't let it come to anything, but . . . just let the truth come out."

She felt the earnestness of his whispered prayer in his breath on her face, and in her heart. "Amen," she whispered.

God, help me to trust my husband. And please . . . let him be trustworthy.

9

Daddy, will you come down to the climbing tree with me and Sadie? Poppa said he's too old to climb trees."

Jesse laughed. Sari asked so sweetly that he hated to turn her down, but he'd promised to help Grant at the grill. "Not now, sweetie. I'm going to help Poppa with the steaks."

Right now climbing a tree sounded pretty good. He would like nothing better than to go hide out by the creek. And climbing a tree sounded like a good way to escape the scrutiny of Corinne's family. Much as he loved them, it could be disconcerting how well they read each other's moods—including his. And he wasn't ready to talk about what had happened at work. He was still hoping that the whole ugly mess would just go away and he'd never have to tell a soul. He and Corinne had agreed they wouldn't say anything tonight, but he knew it would be a tense evening for both of them.

"Did I hear something about climbing a tree?" Corinne's brother snuck up behind Sari and scooped her into his arms.

She giggled and twined her arms around his neck. "Will you go with us, Uncle Link?"

Link turned to Jesse. "You okay if I take them down to the creek?"

"Sure. I have no doubt you'll hear the dinner bell."

"Wouldn't miss it. And by the way, I already have dibs on the biggest steak."

"Not if I'm helping your dad man the grill, you don't." Jesse and his brother-in-law had been ribbing each other since the first time Jesse had driven out to pick Corinne up for their first date on a hot Fourth of July. Link had been a smart-aleck fourteen-year-old then, and in the process of showing off, had accidentally launched a firecracker at his sister's date. The Black Cat had somehow landed inside Jesse's collar before exploding, and he still had the burn scar on his chest to show for it. Corinne always said she would never have forgiven her brother if he'd scared off the love of her life.

He looked across the yard to where Corinne and her mother were talking on the front porch. Even from the distance, he could see the worry etching new lines on his wife's forehead. But she still looked beautiful to him. It would have taken a lot more than a wayward firecracker to change his mind about Corinne Whitman. Oh to go back to those simpler days.

The heady aroma of beef steaks on the grill reminded him of his promise to Grant, and he gave Link a quick salute and ambled to the grill where Grant was taming flames with a spray bottle.

"What can I do?"

"Hey, Jesse." Grant aimed the spray nozzle beneath the grate that held a dozen juicy steaks. He squeezed the trigger, and the flame sizzled and died down. "I think I just about have this fire whipped into submission, and the steaks will be ready in a few minutes. Audrey wanted to put some hot dogs on too; if you want to go in and get those, that'd be great."

"Will do." He was grateful for an excuse to escape. He'd tried to avoid his father-in-law tonight because usually the topic of conversation between the two of them was business. If he told Grant that things at Preston-Brilon were going well, it would be a lie, and if he said work was awful, there was no way he could avoid explaining why. He wasn't ready for that. Not until he and

Corinne got a chance to talk things over. If only this whole mess would just fizzle out . . .

Audrey and Corinne had disappeared from the porch, but he followed their voices into the kitchen where they were loading trays with condiments and bowls of potato salad and baked beans. They abruptly quit talking the minute he appeared. He tried to catch Corinne's eye, but she turned her back and busied herself with something at the sink. Surely she hadn't told her mother . . .

"Grant's ready for the hot dogs," he said.

"Oh . . ." Audrey motioned toward the fridge. "They're in the meat drawer. There should be a few brats in there leftover from last Tuesday if you want to put those on too."

Corinne moved to get something out of the cupboard, and he tried again to catch her eye, to give her an everything-will-be-okay look before he went back outside. She seemed determined not to see him. She and her mom had to have been talking about what had happened. Corinne hadn't agreed not to tell anyone, and he knew she and her mother were close. Still, he felt somehow betrayed. Neither of them knew enough about what Michaela's accusations—her intentions—even were to be talking about this outside of their marriage.

A fleeting thought nagged at him and he examined it as he walked back to deliver the hotdogs and brats to Grant.

What would his relationship with Corinne be like when the dust finally settled from Michaela's accusations? Could his wife forgive him? And if the situation had been reversed, would he forgive her?

<hr />

Corinne carried a tray laden with paper plates and cups full of ice out to the backyard where Dad had twinkle lights strung up in the trees and woven through the pergola. It was a perfect evening and she would have relished the chance to be with her extended family if not for the awful knowledge hanging over her head.

She'd managed to avoid Jesse's scrutiny—or at least to avoid meeting his gaze—most of the evening, but she was on pins and needles, afraid the subject of his job would come up as it nearly always did when the men started exchanging war stories.

The little girls had finished eating and begged permission to go play on the new tire swing Dad had put up in a corner of the yard. She glanced over and saw Simone toddling between the fence and the edge of the deck, chirping happily to herself. Sari was swinging, pumping with her spindly legs and leaning back so far her long honey-colored hair brushed the grass.

Corinne didn't see Sadie. She pushed her plate toward the center of the table. "I'm going to go check on the girls. Anyone want anything while I'm up?"

"I'll go," Jesse said. "Anyone need—" His cell phone rang before he could finish.

"I'll go." Corinne told him, trying not to roll her eyes at that infernal phone. And wondering suddenly if it was Michaela Creeve on the other end.

She slipped out of the picnic table bench seat and followed Jesse toward the house. She watched him check his phone and thought he looked puzzled—or was it distress on his face? He lowered his voice and she couldn't hear what he was saying, but guessed it must be about that woman's accusations.

She kept walking toward the house, her mind reeling. What was going on that they would call him after work hours? Or was it Michaela herself calling?

Her stomach clenched. Could there really be something going on between Jesse and that woman? She heard her daughters' voices and went around the side of the house to check on them. Simone was sitting on the ground, and Sari and Sadie stood over her doing something to her head. Imagining the girls' with Gram's scissors and Simone with a patchy haircut, Corinne jogged to where they were standing. "What are you guys doing?"

"Look at Simone, Mommy. She's a princess!" Sari stepped back to reveal the baby with a wreath of Virginia Creeper and wild-flowers on her head. Simone giggled and reached up to touch her crown.

Corinne laughed and curtsied. "Don't you look beautiful, Your Highness."

The older girls giggled and helped Simone to her feet. She toddled over to Corinne, but the wreath fell over her eyes and she stumbled. Corinne caught her and righted the wreath. Then gasped as she recognized a suspicious three-pointed leaf in the mix.

"Sadie, that's poison ivy!" She tossed the wreath to the ground.

"No, it's not, Mama. It's 'Ginia Creeper."

Corinne found a branch and hooked the wreath with it. "See the leaves. Remember about the points? This is Virginia Creeper . . . it has five leaves. See?" She counted aloud, pointing to each leaf tip. "But poison ivy has three leaves."

The girls counted them with her, keeping their distance from the leaves.

"When I was a little girl, Gram taught us how to remember." She recited the little chant in a sing-song voice. "Leaves of three, leave them be. Might be poison ivy." Wielding the stick like a fishing rod, she flung the wreath into the woods.

Simone burst into tears. "I want my *pwincess cwown.*"

Corinne knelt beside her, careful not to touch her skin. "Sweetie, we can't keep the crown. It might make you itchy and sick."

She looked to Sadie, suddenly suspicious. "Where did you girls get these vines? Poppa wouldn't let poison ivy grow near the house." She leveled her gaze between the two older girls. "You didn't go down by the creek, did you?"

"No, Mommy. We found it up here."

The look Sari gave her told all.

"Sadie. Look at me." She knelt and made her four-year-old look at her. "Did you go down by the creek?"

"No, Mommy. I told you—"

"Sadie, don't tell a lie." Sari propped her hands on her hips.

"I'm not," Sadie spat. "We didn't go by the water, Mommy. We just got the pretty leaves."

"She did too," Sari said, in full tattletale mode.

"Sadie, what have we told you about telling the truth?"

"We didn't go by the water."

"I don't care. You know you are not supposed to go anywhere near that creek without a grownup. And when I ask you a question, I expect you to tell me the truth." They'd caught Sadie in several lies recently. She didn't remember Sari going through that stage, but then Sadie seemed to invent stages as she grew.

"But Huckleberry was with us, Mommy. So we were safe."

"You listen to me." She drew the other two girls into the circle with Sadie and shook her index finger at each one of them. "You are not to go near that creek without a grownup. You could drown if you fell in the water." She shuddered at the thought. "Do you know what it means to drown?"

"It means we would be dead," Sari said soberly.

"But Mommy, Huck would save us. He would!"

"No, Sadie." She made her voice sterner yet. "Huck might be able to swim, but he is not a lifeguard."

Simone was still fussing about the loss of her *cwown*. "Don't cry, sweetie. We can make you a new crown that won't hurt you." She inspected the baby's forehead. No sign of a rash. *Yet.*

She turned to the older girls. "Hold out your hands. All three of you need to get in the house and in the tub. Don't you remember when you had poison ivy last summer, Sadie?"

Huck bounded up from the creek and ran circles around them. Corinne herded the three of them toward the house, but first Sadie raced over to where the wreath had landed and snagged it up.

"No, Sadie! Leave that alone. Those leaves will make you itch." She tossed the wreath aside again, which set Simone crying harder.

Corinne scooped her up, trying desperately not to get any of the sap from the leaves on herself. She'd never had the rash before, and as much as she and her siblings had played down by the creek when they were kids, she'd surely come in contact with the vine before, but there was always a first time. And that plant could be vicious.

Coming up the hill, she saw that Jesse was still on the phone. He looked up and noticed them, but was so intent on his call that he didn't acknowledge them.

"I need help, Jesse," she yelled.

He waved and, still talking into the phone, started for the house.

She had the bathtub in her parents' bedroom almost filled and had the girls stripped down by the time he finally showed up.

"What happened?"

"They got into poison ivy. Down by the creek."

"What were they doing down there?" The way he said it made it sound like he thought it was her fault.

"Can you please help me get them washed up? I wish I had some of that oatmeal soap. The one with tea tree oil."

"Do you want me to go ask your mom if she has some?" He swished a hand through the water, testing the temperature, then lifted the girls into the tub, one by one.

"No, there's probably something in here that will work." Corinne found washcloths in a cupboard along with a bar of one of Mom's fancy goat's milk soaps. The package claimed oatmeal as an ingredient. She started with Simone, gently washing her skin, hoping to get rid of every trace of poison ivy oil before it did any damage.

"Who were you talking to?" she asked Jesse, not looking up.

"On the phone?"

She nodded.

"Work stuff," he said. "I'll tell you later."

"Work work or . . . the other?"

"Not now, Corinne."

Which pretty much told her it was "the other." Was it Michaela he'd been talking to? Surely he wouldn't have stayed on the phone that long if it was her. Unless there really was something between them. She hated the suspicion that crept in again. She couldn't let herself think that way.

Jesse might be a bit of a flirt—that was just his personality—but she knew he wasn't even aware of how he came off sometimes. It was one of the things that made him a successful salesman. But she'd warned him more than once that some women might misinterpret his "friendliness" for something more.

She'd always been proud that her husband was usually the most desirable man in the room wherever they went. She'd secretly enjoyed the jealous looks other women gave her. She felt blessed that of all the women he could have had, Jesse Pennington had chosen her. But now she wasn't so sure.

And even if there wasn't anything between him and that woman, Jesse should have known better.

Mom popped her head in the door and frowned. "What happened?"

"They got into poison ivy."

Her mother huffed. "I told your dad he needed to get that taken care of."

"It was down by the creek, Mom. Not anywhere near the house. And they are in big trouble." She looked at the girls pointedly.

"Sari's gotten into it before without any reaction," Jesse said.

"I don't know about Simone though." Corinne searched under the sink for something to rinse the toddler's hair with.

"Hang on—" Mom disappeared and returned a minute later with a plastic pitcher and fluffy towels Corinne knew were meant for guests of the inn. She'd have to stay long enough to do laundry and scour the tub.

"Do you want some calamine lotion?"

"We have some at home," Jesse volunteered. "It won't do any good until they break out, will it?"

"Can we say unless they break out, please?" Corinne gave him a stern look. She finished rinsing Simone's hair, lifted her from the tub, and wrapped her in a towel. For a child who usually screamed while she got her hair washed, Simone was being strangely compliant. She wrapped her in a towel and gently combed through her damp, tangled locks. "What happened to your hair ribbons, baby doll?"

"She still had 'em when we were down at the creek," Sadie offered.

"Didn't you use Simone's ribbons to tie up your crown wreaths, Sadie?" Sari asked.

"Don't blame me," Sadie pouted. "I already got in trouble once."

"Well, you shoulda done what Mommy said and then—"

"Shh . . ." Corinne shushed them. "Stop fighting. It's no big deal. We don't need the ribbons right now anyway. Maybe Gram will find them when she cleans." Corinne stood Simone on the counter and finished drying her off, while Jesse dried the older girls.

"I'll go get these little yahoos into pajamas," he said, picking up a towel-clad daughter in each arm.

Sari squirmed and giggled. "We're not little yahoos, Daddy. We're little girls."

"You're big trouble is what you are."

"No, we're girls! Little girls." Sadie took up the cry.

"Well, you are little girls in big trouble."

"Huh-uh. We're not in trouble."

"Yes, you are." He turned serious. "Understand?"

They both nodded, appropriately subdued.

"I think you know why you're in trouble," he said. "But we'll talk about this later."

Corinne curbed a smile. She loved Jesse's way with their daughters.

But before he reached the bathroom door, Jesse's phone rang again, and Corinne quickly sobered. If only poison ivy was their worst problem.

Thankfully, he ignored the phone and let it go to voicemail.

A week ago that fact would have made her heart sing. Now it only made her wonder if it was Michaela Creeve on the other end.

10

The shower droned on the other side of the bedroom wall, and Corinne propped herself on one elbow in the bed and stared at Jesse's cell phone charging on his nightstand.

They'd never kept secrets from each other—at least she hadn't thought so—but they'd also never read each other's text messages or e-mails. There just wasn't any reason for it. But she was tempted now.

On the way home from her parents' last night she'd asked him again about the mysterious phone call, but he'd brushed off her question. The girls had been awake in the backseat, so maybe he just hadn't wanted to talk about it in front of them. But even though she'd pressed him, he'd claimed fatigue after they got home and had gone to bed early. Something wasn't right.

She reached for his phone and clicked the power on. Holding her breath, she listened again to be sure the shower was still running. Feeling like she was betraying a sacred trust, she pressed the phone icon and scrolled through a short list of voicemails. Jesse's penchant for tidiness applied to his computer and his phone, and there were only a handful of messages in the queue, including several from her.

She pressed the e-mail icon and scrolled quickly through those messages. Again there were only a handful, dating back a month or so. A few from the Preston-Brilon e-mail account, but all those were from other sales staff—men—whose names she recognized.

She scrolled further, letting relief replace angst when she found nothing to confirm her suspicions. But her heart dropped when Michaela Creeve's name appeared in the From field. She clicked to open the e-mail, feeling as guilty as she had the night she and Heather Garber had snuck out with Heather's big brother and driven over an hour to a forbidden movie at the drive-in in Piedmont.

Hey, Jess, some of the sales team is going to eat at Buca di Beppo tonight. Meeting in the lobby at six to walk down there, but if you'd rather just grab something in the hotel bar let me know.

M.

Jess? Maybe it was just a typo, but Corinne was the only one who had ever gotten away with shortening Jesse's name. He didn't like the nickname and usually politely corrected anyone who tried to use it.

She read the e-mail again and checked the date. It was the first time he and Michaela had been in Chicago at the same time. The message had come through Michaela's Preston-Brilon e-mail address and included her work signature, but that M. was in the same font as the typed message. It felt terribly personal. And why had Jesse not deleted this message? There were no other e-mails from that date saved—not even hers—and there was no address or other information in the message that Jesse would have needed to save.

Had Michaela been coming on to her husband, suggesting an intimate dinner for two? Or was this an innocent invitation to an alternative that several of the staff were opting for? There was no way to tell for sure, but it could easily be read either way. She scrolled further in the queue, searching for clues. Finding none, she clicked over to Jesse's text messages and began scrolling.

Many of them were merely phone numbers without names. She sat cross-legged on the bed, searching back through e-mail for Michaela's number to compare.

"What are you doing?"

She started at Jesse's voice and quickly slid his phone back on the nightstand.

He stared at her. "Is that my phone?"

She wracked her brain for a plausible excuse and came up empty.

"What are you looking for?" His tone was thick with suspicion.

She opened her mouth, but nothing came out.

He ran a towel over his wet hair. Barefoot from the shower and wearing only flannel pajama bottoms, he looked handsome and vulnerable. She was suddenly overwhelmed with love for him, and it broke her heart to think of confessing her distrust, of seeing the pained look in his eye when he realized that she'd doubted him.

And yet, looking at him, she could imagine what Michaela must feel for him. Strangely, she could even understand how easy it would be to be reeled in by the flattery of such a woman. To succumb to the temptation of someone who wanted him so desperately. Someone younger, more beautiful . . .

"I was reading . . . your e-mail." It came out in a squeaky whisper.

"Why? What are you looking for?" His voice was hard.

"I wanted to see what kind of stuff she's been sending you."

"What do you think she's sending me?"

She noticed he didn't hesitate to assume that *she* referred to Michaela Creeve. He picked up his phone and brought it to life, scrolling through as if it would show him what damage Corinne had done.

She let anger take over. Might as well get this discussion over with. It had to happen eventually. "All her phone calls to you . . . I just wanted to know what they were about."

"I told you what they were about. You couldn't take my word for it? And you say 'all her calls' as if there were dozens. She called me twice outside of work."

"Maybe we need to define outside of work." She looked pointedly at the phone in his hands. "You don't count her dinner invitations while you were in Chicago together."

"What are you talking about?" he said again.

She took the phone from him, quickly located the e-mail she'd read earlier, and handed the offending missive back to him.

He skimmed it, then met her eyes. "I ordered room service that night. And skyped with you and the girls."

She thought about the date. May 16. He was right. She remembered because Sari had been excited about the kindergarten field trip to Discovery Playhouse downtown.

"And you didn't go out with her later?"

He stared at her. "Are you actually accusing me of cheating on you?" There was the pain she'd dreaded seeing in his eyes. His beautiful blue-gray eyes.

"I'm not accusing. But what am I supposed to think?"

"What are you supposed to think?" His voice rose. "You're supposed to think that when I stood in the front of that church and promised to love you till death do us part, that I would keep my vow. That's what you're supposed to think. Have I ever given you reason not to trust me? Ever?"

"I'm not accusing, Jesse," she said again. "But . . . a woman doesn't just file a lawsuit like that without some reason."

"It's not a lawsuit. She hasn't even filed an official complaint. It's—" He threw the towel on the bed. "I don't have to stand here and listen to your accusations."

"Jesse, I said I'm not accus—"

"Save it." He turned on his heel and stormed from the room.

She watched his broad, tanned back disappear behind the slammed door. And she realized she didn't have a clue if his anger was that of a man betrayed by his wife's lack of trust or that of a traitor riddled with guilt.

He found her in the laundry room, stuffing damp towels into the dryer. She straightened and started, as if she hadn't heard him come in. Maybe she hadn't. It didn't matter, really. Except everything felt like a game now, and he was tired of playing games.

"Sorry," he said. "Didn't mean to scare you."

She ignored him and picked up the laundry basket, then glanced at the clock. "Aren't you going to work?"

"I'm going in a little late today. Can we talk? Please?" He took the laundry basket from her hands. "Where are the girls?" Sari had already left for school in the neighborhood carpool but he didn't hear the other two. "Is everybody still rash-free after their run-in with poison ivy?"

"Yes, I think we dodged that bullet. Simone's still sleeping. I let Sadie watch cartoons." She looked guilty.

"That's good. Can we talk this out, Corinne? I don't want this hanging between us."

She nodded. "I'll make coffee."

He put the laundry basket away in the hall closet and followed the smell of fresh-ground coffee to the kitchen.

She set up the coffeemaker and waited for it to brew. A few minutes later, she poured him the first strong mug and handed it to him. She set her own cup down on the kitchen bar and slid onto a bar stool, waiting for the machine to finish brewing.

He pulled out a stool and perched beside her.

She studied him like she was trying to predict their future. She looked like a scared puppy.

He wanted to set her mind at ease, and yet, remembering how he'd found her there on their bed, checking his phone messages as if he needed supervision . . . He fought the temptation to make her sweat a little. To get revenge for her distrust. Instead, he brushed a strand of hair from her forehead. "I understand why you might have questions. I'll answer anything you want to ask.

I'm an open book." He held out his hands and waited, watching her intently.

"I'm sorry, babe." Tears sprang to her eyes. "I shouldn't have said the things I did. And I'm sorry I got into your phone without asking. I really didn't mean to accuse you. I know you wouldn't do that to me. Or to the girls . . ."

"But?" There was obviously a "but" waiting.

"I guess I just want to know that you didn't do anything that she—Michaela—" She spoke the name as if it tasted bitter in her mouth. " . . . that she could have interpreted the wrong way."

"Maybe I'm clueless, but I honestly don't think so." He rehashed the events of the weekend leading up to Michaela's accusation, hating having to even remember it, yet knowing that Corinne needed to hear it. Again. And he tried not to leave anything out or candy-coat it. Because maybe he needed to examine his actions more closely, too.

When he finished, Corinne nodded. "Thank you. I suppose you need to be more careful, especially with women like her. But it honestly doesn't sound like you did anything that she should have interpreted the way she did."

"Well, if I did, I'm sorry. I know you've said before that I need to be more careful about stuff like that."

"Well, if you weren't so stinkin' good looking, you wouldn't be in this mess." She narrowed her eyes, but she was smiling that ornery smile he loved so much.

He opened his mouth to broach another subject, but immediately thought better of it.

But too late.

"What?" Corinne said.

"Nothing." He waved her question away.

"No . . . What were you going to say?"

"It can wait. It was a whole different subject. Let's get through one crisis at a time."

"You mean there's another one waiting when this one is over?" She looked truly distressed.

He laughed. "No. Not a crisis. Just an idea I've been toying with. But seriously, it can wait."

Simone's cries floated from the baby monitor on the counter.

"Saved by our little belle," he quipped.

Corinne slid off the high barstool. "Fine, but don't forget what you were going to say."

"Don't worry. I won't."

She cocked her head and studied him again.

"I won't forget. And seriously it's no big deal."

She shrugged and headed upstairs to get the baby.

Jesse sat at the bar counter listening to his wife chirp at Simone through the scratchy speaker of the monitor. Corinne was a wonderful mother to their daughters. She'd always wanted to be a stay-at-home mom, and—scary as it was financially—after Sari was born, he'd agreed it was a good thing for her to stay home with the baby.

Thankfully, by that time, his job allowed her to do that quite comfortably. And he was proud of that fact. But this whole thing with Michaela had only emphasized how trapped he felt in his job. How much he wished he could get out of sales. Change direction. In a very specific way.

But that was impossible. He never should have brought it up. And Corinne wouldn't forget. She'd ask him about it. And if he didn't have an answer, she'd think he was hiding secrets.

When would he ever learn to keep his mouth shut and keep his dreams to himself?

11

Corinne started to open the car door but caught a glimpse of her image in the rearview mirror and threw up a quick prayer that she wouldn't run into anyone she knew at the grocery store. She really was trying to do better about taking care of her appearance, but she'd been in the middle of a baking marathon when Jesse called to say he'd be a little late getting home from work and wouldn't be able to pick up Sari at her friend's house like they'd planned.

Sari had spent the night at Kaylee Morgan's house, but Kaylee's mom wasn't planning on Sari for supper, so she'd quickly loaded the two younger girls in the car and stopped at Schnucks to get a few groceries before heading to pick up Sari.

She and Jesse had reached a tentative peace, but she knew they wouldn't really get back to normal until the accusations hanging over him were resolved. She hated having to keep the ugly secret from her family. Jesse had accused her of talking to her mother about it, which she hadn't, but she had asked him for permission to share with her sisters. "I need someone to talk to about this, Jesse. Not to mention I feel like I'm lying to them every time I'm with them."

"Not saying anything isn't the same as lying," he'd argued at first. "You don't owe your sisters every detail of our lives."

"I'm not saying I owe them. I'm saying they know me well enough to know when something's not right. I'd just feel better if they knew what was going on with us. Besides, we could use their prayers. I trust my sisters completely not to tell anyone."

"Except their husbands. And then their husbands will trust *their* siblings, and sooner or later somebody in the chain will forget it's supposed to be a secret. I don't want this getting back to Mom."

"I don't think telling my sisters is going to get the news all the way to California. Besides, it's not like you did anything wrong, Jesse. Keeping it a secret makes it seem like you have something to feel guilty about."

"Well, I don't. But you know how rumors are in this town. And in the company. My department's sales depend a lot on my reputation, Corinne. You know that."

He'd finally relented, albeit reluctantly. But she hadn't wanted to tell Danae and Landyn over the phone, and between Landyn's understandable preoccupation with the twins and Danae's work schedule, she'd yet to find a time to get together with them.

Inside the grocery store she rejected two wobbly-wheeled carts before finding one that worked. She put Simone in the child seat and buckled her in and instructed Sadie to stay beside her. The girls behaved, but the logistics of trying to shop with two kids in tow were daunting. By the time they got to the produce aisle, she wished she'd just driven through for burgers and saved the grocery shopping for another time.

She gave Sadie the assignment of choosing half a dozen apples and held open a flimsy plastic bag for her to deposit them in. Unfortunately, the first apple her daughter chose was on the bottom of a precarious stack, and three apples toppled from the pile and went rolling on the shiny tile floor.

She was stooped over trying to corral three Honeycrisps and a Gala when she heard her name. She hoped she didn't have a hole in her yoga pants.

She looked up to see Michaela Creeve smiling down at her. "Don't you just hate it when that happens?"

She struggled to her feet, heaped the apples into her cart, and instinctively pulled Sadie to her side. She couldn't find a single appropriate greeting for this woman.

Michaela didn't seem to notice and held out a hand. "You probably don't remember. I'm Michaela Creeve. I work with Jesse."

Jesse had told her that Michaela was traveling this week, a fact that had seemed to greatly relieve him. Yet, here she stood. It was Friday, so maybe she'd caught an early flight, or come home late last night. But did that mean Jesse'd had to face her at work today? He hadn't mentioned the possibility.

Michaela wore dressy black pants with a pale pink tank under a white nubby silk jacket. And more bling than most women would wear to the office, but she supposed it could have been office attire.

Corinne wrangled the bruised apples into the bag one by one, pretending she didn't see the woman's outstretched hand.

"Looks like you have your hands full there," Michaela said. She tossed her head to send a strand of shiny blonde-streaked hair off her forehead, then bent to coo at the baby. "Hello there, sweet pea. You must be Simone."

Simone giggled and reached for the sparkly necklace dripping from Michaela's coppery neck.

The woman dodged her grasp, took a step back, and looked up at Corinne with a smile that was all sweetness and light. "Boy does this one ever look like her daddy. Just look at those eyes."

Seriously? Was this woman for real? Corinne tried to catch her breath. Had she somehow missed a memo? This was the woman who'd just filed a complaint of sexual harassment against Jesse, right? Was she now going to stand here and make nice, as if she hadn't tried to destroy their lives? Corinne was speechless, disoriented even, as if the blood had all run to her head while she was on her knees chasing apples.

Sadie tugged on the hem of Corinne's shirt—the garish green tie-dyed shirt that made her look like a watermelon with arms.

"She's pretty, Mama," Sadie whispered.

Great. Just great. Corinne met Michaela's gaze, willing her lip not to tremble and her eye not to twitch. The words that wanted to come forth strangled her. It took a supreme effort to travel the high road. But she looked Jezebel in the eye and forced her voice to remain steady. "Excuse us, please."

Trembling like the proverbial leaf, she put one hand on Sadie's back, and with the other, she steered the grocery cart past Michaela Creeve.

Before she did something she'd regret.

———

Corinne started out of the Schnucks parking lot, but she quickly realized she was in no shape to drive yet. She still could hardly believe that Michaela Creeve had been so brazen as to come up to her and act as if nothing in the world had gone on between them. She wanted to call Jesse, but she was afraid she'd just burst into tears the minute she heard his voice.

She opted to call her sister instead.

Danae answered on the first ring. "Hey, Corinne, what's up?"

"You will not believe what just happened."

"You won the lottery?"

"Ha ha, very funny. But seriously, are you home? Can I come over? There's something I have to tell you."

"Sure, I'm home, but what's going on? Are you okay, sis? You sound shook up."

"You could say that. But it's too long to explain on the phone. I don't suppose you could get Landyn over there, too?"

"Corinne! Are you pregnant?"

"Danae Brooks, shut your mouth! No! Oh, heaven's no." She instantly regretted her words. Danae and Dallas had tried for so long . . .

But her sister seemed—or pretended anyway—not to notice and only said, "What is going on, Corinne? You're worrying me."

"It's no big deal . . . Well, it is a big deal—a huge deal, actually, but—"

"Quit talking and get your tail over here. I'll call Landyn."

Corinne hung up, then called Kaylee's mother to see if Sari could stay there for another hour while she went to Danae's. Ten minutes later when she pulled into the Brooks's drive, Landyn's SUV was already parked in the driveway. Both her sisters met her on the front porch, eyebrows knit in identical frowns. She couldn't help giggling.

"What is going on?" Landyn asked, sounding a little miffed.

"Where are those babies?"

"They're sleeping. Chase is watching them, but I can't stay long. Spill, sister. What happened?"

"It's a long story and it will require caffeine. Can the girls play out back?"

"Sure."

Corinne called to Sadie and Simone who were turning cartwheels on the perfectly manicured front lawn. "Go around to the backyard to play, girls. Sadie, help Simone with the gate."

Sadie took the toddler's hand, and they ran around the side of the house, well familiar with Uncle Dallas and Aunt Danae's backyard with its garden shed Dallas had built and Danae had fixed up as a playhouse—one still waiting to be filled with children.

Corinne followed her sisters into the house and went to check out the back window to be sure she could see the girls. They were already on the front stoop of the little shed, chattering happily.

She plopped on the sofa in the cozy family room adjoining the small kitchen. "I don't even know where to start."

"Just start already," Landyn said. "What happened?"

While Danae brewed a pot of French press coffee and poured for the three of them, Corinne told her sisters about the accusations against Jesse. When she got to today's encounter with

Michaela, her sisters' incredulous yelps reassured her that she was justified in being so taken by surprise at the confrontation.

"I can't believe you didn't just smack her a good one right in the middle of Schnucks." Danae batted a sofa cushion to emphasize her point.

"Believe me, I wanted to. I wanted to run over her pretty little tush with my cart."

"What did Jesse say?" Landyn scooted to the edge of the overstuffed chair, in rapt attention.

"I haven't even told him about today. But hey, please don't say anything when we're together Tuesday night. He's embarrassed by this whole mess, and he won't want to talk about it in public."

Danae frowned. "I thought he was acting kind of weird last Tuesday."

"Yeah, me too," Landyn said.

"What do you mean? Weird how?"

Her sisters looked at each other, as if they'd already discussed this. Odd, since she thought Jesse had handled the evening pretty well, given the circumstances.

"He was just kind of . . . cool," Landyn said.

"*Cold* is more like it." Danae's frown deepened. "Even CeeCee noticed. You know how Jesse usually is—making the rounds to hug everybody before you guys leave. I didn't even know you'd gone home Tuesday night until Dad said something."

"Well, we were dealing with the girls getting into that poison ivy. That was probably why he didn't say good-bye." But she wondered. Was Jesse afraid even to give her sisters a brotherly hug now? It made her all the more furious at that woman. But the thought brought her up short. She was the one who'd lectured Jesse—again—about being too friendly. And Michaela Creeve proved her point. Still, anyone who knew Jesse knew he wasn't really a flirt. He was just friendly. And thoughtful and sweet and—

"Corinne?"

94

She realized Landyn had been saying something. "Sorry, what?"

"I asked if the girls were both okay. They didn't break out or anything?"

"What?"

"The poison ivy, silly."

"Oh . . . No, they're fine." Tears she couldn't seem to control flooded her throat.

"Corinne? What's wrong?" Danae put a hand on her shoulder. "Is there something else? What's going on?"

She fanned a hand in front of her face, trying to get a grip on her emotions. "I just feel like . . . Maybe I've made Jesse feel like this whole thing with Michaela was somehow his fault. Because he is always so friendly. But I don't want him to feel like he can't even hug you guys without feeling like it's some perverted . . ." Her voice broke and she fanned harder.

In a flash, Landyn jumped up and came to sit on the other side of her. Encircled by her sisters, she fell apart. Then just as quickly, she got the giggles. "This is stupid. I don't know why I'm so emotional."

"Of course you're emotional!" Landyn's voice rose an octave. "That stupid little witch messed with your man. Anybody would be upset. And Jesse Pennington is the last man on earth who deserves that kind of an accusation."

Danae clucked her tongue, sounding remarkably like CeeCee.

Corinne gritted her teeth. "I don't see how one woman can mess things up for our entire family! It just makes me furious." She fumbled in her purse for a tissue and blew her nose.

"It'll be okay, sis," Danae said. "Hopefully it'll all blow over and you'll be able to laugh about it someday."

She wasn't so sure about that, but she was comforted by the way her sisters had taken up for Jesse.

"Don't you worry. We've got your back." Landyn patted her shoulder as if to demonstrate the point.

"Thanks, you guys. That means the world. But I'm serious, please don't breathe a word to anybody about this. You know how small towns are. And of course, I don't mean your husbands." Thanks to Mom and Dad's example, Corinne and her siblings had always had an understanding that they'd never ask each other to keep anything from their spouses. "But truly, you guys, nobody else."

In unison, her sisters held up their fingers in a Girl Scout pledge—which sent all three of them into a fit of giggles.

Corinne looked between her sisters, so grateful they were here. The whole thing really did feel much less daunting now that they knew. She should have told them when this whole mess first started.

She glanced up at the clock and gave a little gasp. "Is it really after five already? I'd better round up the girls and go pick up Sadie." She glanced out the windows overlooking the backyard. The door to the playhouse was open and it appeared empty inside. She went to push aside the sheer curtain and peered through the glass, looking as far in each direction as she could see through the window. No sign of the girls.

She hurried to the back door off the kitchen and ran into the yard calling their names.

Her sisters joined her a few seconds later.

"Did anyone check in the front yard?"

"I'll go," Landyn said, already sprinting around the side of the house.

"They'd better not be in front," Corinne said. But knowing Sadie's ornery streak, she wouldn't put it past her. Danae's street wasn't busy, but the girls couldn't be trusted to watch for cars. She turned to Danae. "They didn't come inside while we were talking, did they?"

Danae shook her head. "I think we would have heard them. But I'll go check the house."

Corinne took one last trek through the backyard before running to the front.

Landyn stood with her hands on her hips looking down the street. When she spotted Corinne, she shrugged and shook her head.

Danae emerged from the front door with the same shrug.

An ominous knot lodged in the region of Corinne's heart. Where on earth had the girls gotten to?

"They're not in your car are they?" Landyn asked.

Corinne went down the driveway to check. The Pathfinder was empty.

12

I'll have to check on that and call you back, Mr. Hardtner." Jesse shifted the phone to his other ear.

His client launched into another diatribe, his strident voice droning in Jesse's ear. On his desk, his cell phone vibrated in silent mode, taking tiny hops across the blotter where he'd placed it before dialing Jerome Hardtner.

"Mr. Hardtner? Sir, I apologize for interrupting, but I need to let you go. I've got a meeting to get to." Which was true, although the meeting wasn't for another hour. "I'll call you back as soon as I hear from marketing."

He hung up before Hardtner could launch into another tirade on the state of the industry. It wasn't like the fate of the world rested on the sale of another vacuum sweeper.

He picked up his cell phone. It had already quit ringing, but he had a voicemail waiting from Corinne. She must have changed her mind about him picking up Sadie in town. He punched Play.

"Jesse. Call me *right now*."

The alarm in her voice made his heart rate accelerate. He didn't wait for the rest of her message, but punched Call. She answered almost instantly. "Corinne? What's wrong?"

"I can't find the girls!" She sounded frantic.

"What do you mean you can't find them? Where are you?"

"I'm at Danae's. They were playing in the backyard and . . . now we can't find them!"

"How long have they been missing?"

"We got here around four-thirty, and they went out to the playhouse. They were still there . . . I don't know . . . maybe twenty minutes ago. But when I went to get them to go home they were just . . . *gone*. We've searched everywhere."

"Well, they didn't just disappear." He tried to keep his voice steady, but already news headlines were flashing across his mind's eye—too many of them straight off the pages of the local news in recent years. But Corinne sounded like she was near hysteria. He needed to keep his head.

"You looked inside the house?"

"Yes, Jesse. We looked everywhere."

"Well, you couldn't have looked everywhere or you would have found them. Calm down. It doesn't help anything for you to flip out."

"That is not helpful. And I'm not flipping out," she said. "But we've got to find them, Jesse!"

"I know. I know, babe . . . I'm on my way." He grabbed his keys and jacket and headed for the parking lot. "Call me if they show up."

The girls couldn't have just disappeared. There had to be a logical explanation.

He drove like a maniac across town, making a quick call to cancel his meeting as he maneuvered through traffic. References to rush hour were usually a joke in this small city, but right now he would have given anything to clear the four lanes of traffic off the road.

He hit a red light half a mile before Danae's. At the same moment his phone rang. He fished the phone from his pocket, but didn't recognize the number. He wanted to ignore it, but decided that wouldn't be wise under the circumstances. "Hello."

"Mr. Pennington?"

"Yes?"

"This is Joan Morgan, Kaylee's mom? I'm sorry to bother you, but I haven't been able to reach Corinne. I was just going to let her know that we have to go to Poplar Bluff tonight, so we could easily drop Sari off on our way—if you don't mind if she stays for dinner."

"Wait a minute? Sari's with you?"

"Um . . . yes."

"Do you have the other girls? Are Sadie and Simone at your house?" He didn't think that was the plan, but he'd assumed Corinne meant all three of the girls when she said they were missing. She would have picked Sari up by now—unless he'd completely misunderstood. What was going on?

"No . . . " Kaylee's mom hesitated. "Only Sari is here . . ." Her tentative tone told him he was confusing the poor woman.

But no one was more confused than he was. "Um . . . I think that would be fine for Sari to stay for dinner. I'll talk to Corinne and get back to you for sure, but just plan on it unless we let you know otherwise."

The light turned green, and he gunned it, calling Corinne as he drove on.

Again, she picked up instantly.

"Did you find them?"

"No! Where could they be, Jesse? They were right in the backyard. It's like they've disappeared into thin air."

"You're just talking about Sadie and Simone, right? Sari's friend's mom just called and—"

"Sari! Oh, no! I forgot all about her. I was supposed to go pick—"

"No, it's okay . . . I made arrangements." He made a mental note to call the woman back the minute they found the girls. "Listen, I'm almost there. Talk to you in a minute."

He clicked off without waiting for a response. Was Corinne losing it? First she "lost" their two younger girls, and now she seemed to have completely forgotten about their oldest daughter. She was easily distracted when she was with her sisters. It drove him a little nuts, but he was used to it, and besides, the girls often played in their Aunt Danae's backyard playhouse. They knew to stay in the yard and away from the street.

An image flashed on the screen of his mind: the girls down by the creek behind the inn on Chicory Lane. They knew better than going near the water by themselves, too. But Corinne said Sadie had done so anyway—and then tried to lie about it. The memory gave him strange comfort. Maybe this was the same, and they'd just ventured outside Danae's yard and gotten lost in the neighborhood.

A minute later, he turned into Dallas and Danae's neighborhood, winding his way through streets where tricycles and skateboards littered every other driveway and children played on front porches.

He started to crank the steering wheel to turn onto the cul-de-sac where Corinne's sister lived, but something made him look down the street running the opposite direction.

He did a double take. *What in the—*

⊙━✦━⊙

"Where *is* he?" Corinne wrung her hands and resisted the urge to call Jesse again.

Danae and Landyn had gone back inside to search the house once more. But they'd already searched from top to bottom, even to the point of looking under mattresses and inside the laundry hamper. But there was no way the girls could have come in without her and her sisters hearing.

Hot tears stung her eyes. "Oh, God, help us! Help us find them." It had only been thirty minutes, but she was about ready to call the police. If they didn't find the girls by the time Jesse got here, she would. And she'd have to be honest about how distracted she'd been because of the encounter with Michaela. She should have checked on them more often. Sadie was only four. It was one thing to let them play outside if Sari was with them. But even in Danae's safe, fenced-in backyard, it hadn't been wise to let the two little ones play alone.

Landyn came out the front door, purse on her arm. "Corinne, I *hate* to do this, but Chase called and the babies are awake. I didn't leave any formula for him and besides, I'm about to bust." She crossed her arms over her chest.

"I understand. You go."

"Call me the minute you find them."

"I will."

"I'll be praying." Landyn jogged to her car and pulled away from the curb without looking back.

"Sure," she whispered. Corinne understood her sister needing to get back to her nursing babies, and yet resentment stabbed at her. How could Landyn just walk away when for all they knew something unspeakable had happened to Sadie and Simone?

She felt another wave of hysteria coming on and shot up another prayer. She could not fall apart. She had to keep looking. Like Jesse'd said, the girls had to be out there somewhere. Tonight they'd be shaking their heads at the whole ordeal—and likely doling out some serious consequences for two disobedient little girls. She grabbed onto that thought as if it were a lifeline.

13

Jesse pulled the car to the curb and threw open the door. "Sadie!"

He scrambled across a manicured lawn, not caring if he'd trampled someone's prize rose bush in his race to get to his daughters. What in the world they were doing out here, at least two blocks from Danae's home, he couldn't fathom. And they had to have crossed the wide street to get to where they were.

A teenager roared through the intersection on a motorcycle without looking one way, let alone both, and a sick feeling roiled in his gut. "Sadie!" Jesse yelled again.

Corinne had to be beside herself by now. He should call her, but he was afraid his little Houdinis would escape again if he didn't capture them and get them in the car.

He sprinted toward the girls. As he came up behind them, huffing and out of breath, he realized Sadie was talking to her sister. He slowed to listen.

"We gots to get back to Aunt Danae's house 'cause Mommy said we should stay in the fence."

Simone toddled beside her, sucking her thumb.

"Sadie."

She let loose of Simone's hand and turned. "Daddy! Are you going to Aunt Danae's house with us?"

He scooped Simone into his arms. Her shoes were muddy and untied, but she seemed fine. He knelt to look Sadie in the eyes. "What are you and Simone doing out here?"

"We just— Simone, quit kickin' Daddy's pants. You're gonna get them all dirty."

"Sadie? Did you hear me? What are you girls doing out here?" The cocktail of terror and relief made his voice sharp, and seeing tears spring to his daughter's eyes, he forced a calm he didn't feel into his voice. "How did you get here?" He looked around, trying to judge how far they must have walked from Danae's.

Sadie followed his line of sight. "That nice lady took us for a ride. We were just walkin' back."

"What nice lady?"

"That *lady*. You know, from the grocery store."

"No, I don't know. What lady are you talking about?"

"That pretty lady that was at the grocery store. 'Cept Mommy doesn't like her. But she's nice and we went for a ride with her, and then she . . . dropped us off. Yeah, she dropped us off."

"What is her name?"

Sadie shrugged.

"Okay . . . let's get in the car. We'll talk about this later."

Sadie seemed relieved to end the conversation, but Jesse didn't have a clue what she was talking about.

He glanced at his watch. He had a meeting back at the office in half an hour. He hoped Corinne could shed some light on how on earth his little girls had ended up almost three blocks away without her knowledge.

⌀—✦—⌀

Corinne made one last trek around the outside of Danae's house. But it was futile. They hadn't turned up so much as a clue, and as the seconds ticked off the clock, she began to lose hope.

Danae was inside calling the neighbors on each side of them and across the street to see if they'd happened to see the girls. If they didn't find them by the time Jesse got here, she was going to call the police. Maybe she should have called earlier, but she'd been so sure the girls would turn up any minute. It had been more than thirty minutes now. And where was Jesse? He'd said he was almost there, but that had been close to ten minutes ago.

She tried to comfort herself with memories of people she knew who'd lost their children briefly in the supermarket or at the park. She didn't think any of those moms had gotten scared enough to call the police, but she wasn't sure.

Mom often told a story about how Tim and Link had scaled the climbing tree one summer and perched among the upper branches. While the entire family called their names and practically tore the property apart looking for them, her brothers had kept silent, hiding, and enjoying the little drama they'd created.

Tim and Link had been older than Sadie and Simone were now, but Sadie just might pull a stunt like that. But she could only get so far with Simone in tow. Still, the thought made her look up into the branches of the oak tree in Danae's front yard.

Nothing. They had to do something. They couldn't keep searching the same places over and over without—

A familiar horn blared from the street. Corinne looked up to see Jesse rolling into the cul-de-sac. As he got closer, she saw movement in the backseat of his car. And when he opened his car door, smiling broadly, the relief that flooded her nearly took her to her knees.

Thank God! Thank you, Jesus. She ran down the driveway to his car and ripped open the back door. "You found them! Where have you been, Sadie?"

"Mommy, Daddy brought us home."

"I know he did." She straightened and looked over the roof of the car at Jesse. "Where were they?"

"Let's get in the house and we'll talk." Jesse's tone said somebody was in trouble.

She nodded and went around to unbuckle Simone from the backseat. Danae met them on the driveway and immediately called Landyn to let her know the girls had been found. Still talking to Landyn, she carried her cell phone into the kitchen, leaving Corinne and Jesse on the driveway with the girls.

"What's the deal?" Corinne asked, grateful for a chance to talk to Jesse out of her sister's hearing. She lifted Simone and hitched her up on one hip.

Jesse gave her a look before squatting down on the concrete drive. He pulled Sadie close. "Tell Mommy what you told me."

She shrugged. "I don't know."

"Sadie, look at me." He took her face between his palms. "This is important. Tell us why you weren't in Aunt Danae's yard when Mom came looking for you."

She glanced up at Corinne with a look Corinne couldn't decipher, but guessed was guilt.

Sadie turned back to Jesse. "I already told you. That lady took us for a ride."

"What lady?" Jesse shot Corinne a just-listen-to-this look.

"I *told* you, Daddy—the lady in the grocery store."

Corinne set Simone down on the drive and knelt beside Jesse. "What lady, Sadie?"

Sadie couldn't seem to look either of them in the eye. "That lady you were talkin' to. That pretty one."

"Which lady? The clerk?" Fear slithered up her spine and coiled in the center of her chest. *It couldn't be. Could it?*

Jesse frowned and looked to her for answers. She rose, not sure her legs would hold her. "We saw your . . . *coworker* at Schnucks this morning."

Jesse frowned like he didn't get her meaning, but then she saw understanding slip into his expression. "Sadie, are you saying Michae—that lady—came to Aunt Danae's house and took you girls? In her car?"

Feeling physically ill, Corinne knelt to be eye level with Sadie again. "Are you sure she came here, Sadie? You saw her?"

Their daughter nodded.

"What did she say to you, sweetie?" Corinne asked, working to keep her voice level as fury rushed in to crowd out her fear.

"Wanna go for a ride? That's what she said."

"And you said *yes*?" Corinne's voice rose. "Sadie! You know what we've told you about talking to strangers. You shouldn't even—"

"But she *wasn't* a stranger, Mommy. I saw her when we were gettin' groceries. She talked to me and Simone, remember? She was nice. And she was pretty."

"I don't care how pretty she was." It was all Corinne could do to keep it together. "Why on earth would she do that?"

She'd meant the question for Jesse, but Sadie shrugged and replied. "I don't know—"

"I wasn't talking to you." It came out harsher than she intended and Sadie's face crumpled.

Simone toddled over and looked up from one to the other, obviously confused by their strident voices. Corinne embraced a daughter with each arm. "I'm sorry, Sadie. I didn't mean to snap at you."

Danae came down the sidewalk from the house, and Corinne stood quickly, avoiding Jesse's questioning look. She scooped Simone up and handed her off to Danae. "Would you mind taking the girls inside for a minute?"

"Sure. Is everything okay?"

"I'm not sure. I . . . need to talk to Jesse," she whispered. "Sadie claims that Michaela Creeve put them in her car and took them for a ride." Putting it into words like that made it sound completely crazy.

"What!" Danae apparently thought so too. "You have got to be kidding me! You need to call the police, Corinne. She must be insane!"

"The girls are fine. See if you can get Sadie to give you some details. I have to tell Jesse what happened at the store first."

"Okay," Danae said reluctantly. "Come on, girls, let's go inside."

Feeling like she was walking to the gas chamber, Corinne turned to face Jesse.

He waited by the car with his hands tucked in his pockets. "What's the deal?"

"Michaela Creeve came up to me in the grocery store this afternoon. She acted like there was nothing in the world between us and was making goo-goo eyes at the girls and telling them how much they looked like their daddy. It was all I could do not to punch her out."

"She didn't say anything about the complaint she's filed?"

Corinne shook her head. "Not a word. She was sickeningly nice."

"You didn't say anything to her, did you?"

"No . . . I was nice." She rolled her eyes. "Far be it from me to say anything harsh to the woman who's accused my husband of sexual harassment."

"Corinne . . ."

"Don't worry. I was nice. But it was hard."

"Wait a minute. Sadie's saying it was *Michaela* who took them for a drive?"

"Yes, I think that's exactly what she's saying."

Jesse shook his head. "Why would she do that? And then drop them off three blocks from Danae's? That doesn't even make sense."

"Does anything that woman has done make sense?"

He released a breath. "Good point. But this is . . . over the line."

"You don't have to tell me that. And I thought you said she was out of town this week." She hadn't meant to sound accusing, but she knew it had come out that way.

"She was." His eyes narrowed. "I haven't seen her in the office all week, if that's what you're implying."

"I wasn't implying anything. But why is she suddenly back in town . . . *abducting* our daughters? I think we should call the police, Jesse."

He raked a hand through his hair. "But what if it wasn't her? It would look like I'm just trying to get back at her for her accusations against me."

"Who else could it be, Jesse? Sadie was gushing about how pretty Michaela is. She even told her that at the grocery store. And that's exactly how she described her."

"We need to grill Sadie. Find out what kind of car it was. Maybe find a picture of Michaela to show her."

"Jesse," she said again. "Who else could it be? It's too weird to be a coincidence."

He nodded. "I guess it is. But let's talk to Sadie again before we do anything rash. We have to be sure before we go making accusations."

She stared at him. Was he so determined to keep this business about Michaela under wraps that he would put his own daughters in jeopardy? If Michaela Creeve would do this, who knew what else she was capable of?

Maybe this was only a warning. What if that woman—she gasped. "Sari! I was supposed to pick her up"—she checked the time on her phone—"an hour ago!"

But Jesse put up a hand. "No, it's okay. I talked to Kaylee's mom. They invited Sari to have supper with them. But they're bringing her home afterwards, so we'd better touch base and see what time that will be."

"Call her right now, Jesse. What if that woman—" She exhaled. She could not bring herself to use her given name. "What if she goes after Sari too."

"How would she even know where Sari is?"

"How did she know the girls were *here*?"

"She probably followed you from the store."

"That is just creepy, Jesse. If you're not going to report this, I am!"

He panned the cul-de-sac street as if he'd find a solution there. "Maybe we should talk to some of the neighbors . . . see if they saw anything. Why don't you and Danae do that, since she knows them. And I'll see what I can get out of Sadie."

"No, I think I should talk to her. You weren't at the store, so you won't know what . . . *Michaela* . . . was wearing or what she said to the girls."

"You're right," he said. "Maybe Danae won't mind talking to the neighbors while we question Sadie together."

As they headed into the house, Corinne couldn't help but think that her having told her sisters would be the least of Jesse's worries now. Once they contacted the police, Jesse's "secret" would be all over the news.

14

"Where are you going, Aunt Danae?" Sadie asked.

"I'm just going next door for a few minutes. I'll be back, sweetie."

"Can't I go with you?"

"No, you stay here," Jesse said. "Mommy and I need to talk to you."

"No fair! How's come Simone gets to go with Aunt Danae and I don't?" She pooched out her bottom lip.

"Come on, Sadie. Right now." Jesse grasped her shoulder, more roughly than necessary. "Thanks, Danae."

With Simone in tow, Corinne's sister waved and ducked out the back door, looking relieved not to have to be involved in Sadie's questioning. Jesse couldn't blame her. The whole scenario was so bizarre he wished *he* wasn't involved. In any of it.

But he was. And he was at least partly to blame. He sighed. If only he could go back and turn a cold shoulder to Michaela Creeve the very first time she'd batted her curly eyelashes in his direction. But he'd never dreamed she would take her flirtations this far—to the point of stalking his family. For all he knew, she may have been following him or eavesdropping on his conversations.

That she might have harmed one hair on the heads of his precious daughters . . . The thought took the very breath from him.

He stretched out his arms and pulled Corinne and Sadie into a hug. "Let's go sit in the living room."

He and Corinne settled on a sofa and Sadie climbed into the overstuffed chair across from them. She looked so small and vulnerable. Feeling the need to proceed with great care, he took Corinne's hand and one of Sadie's. Corinne took Sadie's other hand, closing the circle.

She wrinkled her nose. "How's come we're prayin'?"

Corinne squeezed Jesse's hand, then leaned across the coffee table. "I know it's hard to understand what's going on, sweetie, but we need to help you understand. That woman should not have picked you up in her car. And you know better than to go with strangers!"

"But, Mommy, she wasn't a stranger. *You* talked to her. At Schnucks."

"That doesn't—"

"Sadie . . ." Jesse gently touched Corinne's arm. "I already talked to you about that. Just because Mommy or Daddy talk to someone doesn't mean they aren't a stranger. You should not have gone with the lady from the store. But we're not going to talk about that right now. Mommy and I need to ask you some questions and we need you to think really hard before you answer. It is very important that you think about your answers and be sure about what you tell us. Do you understand?"

She nodded soberly, and he despised what Michaela's actions were putting them through.

"First of all, did the lady tell you what her name was?"

Sadie shook her head.

"What did she look like?"

Sadie huffed. "I told you. Like that lady at Schnucks. The one Mommy doesn't like."

Corinne frowned. "Sadie, why do think I don't like her? I never said that."

"'Cause you were goin' like this—" Sadie furrowed her brow and stuck out her jaw.

Corinne glanced at Jesse and cringed.

He ignored her and turned back to Sadie. "Tell us what the lady looked like."

Sadie launched into a detailed description, right down to a spangled watch Jesse had seen Michaela wear to work often. One glance at Corinne told him Sadie had it spot-on. Of course, they'd seen Michaela earlier today, so the grocery store encounter might be where she'd gotten her accurate details from.

"Did she come up to the fence and talk to you, or did she come into Aunt Danae's yard?"

"She'd better not have!" Corinne huffed under her breath. "She'd have had to walk in front of the house in broad daylight to go in by the side gate."

Corinne was right. Other than going through the garage, there was only one easily accessible entrance to the backyard. But he nudged her. He didn't want to sway Sadie in either direction. They needed to get to the truth here.

Sadie looked from Corinne to him and back. "Me and Simone were just playin' in the playhouse and she came up and said, 'Ya wanna go for a ride?' and so we did."

"She came in the yard?"

Sadie nodded. "She was smilin' and talkin' about how cute Simone was and then she said 'Ya wanna go for a ride?'"

He and Corinne exchanged a look.

"Where did she say she was taking you on this ride?" Jesse asked.

Sadie shrugged with an expression that was quickly growing exasperating.

"She didn't say?"

"I don't know. I can't 'member." She put her thumb in her mouth, a habit she'd abandoned before Simone was born.

He gave her arm a gentle tug. "Sweetie, take your thumb out of your mouth so we can understand you."

Sadie complied with her head bowed.

"What did you talk about while you were riding with her?"

"Did she buckle Simone up?" Corinne asked.

Sadie pounced on that, scooting forward in the overstuffed chair. "No, she didn't buckle neither one of us. That was bad, wasn't it, Mommy?"

"What did you talk about with her?" Jesse repeated, bracing himself for what the answer might be.

"She just said how Simone was cute and how she looked like you, Daddy."

"That's what she said at the store," Corinne whispered. "How much Simone looked like you."

"Did she say where she was planning to take you?"

"Just—for a ride."

"I know, but where to?"

"I dunno."

"Why did she drop you off across the street?" He pointed through the front windows in the direction where he'd found the girls wandering. "Did you go anywhere first?"

Sadie shook her head.

"Did you ask her to drop you off?"

"No. She just did."

"Did she show you how to get home?" Corinne asked. "Did she point toward Aunt Danae's house or give you directions?"

"No. She just drove off."

Jesse floundered to think of questions that would help them decide what to do. "What color was her car, Sadie?"

"Um . . . I think it was . . ." She looked at the ceiling. "Do you mean inside or outside?"

"Either one."

"It was . . ." Again, she looked at the ceiling as if the answer might be up there. "It was white. Yeah. It was white."

Corinne raised her eyebrows in question at Jesse. He gave a half nod. Michaela drove a cream-colored Chrysler sedan, but Sadie might consider that to be white.

"White on the outside?"

"Uh-huh." Her thumb headed toward her mouth, but she caught herself and put her hand back in her lap.

"What color was the inside?"

"I don't know. I think . . . I think it was . . . pink?"

Jesse frowned. "The inside of her car was pink? Are you sure?" He'd never ridden in Michaela's vehicle, but he was pretty sure it wasn't pink.

"Sadie, where did you sit in the car? And where did Simone sit?"

"Um . . . I sitted in the backseat and Simone sitted in the front."

"And Michae—" He stopped himself. "The *lady* didn't buckle either one of you in?"

"Well, maybe she buckled Simone in. I can't 'member. She got the ribbon out of her hair."

He and Corinne exchanged looks.

"What do you mean, sweetie?"

"Simone's ribbon was fallin' out and she got it. So it wouldn't get lost."

"Who got it? Do you mean the lady took the ribbon out of Simone's hair?" Corinne pressed.

"It was *fallin'* out," Sadie repeated.

"Did that lady tie it back in Simone's hair?"

"I don't know." The thumb went back in her mouth.

Simone was constantly losing hair ribbons. Jesse remembered Corinne putting Simone's hair in a ponytail this morning—with a lime green ribbon to match her outfit. "Did she have the ribbon in her hair when you got here to Danae's?" he asked Corinne.

She pursed her lips, thinking. "I don't remember. I think I would have noticed if it had fallen out, but I couldn't be sure."

He made a note to look for the ribbon.

"Did the lady talk to you?" Corinne asked Sadie gently. "Did she ask you any questions?"

Jesse couldn't tell from her tone whether Corinne was beginning to doubt Sadie's story, but he certainly was.

"Did she ask about me and Daddy . . . ? While you were in her car?"

Jesse cringed. She was making this too personal. He wished Corinne would just let him ask the questions. Poor Sadie was confused enough as it was.

"I don't know," Sadie said. "I think she did."

"What did she ask?"

The shrug again.

Jesse patted Corinne's hand. "That's probably enough for now, babe."

"Jesse, we have got to—"

"Corinne, that's enough." He saw in the taut line of her jaw that he would pay for speaking to her that way—but she was just complicating things, and he was starting to think Sadie was inventing things as she went.

Corinne shot him daggers, then rose and went to Sadie. "If you think of anything else—anything the lady said or did—you need to let us know, okay?"

Again, that shrug.

Corinne knelt in front of her daughter. "This is important, Sadie. Do you understand?"

"Can I go play with Aunt Danae now?"

"Sadie, look at me. This is very important. Do you understand me?"

"Yes. Can I go play now?"

Jesse stepped in. They'd grilled her enough. "Yes, go play, but you stay in the backyard—"

"I'll get the crayons." Corinne looked at Jesse like he'd just suggested their daughter go play in traffic. "You can color at the kitchen table."

"Mommy and I will be right in here if you need anything, okay?"

Sadie nodded and followed Corinne into the kitchen.

When she came back a minute later, she was in full attack mode. "What are you doing?" she spat. "Why did you stop ask—"

"Grilling her?"

"What's that supposed to mean?"

He didn't want to fight. This was not the time. He made an effort to soften his tone. "It seemed like she was just—making things up."

"What? You don't believe her? Seriously?"

"I don't know what to believe. But I'm pretty sure the interior of Michaela's car isn't pink."

"Could it be—tan? Sadie might call that pink. And you know . . . she was wearing a pink shirt. Michaela, I mean. Maybe that's where Sadie got the pink."

He shook his head. "Exactly. Except for the car, all the details Sadie is 'recalling' could apply to your encounter with Michaela at the grocery store. I'm starting to think she just pulled someone out of the hat to blame, and Michaela was the most convenient— most recent—person she remembered. Especially if she sensed you didn't like Michaela."

"So how did the girls get all the way out there?" She punched a finger in the direction of where they'd had been found.

"They probably walked."

"Sadie maybe, but could Simone have walked that far?"

"Are you kidding? Twice." He gave a humorless laugh. "You've said yourself that you couldn't catch her if she got too much of a head start on you. I hate to say it, Corinne, but I'm starting to think our sweet daughter made up an elaborate story to keep from getting in trouble for running off."

Corinne seemed to consider that. But then her expression turned resolute again. "But you were leading her with your questions, Jesse. She felt threatened. Shoot, *I* felt threatened."

"If anyone was leading her, it was you. *I* was just testing. Trying to catch her in her lies if indeed they were lies. I haven't been in Michaela's vehicle, but I can tell you, it's not pink. And why would

Michaela put Simone in the front seat? And not buckle them in? Too many things don't add up."

"The question is, why would she kidnap them in the first place?"

He glanced toward the back of the house. "I'd be careful throwing that word around."

"Well, it's what she did, Jesse. For all we know she had no intention of bringing the girls back. Or maybe she was going to use them as a bribe. Who knows what she's capable of?"

"I'm just saying we need to be sure before we make any accusations. This is already a sticky situation. If we take our four-year-old daughter's word for this and accuse Michaela of 'kidnapping' our daughters—and it turns out not to be true?" He blew out a long sigh. "That could have serious implications, Corinne."

"And *this* doesn't?" She stood looking at him as if he were out of his mind. "Why would Sadie lie about this, Jesse?"

"Why did she lie about the poison ivy, down at the creek? She's afraid she's in trouble. We've both yelled at her. Not that she shouldn't be in trouble. Remember how she told you she didn't go near the water, and then when you caught her in her lie, she changed her story to 'Huckleberry could have saved us'? She's a pretty creative little storyteller, Corinne. Especially if it will get her out of hot water." He found great comfort in the realization.

"Yes, but what if you're wrong, Jesse?"

He opened his mouth to respond, but the back door opened just then, and Danae came in with Simone, shaking her head. "Nobody saw anything. All but the Hodges were at work when it happened."

"Mommy!" Simone lurched for Corinne.

"Hi, sweetie." Corinne took the toddler from her sister's arms.

Jesse looked at his watch. "I'm not sure what to do. We can't accuse somebody of kidnapping on the word of a four-year-old. Especially when the girls are safe with us."

"We can't just do nothing either, Jesse."

"I know. I'm not saying do nothing. But I don't think it's quite so urgent since the girls *are* okay."

"Then what do you propose we do?"

He scrambled for an answer. The truth was, he didn't have a clue what to do. If the whole mess with Michaela's charges against him hadn't been an issue, he would likely be, at the very least, questioning her. But that mess *was* an issue. A big one.

He scratched his head. "Maybe I should talk to people farther up the street between here and where I found the girls. See if anyone might have seen them walking."

Danae's puzzled look reminded him that she didn't realize his doubts about whether Sadie was telling the truth. He filled her in.

"You could take one side of the street and I'll take the other," Danae suggested. "Or I can stay with the kids if you'd rather go, Corinne?"

"No. I'm too emotional."

"Of course you are," her sister said. "I'll go. I'm glad to. I don't know many people on down the street, but it's a pretty friendly neighborhood."

"Okay," Jesse agreed, dreading having to explain the situation to strangers. But it was better than risking a false accusation—and having to make the news public.

Corinne put her hand on Simone's head and gave a little gasp. "Jesse, look." She brushed Simone's hair back from her face and pivoted so Jesse could see where she was pointing. She turned to her sister. "Danae, do you remember if Simone had a ribbon in her hair when we got here?"

Danae closed her eyes as if trying to recall the image. "I really don't remember. What color was it?"

Jesse looked at his daughter's flyaway hair and knew exactly what Corinne was getting at. The thin strand that was left of her ponytail was barely held in place by a tiny covered rubber band. No green ribbon. No ribbon at all.

A chill went through him. But he tried to reassure Corinne. "It doesn't really prove anything, Corinne. She's always losing her ribbons."

"Maybe. But are you willing to just dismiss it? This scares me to death, Jesse."

"I know." He pulled her and Simone into a hug. "I know, babe. It scares me too. But the girls are okay. They're safe. And we're going to get to the bottom of this. I promise you."

15

Jesse went in to the office the next morning to make up for the work he'd missed yesterday, and Corinne decided to drive out to the inn and let her parents know what was going on, in case things escalated with Michaela.

She kept her eyes on the familiar country road that led to her parents'. In the seats behind her, the girls giggled and chattered at a high-decibel level. But that wasn't the source of the confusion that nearly paralyzed her. A quiet, peaceful vehicle wouldn't have changed things, since she and Jesse could not seem to agree on what their next step should be.

Even though Jesse wanted to keep the whole thing on the down-low, she valued her parents' opinions about whether they should report the incident with Michaela kidnapping the girls.

Jesse didn't like her using words like *abduct* and *kidnap*. Especially since he didn't seem convinced it had even happened. But if that woman drove off with their daughters in her car, then they were apt words. Regardless of whether she ultimately let them go. He'd promised her they'd "get to the bottom of this," but his and Danae's canvassing of the neighborhood yesterday had not yielded any results until the last house on the block, where Danae talked with an elderly woman who said she'd seen two little girls walking on the sidewalk across the street headed toward the main road. She'd thought they were visiting at her neighbor's across the street, but Danae had inquired at that house and discovered there hadn't been any visitors there.

To complicate matters, the old woman's description of the girls she supposedly saw didn't exactly fit Sadie and Simone. She'd said both girls had long, brown hair. Her girls' hair was actually more honey colored, and shoulder length. The woman had also thought the girls she saw were both wearing yellow. Corinne supposed if the woman's eyes were bad, she might have mistaken lime green for yellow.

Yet, even if the woman had described Sadie and Simone with undeniable accuracy, it still wouldn't have proven anything for certain. Michaela could have abducted the girls at Danae's and dropped them off a few blocks up the street from her sister's house. What her motive might have been for such a crazy action, Corinne was afraid to guess. Probably just to scare them.

Well, she'd certainly done that. Corinne checked the girls in the rearview mirror. Would she ever again feel comfortable letting her daughters out of her sight?

After talking late into the night, it seemed the only thing she and Jesse had been able to agree on was that they would give it another day and hope Sadie came clean. *If* she was lying.

She and Jesse had tossed and turned, neither of them able to sleep more than a few hours. He seemed convinced this was just another of Sadie's tall tales to keep from getting in trouble. Corinne wasn't so sure.

Despite her hesitance to share all the details with her parents, Corinne was thankful to not be home alone with the kids today. For the first time since they'd moved into their house, she'd felt vulnerable at home last night, imagining sounds that Jesse promised her weren't there and having flashbacks to scenes from that movie—*Fatal Attraction*, was it?—that she and some high school friends had rented at the local video store. And regretted ever since. She shuddered, thinking about the depiction of a woman scorned exacting her revenge on the man's family.

She topped the hill on Chicory Lane, and the inn came into sight. Grateful for the haven her childhood home would be today, she rehearsed once more how she could tell her parents what had happened without alarming them.

And she prayed again that there was *no need* for alarm.

∘━━✦━━∘

Audrey walked up the drive from the mailbox, relishing the warm June sun on her back. The chicory was starting to bloom in the ditches on either side of Chicory Lane, adding lively daubs of purplish blue to the native grasses that waved in the breeze.

Spring was her favorite time of year—well, at least until autumn came along. Grant always accused her of being fickle about the seasons. But the niggling fears she was entertaining today were spoiling her enjoyment of the season.

Corinne had called and asked to come out and talk to her and Grant. Since when did her kids need "permission" to come out to the inn? Something was up with Corinne. She hoped they hadn't gotten in over their heads financially. Heaven knew she and Grant weren't in a position to help them out right now.

The thought had crossed her mind more than once that Corinne and Jesse might be having marital problems. They'd seemed rather tense the last few Tuesday nights when they'd all gathered. But she couldn't let her mind go there. Whatever it was, they'd work it out. For the sake of those precious little girls, they'd work it out. *Please, Lord.*

She heard a car on the gravel drive behind her and turned to see Corinne pulling in. Audrey had to smile at the swirl of activity visible through the windshield. Those three girls made her tired just thinking about them.

She'd never thought she'd see the day, but she had to admit she was thankful to be where she was in life—even if it did mean she was pushing sixty (as Link loved to point out). She simply did not have the energy to wrestle a handful of kids the way she had

125

when hers were young. God certainly knew what he was doing when he gave kids to young people.

She waved at Corinne and the girls, ran in to put the mail on the kitchen desk, then hurried back out to meet them on the drive. She and Grant had guests arriving at the inn later today, and the house was clean and tidy. In an effort to keep it that way, she would steer this gathering to the back deck. Thank goodness the weather was perfect for sitting outside.

Audrey bent to look into the van. "Good morning! How are my three favorite girls?"

"Hey!" Corinne affected a pout. "What am I? Chopped liver?"

"You want to go out back? It's such a beautiful day."

Corinne tilted her head. "Why don't you just say what you mean, Mom: *don't you dare mess up my spotless house.*"

Audrey laughed. "Well, maybe there's a little of that." But she took comfort in Corinne's teasing. Whatever she'd come to tell them couldn't be too bad if she was in a joking mood.

They walked around the side of the house, Corinne exclaiming at the riot of color Grant's flowers provided. "What's that red one called?"

Audrey turned to see the plant Corinne was pointing at. "You'll have to ask your dad, honey. The only ones I recognize are the roses and the geraniums. Besides, your dad will have fun hearing you ooh and aah over his hard work."

"Where is Dad? I want to talk to him too."

Audrey gave her a searching look. "He's in the wood shop. But he knows you're here. He'll be out. Is everything okay?"

Corinne looked pointedly at the girls. "I'll explain. Later."

"Okay." She furrowed her forehead. "But you're worrying me," she whispered.

"Don't worry, it's nothing … . fatal."

The shadows under her daughter's eyes didn't comfort her.

Corinne slung her purse over the back of a chaise lounge and pulled a tube of sunscreen from her jeans pocket. "Come here, girlies."

The girls lined up like stair steps, and Corinne slathered the lotion on three noses and three pairs of cheeks, ears, and bare arms. She was just finishing their already bronzed legs when Grant appeared around the opposite side of the house.

"There're my girls!" He held out his arms.

Three identical squeals of "Poppa!" and they escaped to take turns getting tossed in the air by their doting grandpa.

"Careful, Dad. They're all slick with sunscreen."

"They are?" Grant threw Simone into the air and pretended to let her slip through his hands, catching her at the last possible moment. "Wow, you're right, they're slippery little eels."

Simone giggled and got in line for another toss.

"Be careful, Grant."

"I wouldn't hurt these little eels for the world."

"I don't think it's the eels Mom's worried about," Corinne said wryly.

He gave her a sidewise glance. "Hey, don't you be calling your old man *old*."

Corinne and Audrey exchanged grins. It still warmed her heart to see Grant with his granddaughters. He'd been a wonderful father to their girls, but as "Poppa" he was in his element.

Sadie trotted over to Corinne. "Put more on me, Mommy. I'm not slickery enough."

"You are plenty slickery."

"Please?"

Corinne squeezed out an all-but-invisible amount of lotion and "slathered" it on her daughter. Of course, Sari and Simone had to get in line for extra "slickery."

After ten minutes Grant was worn out. He shooed the girls off to the meadow between the deck and the creek. "You can play on the tire swing, but you stay where we can see you now, you hear?"

He limped over to where Audrey and Corinne were ensconced in red cushioned lawn chairs at a round table, and plopped into a lounge chair across from them. "You Whitman kids better hurry up and get your quota of grandkids delivered up because I'm not getting any younger."

Corinne made a cross of her index fingers and held them up as if warding off a vampire. "Don't look at me. I'm done delivering."

Audrey and Grant laughed.

He jumped up again. "I need something cold to drink. You ladies want some sweet tea?"

"Sure, I'd take some," Corinne said.

Audrey declined, eager to get this mysterious conversation going.

A few minutes later, Grant returned with two tall glasses and a box of store-bought cookies. This time he moved to a chair at the table between her and Corinne.

He patted Corinne's hand. "So what's going on, kiddo?"

Their daughter looked at the table, fingering the edge of the paper napkin her drink was resting on. "I'm not sure where to start."

◦━◆━◦

Tears welled in her eyes, but Corinne swallowed hard and blinked them away. She'd hoped to keep this as low-key as possible, but the concern mirrored on her parents' faces as she'd shared the details of the ordeal made it seem more serious even than she'd dared believe.

"You've got to put a stop to this," Dad said, gripping the edge of the table before pushing himself to standing. He paced the patio, fists balled at his sides.

"I agree, Corinne." Her mom shook her head. "That woman has to be stopped before she ruins your lives."

"Unfortunately, I don't know what we can do. Jesse feels pretty certain Sadie just made up the story about Michaela taking her and Simone in her car. As much as I'd like to believe Sadie so we *could* press charges, it does seem a little far-fetched. And if we accused Michaela and she turned out to be innocent—"

"No, that wouldn't be good," her dad agreed. "But you can't just let her manipulate the situation this way."

"It's her word against Jesse's, Dad."

"Well, that's easy," Mom said. "There's not a person in this town who wouldn't defend Jesse Pennington to the death."

She bit her lip. "If it goes before a judge or a jury"—she shuddered at the thought—"they won't necessarily know Jesse."

"Oh, surely it won't go that far." Mom rose and started gathering tea glasses.

Just then the girls came up from the meadow. Corinne gave a halting nod, meant to signal her parents not to discuss this in front of the girls, but Sari eyed her suspiciously.

"Are you talkin' about that lady you and Daddy don't like?"

Corinne sputtered and tried to change the subject. "Are you girls ready to go home? You need to gather up your things and—"

"No! Not yet."

"Not yet home, Mommy," Simone parroted.

"Just a few more minutes, girls."

Sadie spied the cookie box on the table. "Can . . . *May* we have a cookie, please?"

"Of course." Mom doled out cookies while the girls climbed up on the picnic bench. "Let Gram get you some juice to go with that, too." She hurried in to the kitchen.

While Corinne got the girls settled at the table, her dad teased the girls like always. But it was clear he was distracted.

It disturbed her that the girls—Sari at least—had overheard more than they realized. She'd have to talk to Jesse tonight and decide what they were going to tell *them*. She recalled when her uncle and aunt, Mom's brother and his wife, had gone through a divorce when she was seven or eight. The whispered conversations her parents had then had frightened her and made her worry that something was wrong between them. She didn't want her girls to think something similar.

Her dad came up behind her and put his hands on her shoulders. "You hang in there, honey. Mom and I will be praying."

"Are you praying for that lady?"

Corinne turned to see that Sadie had wedged herself between her and her dad's legs.

Dad gave Corinne an apologetic look. "We're praying for all our kids, pumpkin. We always do."

"And that lady, too?" Sadie pressed.

He hesitated, then, "Yes. That lady too."

"She needs it," Corinne mouthed over her daughters' heads.

The smile her dad gave her made her feel a little better.

A little.

16

Jesse knocked on the jamb of the open door and stepped into Frank's office.

His boss was on the phone and Jesse gave him an apologetic look and turned to leave. Monday was never the best day to try to meet with Frank. But he held up a hand and motioned for Jesse to have a seat. He quickly ended his phone conversation and turned his attention to Jesse.

Jesse glanced toward the still-open door. "Mind if I close this?"

"Sure."

Jesse leaned and gave the door a gentle push. It closed, but he kept his voice low. "I wanted to ask if there's been anything new with Michaela's . . . charges against me?"

Frank shook his head, looking somber. "Nothing's changed as far as I know. Either way. Why?"

"She stopped and talked to Corinne in the grocery store last Friday. Acted like nothing had happened. Like they should be on friendly terms."

"You're kidding?"

"I wish I was, Frank. Unfortunately, that's not all. I hesitate to say anything because we can't prove it, but . . ." He bit a corner of his lip, still unsure how much he should tell his boss. He gave him the short version of what had happened at Corinne's sister's house.

Frank raised a brow. "That seems a little out of character—even for Michaela, don't you think? I mean, really . . . *kidnapping*?"

"Well, I'm not ready to label it that yet. I . . . I don't know what to think. But then, I never thought she'd file such ridiculous charges against me either."

"I won't tell you what to do, Jesse, but if I were you, I'd want to be pretty certain she actually did something like that before I went making any accusations."

"I know. But as you can imagine, my wife is pretty freaked out by all this."

"Understandably so."

Frank rose and came around the corner of his desk, and Jesse sensed he was being dismissed. Had his boss decided to just distance himself from the whole situation? Or had something else happened to turn Frank cool toward him?

Jesse followed suit and stood. "I just wanted you to be aware."

"Okay. I'll let you know if anything changes."

Reaching for the door, Jesse hesitated. "One more question. How, exactly, is this being . . . handled?"

Frank glanced pointedly at the clock. "Unless she files those papers with the State, we're just going to consider that it was her way of warning you, and as long as you steer clear of her, we'll consider it handled in-house. Done and over with."

"Where was she last week?"

"In Chicago. All week. So I was a little surprised to hear that your wife saw her in town Friday. She was traveling with Monica Perez, and I thought they were staying over the weekend, but they must have changed their minds. Or at least she did. But I know she's back in Chicago this week because she called with a question about an order first thing this morning. Carl wasn't in yet, so she talked to me."

"Okay." He took his hand off the doorknob.

"You aren't going to talk to her—about what happened with your daughters?"

Jesse shook his head. "Not yet. I . . . I'm not sure what I'm going to do."

"Okay, well, let me know if you hear from the State or have any other issues with her. I trust this won't affect your working relationship here. It won't do anyone any good if we have to tiptoe around each other because of this."

He cleared his throat. "I understand. And I don't want to make a big deal about this, but as you can imagine, it's a little tense working in the same office with her as long as this threat of a lawsuit is hanging over me."

"Well, what do you want me to do about it?"

"I don't really know that there's anything you could do." *Except maybe transfer her to the Toronto branch. Or fire her sorry, sue-happy butt.* "To be honest, I'm more concerned about what will happen the next time we're both scheduled to travel to the same trade show or sales meeting."

Frank shook his head and all but rolled his eyes. "I have enough trouble keeping everybody happy with the travel schedule. I can't let something like this dictate the rest of the office's travel schedules. This is something you're simply going to have to work out."

"Of course." Jesse studied his boss. Maybe it was his imagination, but he felt Frank's loyalty fading by degrees. "Well . . . Thanks. I wish this whole thing had never come up."

"Believe me, we all do." Frank turned his back and walked around his desk.

A little shell-shocked, Jesse started down the hall back to his own office, but he was afraid he saw writing on the wall. He couldn't quite read it clearly, but he feared it said something about his days at Preston-Brilon being numbered.

He couldn't fathom traveling with Michaela Creeve again, given the circumstances. But after the way this meeting had gone, it wouldn't surprise him if Frank forced the issue and scheduled him on a trip with Michaela. Just to smoke one of them out.

And it wouldn't be Michaela.

Back at his desk, he plotted the possible scenarios and came up with one conclusion. He could not stay at Preston-Brilon. Even if Michaela left, he sensed that Frank's estimation of him had taken a nosedive.

He examined the emotions he was feeling. He should have been stressed and upset, but instead he felt a strange elation.

And he knew why. It appeared he'd been handed a golden opportunity for the change he'd been looking for. Longing for.

Now all he had to do was break the news to Corinne.

⊶✦⊷

"You're not serious?" Corinne shook her head, trying to shake off the bombshell Jesse had just dropped. "Why would you quit your job? *She's* the one who should be quitting." Corinne refused to utter that woman's name in their home again.

Jesse cleared his throat and looked at the floor like a shy little boy. "This isn't about her, Corinne. It will probably take some getting used to, but—this is something I've been thinking about for a long time, and well . . ."

"What? What is it, babe?" He was scaring her. What could be so hard to spit out?

"I want to change careers." He blurted it out like a confession. "I've wanted to for a long time."

"Change careers?" She narrowed her eyes. "To what?"

"I'd like to go back to school and get my teaching degree."

"What?" She couldn't help it—she physically reeled backward.

"I think it's what I'm . . . gifted for. I'm tired of being in a job that doesn't make a real difference in the world."

"Your job makes a difference," she argued, scrambling for a reason to hang her comment on—and failing to come up with one. "Besides, you *do* make a difference in the teaching you do in our church. With the kids there," she finished lamely.

"That's part of what got me to thinking this way. Teaching the kids at Community Christian, that's when I feel like I'm making

134

a difference. That's when I feel . . . *alive*. I'd like to feel that way about my job. What I do every day. Like I said, this isn't just a whim. I've been leaning this way for a long time."

"Define 'long time,' please."

"Years."

"Whoa." Where on earth was this coming from? "You've been wanting to quit your job for *years*? How could I not have known this, Jesse? How could this have *not* come up in conversation?" She wouldn't accuse him now, but she felt certain this was merely a reaction to the situation with Michaela Creeve. A defense mechanism of sorts. A way out.

But Jesse was so touchy lately. How could she make him see his reaction for what it was without accusing him of lying?

"I didn't tell you because I didn't think it was possible. But I see now that it could be. It wouldn't be easy. But I've thought this through. I don't have my head in the sand . . ."

But he did. He had his head so deep in the sand that Corinne didn't know how he could even see that it was her he was talking to! "Babe . . . Jesse. We'd have to sell the house. I'd have to go back to work. Leave the girls in daycare." The thought made her sick to her stomach.

And just as quickly sick with guilt. She was privileged to get to have her dream job—staying home with the girls. Privileged to have this beautiful home they lived in. They lived well on Jesse's salary when few families could afford to live on one salary in this economy. Why did she think she was above that?

"I've thought about this a lot, Corinne. Yes, you might need to take part-time work, a couple days a week. But with Sari and Sadie in school, you could find something during the hours I'm home—so we wouldn't have to leave Simone in daycare."

"And what about during the summer?"

"I'd be home then."

"So you're not working at all?"

"No, I would." He looked sheepish. "I'd work as much as I could. We might have to work on the scheduling. But if we sold the house, we could buy something else and get rid of the mortgage altogether. We'd have to downsize. And maybe trade in the Nissan for something more economical. I'm not saying it would be easy. For a couple of years it will be a little crazy. But I think we can make it work."

Will be a little crazy . . . He was talking like this was a done deal. "When were you going to tell me this, Jesse?"

"What do you mean?"

"If this whole thing with Michaela hadn't happened, when were you going to tell me that for years you've wanted to quit your job and become a teacher?"

He shrugged, but his eyes never left hers when he said, "Probably never."

"What? That's crazy."

"I didn't think it would make any difference. It never really seemed like a possibility. But now . . ."

"How long have you been miserable?" She wasn't sure she wanted to know the answer to that.

"I never said I was miserable. But I've never felt fulfilled in my job at Preston-Brilon either. You know that."

"Never?"

"No. Not really. I mean, it was nice to hand you that healthy deposit slip every payday. And it was worth it to me to have you at home with the girls. That's important to you, I know, so I'm glad this job made that possible."

"It's still important to me." It struck her that he was speaking in the past tense. "Have you already given notice?"

"I wouldn't do that to you." He rose and went to the window, his shoulders slumping lower with every step. He looked out toward the backyard, speaking with his back to her. "Maybe it was a crazy idea. I guess I'll just gut it out. Maybe Michaela will leave."

"Jesse, I'm not saying I wouldn't even consider it. But . . . it's not like you to run from trouble like this."

He whirled and glared at her. "I'm not running away from any-thing. Like I tried to tell you—" He huffed and strode toward the dining room. "Just forget I said anything."

"No, Jesse . . . Wait."

He turned back around and she saw something in his demeanor she'd never seen there before. Defeat. She hated seeing him this way. Especially when it felt like she was to blame.

She had a sudden memory of her mother talking about what a great teacher Jesse would be. Did everyone but his own wife see his dreams, his longings? She went to him and put her arms around him, laid her head on his chest. "Let's talk this out."

He stood stiffly, not melting into her embrace like he usually did. Still, this wasn't something they could just enter into lightly. "Babe, let's talk about this. I want to know what you're thinking."

He relaxed a little.

She drew back to study him and recognized a spark in his eyes. Hope? "I'm listening. Talk to me."

He gave her a quick hug and pulled out a kitchen barstool and straddled it. "It would be hard, like I said. I haven't checked into it, but I'd probably need to go at least two years to get all the classes I'd need for a second degree. But maybe I could do some substitute teaching in the meantime. Or . . . something." He picked up a ballpoint pen from the counter and twirled it through his fingers.

"What level are you thinking of teaching? What subject?" She still could hardly wrap her mind around this career change he was contemplating.

"High school. Or maybe even college. I'd probably teach math or science. Maybe chemistry. I was pretty good at that in college. But I could teach about anything—except English or literature. That's not my strong suit. You know that."

"Wow." She shook her head. "This is . . . I'm sorry, but I'm just struggling to . . . process this."

"I know. But . . . do you think you could support it? Eventually?"

"It would change our lives. Me working. The kids in daycare."

"Only Simone. The other girls would be in school."

"Not in the summer."

"Well, yeah . . ."

It didn't seem like he'd thought this through quite as well as he claimed he had. "Are you sure it would be wise to teach at that level—high school? College?"

"What do you mean?"

"I know you don't want to hear this, but after this whole Michaela thing, I think you—we—need to consider it carefully about you teaching at that level."

"What do you mean?" He looked genuinely puzzled.

She took a deep breath and willed her words not to sound like an accusation. "Jesse, it's one thing to have a coworker accuse you, but if it had been a high-school girl making the accusations that woman did, we'd be in a very different situation right now. If you were a teacher and one of your students accused you of something like that, you could go to jail."

Immediately, his jaw tensed. "How is that any different than one of the girls in my Sunday school class making a similar accusation?"

"Don't think I haven't thought about that. But it's not nearly as likely that someone from church would do that. Where everyone knows us. Knows me. And our family. But in a public school? Girls are ruthless. It happens all the time, Jesse."

"Really?" His voice took on a sarcastic tone. "When's the last time you heard about that happening?"

She sputtered. "Just . . . just Google it and see if it happens. It's on the news nearly every day."

He blew out a hard breath. "I'm not saying it never happens, but good grief, Corinne, I didn't do anything wrong and I'm not going to walk on eggshells out of fear. You can't let stuff like that dictate your life."

"Well, it sure seems like it's dictating our life right now. You have to at least consider it, Jesse. Especially if it's already happened to you. What if you lost your job? They could take our girls away from us!"

He threw down the pen he'd been fiddling with. "Now you're just grasping at straws. Making things up."

"And you're just in denial. You have to at least acknowledge it's a possibility."

He stared at her. "You still blame me, don't you? You still think I actually did the things Michaela Creeve accused me of."

She bit her bottom lip. She didn't want to explore the answer to his accusation. Maybe she did still blame him. Maybe she was just using it as an excuse. "I . . . I'm scared, Jesse. Our world has already been turned upside down by her accusations. And now you want to change everything!"

"I already told you I wouldn't do this unless you were onboard."

"Yes, but you're not giving me a chance to get onboard. You're already packed for the trip. Shoot, you've practically set sail. And I don't even have my passport yet. You can say you're not going to do anything without me, but I feel like if I don't jump in and start swimming toward your boat, I'm going to get left behind altogether." She gave a bob of her head, rather proud of the whole metaphor she'd just painted. She wasn't sure where it had come from, but it was exactly how she felt.

He looked toward the ceiling, his mouth set in a firm line the way it was when he was trying to control his temper. She braced for him to explode—something he did rarely, but memorably. Instead, he came to her, and took her hands in his. "If we let this ruin us, if we let it dictate our lives, we will be captive to Michaela Creeve forever. Do you want that?"

Her stomach twisted in a knot. "Of course not."

"Then let's forget about her and live our lives as if that whole thing never happened."

"But it did happen. Jesse . . . You can't just pretend it didn't."

"Oh? Watch me."

There was that temper again. She'd seen his temper flare more often in the last month than she had in all the rest of their marriage put together.

He strode from the room leaving her adrift on a stormy sea without so much as a paddle.

17

I hope you'll come and stay with us again." Audrey put on her best innkeeper's smile and walked with the couple to the door.

She returned to the porch and made a show of deadheading one of the huge geraniums that stood in front of the entry columns on either side of the porch. But she was mostly just waiting till the car with the New York tags disappeared from sight so she could jump for joy.

Grant came around the side of the house with a sprayer on the end of a garden hose in hand. "They're gone?"

"Yes, and thank the Lord for small blessings." She sank onto the top step and leaned her head against the column.

Grant dropped the hose long enough to climb the steps and deposit a kiss on the top of her head. "I thought you liked guests who stayed for a nice long time."

She gave a very unladylike snort. "Not when it's the Queen of Cluckingham and her poor slob of a king. Have you ever seen such a diva in your life?"

He laughed and shook his head. "No, and I hope never to again in my life. That poor man. It was all I could do not to pull him aside and help him come up with an escape plan."

"Grant! You *wouldn't?*"

"Of course not, but I was tempted. It seemed like the humane thing to do."

Their guests had arrived four long nights ago and Audrey was certain the woman had talked nonstop from the moment she stepped out of the car and asked if the valet could please park it for them. "Oh, by the way, I hope she left a nice tip for the valet."

"No, but I had a couple of tips for her."

"Grant!" She giggled. "But seriously, I hope you didn't say anything?"

"Ha! Do you think I could have gotten a word in edgewise?"

"Good point. The worst moment was when they were dragging their Louis Vuitton luggage to the car, complaining all the while that they had to do it themselves, and he—"

"I would have thought that was the best moment . . . when they were *leaving*."

"Let me finish. She actually said to me"—she affected an East Coast accent like their guests'—"I do believe we may return here when we're traveling in the South next fall."

"Did you tell her we wouldn't be open that weekend? Whatever weekend that happens to be?"

She smacked her forehead. "Oh, why didn't I think of it? But you can be sure there will be a sticky note by the phone with their names and a 'do not reserve' note."

"I, for one, won't need a reminder," he said with a droll grin.

"If you'd only listened to me when I asked you—ahem, *again*—not to book on Tuesday nights." She clucked her tongue. "I honestly don't know how one individual can be so consistently obnoxious."

"Speaking of which," he said. "You haven't heard anything about Jesse and Corinne's pain-in-the-neck friend, have you? I wonder if they've made a decision about confronting her."

"I haven't talked to Corinne. It's taking everything I've got to keep my mouth shut, so I figure it's best if I don't ask."

Grant sighed. "I know. Whose brilliant idea was it to have a don't-give-advice-unless-asked policy around here?"

"I believe that was you, Mr. Whitman."

He gave her a hangdog look. "Well, it was a stupid idea."

Check Out Receipt

Prospect Library Branch
541-560-3668

Friday, June 17, 2016 3:24:45 PM

Item: 002289039
Title: Snakeroot
Due: 07/08/2016

Item: 002299850
Title: Bloodwitch
Due: 07/08/2016

Item: 002291390
Title: Evertrue
Due: 07/08/2016

Total Items: 3

Thank You!

"Do you think Corinne would even tell us if that woman tried some other stunt?"

"The question is, would Jesse tell Corinne?"

"You don't think there could be anything between him and that girl, do you?"

"Michaela? No! Of course not. Why would you even ask such a thing?"

"It just seems odd that she would randomly single Jesse out."

"Oh, my sweet, innocent husband. There is nothing random about Jesse Pennington. He may not get it, but anyone of the female persuasion will tell you the man is a hunk."

He raised an eyebrow. "Should I be worried?"

She laughed. "If I'd been born twenty years later, maybe."

He gave a little snort. "Sorry to burst your bubble, my dear, but you still would have been an older woman to him."

"Whatever." She winked, but quickly did the math, and it shocked her a little to realize how much older she was by the calendar than she was in her thoughts. "Back to the subject of this evil woman . . . Maybe *she* misinterpreted Jesse's friendliness, but I don't think for one minute that he would do anything inappropriate."

Grant was silent.

She studied him. "You don't know something you're not telling me, do you?"

He shook his head and gave her a wry grin. "I'm still trying to deal with the shock that my wife thinks my son-in-law is a hunk."

"Oh, stop. And that information does not need to leave this house."

He ignored that and turned serious again. "To answer your question: No, I don't know anything that would make me doubt Jesse. But you hear stuff like that all the time. Men doing things in secret that no one ever suspected. I think I would have felt better if it had been Jesse who came and told us about this. He was awfully quiet last night."

"He was . . ." She hated the direction this conversation was taking. They loved Jesse Pennington like he was their own. And she truly couldn't imagine him doing the things that woman had accused him of. "He's probably just embarrassed by the whole fiasco."

Grant looked skeptical. "I hope that's all it is. I just hope they take it seriously enough. If that woman really did take the girls in the car . . ."

Audrey shuddered at the thought. "I know Corinne was feeling nervous that day she was here. I'm sure they're being extra watchful."

"Yes, and it did seem like Sadie was telling a story to keep from getting in trouble."

"I don't know," Audrey said. "Her story sure had a lot of details for being made up on the spot."

"For instance?"

"She named the color of the car, which seat she and Simone sat in . . ."

"Yes, but she said it was a white car. What other color does she know? This whole family owns white cars."

That was true. They'd laughed about it just a few weeks ago, sitting on the front porch after their Tuesday dinner together and looking out on a sea of white and cream-colored vehicles lining the driveway.

"And that little tyke *has* been known to tell some whoppers. Remember the night they got into the poison ivy down by the creek?"

That was true, too. "Well, she comes by it honestly. Her mom told a few tall tales in her day."

"Not to mention her Uncle Tim and Uncle Link."

Audrey nodded. "I just wish that woman would leave town. I don't understand why people get such a thrill out of ruining other people's lives."

"I know. And unfortunately, women like that rarely just disappear."

Jesse tapped the brakes involuntarily at the sight of Michaela Creeve's car in the parking lot. She wasn't supposed to be back until Friday. Maybe she'd just left her car in the lot as she sometimes did when they carpooled to the airport, but he didn't remember it being here yesterday.

He drove slowly past and started to turn into his assigned parking space, but something made him stop. On a whim, he put his car in reverse and stopped just behind Michaela's. He glanced around surreptitiously, and when he was sure no one was watching, he climbed out of his vehicle and went to look through her front passenger side window. The tinted windows and reflections on the glass kept him from seeing clearly, and he didn't want to be too obvious by shading his eyes and peering into the window, in case someone happened to be looking out from the office just now. But he could see enough to confirm that her car had a cream-colored interior just as he expected. At least he could put Corinne's mind at ease.

But when he walked past the back window, headed for his car, a flash of color made him do a double take. Draped over the backseat like a seat cover was a fluffy wooly-looking blanket.

It was pink.

He bit his lip, trying to come up with a plausible explanation. But all he could think of was Sadie insisting that Michaela's car was pink inside—and then remembering her telling them that she'd sat in the backseat while Michaela had put Simone in the front.

Sadie hadn't been lying! His mind reeling, he got back in his car, parked it in his reserved spot, and strode into the building. He muttered a half-hearted reply to the receptionist's greeting and headed straight for Michaela's office. He didn't care what anyone thought. Didn't even care if he got fired. This had gone far enough. That woman had messed with his family for the last time.

She was at her desk, but she was on the phone. Fine. He would wait.

Her eyebrows went up when he entered her office and sat down to wait in the chair across from her. She appeared flustered and turned away from him to finish her conversation. She wrapped up the call, making a flimsy excuse to hang up.

She placed her phone face down on her desk and narrowed her eyes at him. "May I help you?"

"You tell me. Did you—take my girls for a ride last Friday?"

Now she looked him in the eye. Stared him down. "Your girls?"

"Sadie and Simone. Did you take them in your car?"

"Why would I do that?"

"You tell me why!" He hadn't thought about what he'd do if she denied it. Of course, she hadn't exactly done that. "But if you ever go anywhere near them again, I will make you sorry you ever met me."

She looked at her lap and became preoccupied with a thumbnail that wore bright red nail polish. "I'm already sorry I ever met you." She sounded close to tears.

He didn't care. "You just think you're sorry. I'm dead serious, Michaela. I don't know what you are trying to prove, but I *will* prosecute to the fullest extent of the law if I hear you so much as looked at my daughters cross-eyed." He hadn't intended to threaten her. He wouldn't know where to start with "the full extent of the law." But he would not allow her to hurt his family.

She looked up at him, her eyes dry and cold as steel. "Then I suggest you keep your daughters out of my path. Last I heard, it's a free country."

He shot to his feet and took two steps backward. "There is no reason on earth you should ever have any reason to be within spitting distance of my family."

Her face crumpled and pink rose to her cheeks. She swiped at her temple with the back of one hand the way Corinne did when she was crying but didn't want to mess up her makeup. "I don't know what I ever did to make you hate me so much."

Jesse drew back. Where was this coming from? "I—I don't hate you. I never said that. But I will not have you . . . *stalking* my family." He glanced over his shoulder making sure there was no one in the hall outside her door. "What you did was virtually kidnapping."

"I don't even know what you're talking about, Jesse. If I read you wrong or if . . . if you've changed your mind about us, I'm sorry. All I ever wanted was to see where things might go with us."

Again, he all but physically reeled. This woman was insane! "I don't know what I ever did that gave you the impression I was *remotely* interested in—anything of the sort. I certainly never did anything that warranted having charges filed against me."

She waved a hand as if swatting at a fly. "I haven't done anything with that, if that's what you're worried about."

"I'm worried about my family! I want you to stay away from them. Stay away from my wife and my daughters."

"If you're talking about that day in the grocery store, I can't exactly help it if we end up at the grocery store at the same time. Are you going to send me your wife's schedule so I know where not to show up when?"

"That's not what I'm talking about. I think you know what I'm talking about."

"I have no interest in your family. I have no interest in anything beyond getting back to the friendship we once had." She slid her flattened palm across the desk, then repeated it again and again, as if smoothing out a wrinkle. "Jesse . . . Oh, Jesse, I've been miserable ever since that night we came home from Chicago and you left me thinking there was something special between us."

He shook his head firmly. "Michaela, I don't know what I did to make you think that, but I'm sorry. If I somehow led you to believe that—" He swallowed hard. He did not want to put an image with her outrageous words. And didn't think it would be wise to do so, given her history. "I'm very sorry, but you need to know that I am a very, very happily married man and . . . whatever you thought about me, I'm sorry, but it wasn't true."

"I don't know if I can ever believe that. I know what I saw in your eyes. A woman recognizes the signals you were send—"

"Stop!" He held up a hand. "I won't listen to this." He turned and fled, thinking oddly of Joseph fleeing the advances of Potiphar's wife in the Old Testament story. And with every step he took, he felt as doomed as Joseph had been.

Michaela would surely file those charges now. She'd already started the process. That was the hard part. Going ahead and filing the papers she'd already prepared—and showed to Frank—would be an easy task.

He went back to his office, keeping his head down so no one would make eye contact or try to engage him in conversation. When he finally sat down at his desk, his hands were trembling and his heart was a strangling lump in his throat.

He needed a mediator. Someone who would hear both sides of the story and help him reason with this unbalanced woman. She hadn't admitted to taking his daughters from Danae's yard, but neither had she denied it. Anyone else would have been outraged at such an accusation—if it was false. But Michaela had almost toyed with him, as if she wanted him to believe she'd done it.

Yet she was smart enough not to admit to anything.

Maybe she hadn't done it. Maybe she was just sick enough that she would let him believe something like that, take credit for it, just for his attention. Was that it? He couldn't make sense of any of this. It was absurd. And he didn't have a clue what his next step should be.

He knew one thing though. Michaela Creeve was dangerous. He could no longer do nothing and hope this nightmare would go away.

18

The June evening was warm, but a cooling breeze blew across the creek and up to the backyard where the Whitman women sat beneath the pergola on the back deck after another Tuesday family night dinner. Corinne leaned back in her chair and closed her eyes. "Ahh . . . There's just nothing quite like the music of men in the kitchen doing dishes."

"Unless it's a man pushing a vacuum," CeeCee said in her gravelly voice. "Now that is a philharmonic symphony."

"CeeCee!" Corinne couldn't help laughing. "Then I guess I'm extra lucky to be married to a vacuum cleaner salesman."

Her sisters and Bree cracked up, but Mom feigned horror and shushed them. "Pipe down, ladies. You do not want them to hear you gloating, or it could all go up in smoke just like *that*." She snapped her fingers.

"Not for Jesse. It's his favorite part of Tuesday dinners."

"Doing dishes? Seriously?" Bree pulled her feet up under her in the deck chair, settling in for the girl talk that always happened at this point in the evening.

"He'd probably kill me if he knew I was telling you this, but he says there's just something about the teamwork, and standing in a row like they do, that fosters the best conversations."

CeeCee winked at her. "I told you that you got a good one when you caught him."

"Oh, that's so sweet," Bree said.

"He is sweet, isn't he? But don't you dare let him hear you say that, Bree Whitman." Corinne laughed, and was again overwhelmed with gratitude that Tim's wife was still such a dear part of their family, even four-and-a-half years after Tim's death. She knew they'd all mentally tried to prepare themselves for the inevitable day when Bree would find someone else. And of course, they all wanted that for sweet Bree. She was far too young not to marry again and have a family. And yet, it would change everything when she moved on with her life. And it would move them that much further from Tim. From his memory.

She shook off the thought, not wanting to spoil this evening of respite from the stress she'd been under because of Jesse's lunatic coworker.

"I love the way you have it set up out here, Mom." Corinne looked around at the magical space her mother had created under the pergola in the backyard. "I can't believe how fast that trumpet vine has grown."

"It's the one thing I put my foot down about. I usually bow to Dad's decisions when it comes to the flower—and your dad insists that vine is a noxious weed—but I love it."

"Well, it's the prettiest weed I've ever seen." Danae reached to pick a bloom from a stem and put it to her nose.

The lush, green vine had engulfed three of the four pillars of the pergola Dad had built and was just coming into bloom. Mom had woven strands of tiny white lights among the fronds and all through the top of the structure. The lights were set to twinkle softly, giving the effect of a canopy of fireflies. Pots of lemon grass, along with citronella candles, did a decent job of keeping the mosquitoes at bay, and their tang mingled with the honeysuckle that grew along the side of the house. The sweet scent reminded Corinne of the cotton candy CeeCee had always bought for them at the state fair in Sedalia when they were small.

Mom started to say something, then stilled. "Did I hear a baby?"

Landyn settled deeper in her chair. "Chase is listening for them. He'll let me know if they wake up."

"It's probably just the girls playing downstairs that you hear."

Mom scooted her chair away from the table. "I think I'll go check on all my babies. Anyone want anything when I come back?"

They eyed an almost-full pitcher of iced tea sweating on the table and sent up a chorus of murmured *no-thank-yous.*

When Mom had disappeared into the house, Danae took a sip of her tea and turned to Corinne. "Is everything okay with Jesse?"

"Why?" Corinne wasn't sure her sister was referring to the whole thing with Michaela Creeve, and she didn't want to bring up that subject if she could avoid it.

"He just still seems so—*different.* I miss the old Jesse," Landyn said. "I thought maybe I'd said something to offend him."

"What? You have to work pretty hard to offend Jesse." She was genuinely puzzled. "What'd he say?"

Her sisters exchanged looks.

"It's not what he said." Landyn shook her head. "He just isn't himself. Hasn't been ever since that stupid woman—"

"Can we talk about something else, please?" Corinne sighed. "I am sick to death of the subject of that woman."

"Sorry," Landyn said. "I just hate seeing Jesse so uptight."

"I wonder," Danae said, seeming hesitant, "if this whole thing has made him . . . gun-shy."

"You mean about being too friendly?"

Bree nodded. "I could see why, too. That woman has probably made him second guess everything he does."

Without warning, tears sprang to Corinne's eyes.

"Corinne? Are you okay?"

She shook her head, unable to speak just yet. When she'd swallowed back the tears, she tried to put her thoughts into words. "I think that's exactly what's happened, Bree. And . . . I'm sure I haven't helped matters any."

"What do you mean?" Landyn touched her arm gently.

"I've lectured him—for being too much of a flirt. I just don't want him to get in trouble again. It scares me where this could all lead."

"But Jesse's always been a flirt!" Bree clapped a hand over her mouth as soon as the words were out. "I didn't mean that the way it sounded. What I mean is, that's just his personality. He's never inappropriate or crude. It's why everyone loves him so much."

"Exactly. That's just the way Jesse is." Danae agreed. "He's always been super friendly."

Landyn picked up the battle cry. "That's why he's so good at his sales job, too. I wish I had half his charisma."

Corinne looked at her lap and tore at the edge of the paper napkin wadded in her hand. "I hate what that woman has done to our lives."

"Don't let this change him, Corinne." Bree got up from her chair and came to put an arm around Corinne's shoulders.

"I feel like it's too late. He already has changed."

"Do you want us to say something? So at least he knows he doesn't have to change around us?"

Corinne smiled through her tears at the defensiveness in Landyn's voice. But she shook her head. "I don't think he'd like it if you brought it up. We've mostly just been trying to pretend that . . . *witch* doesn't exist. That this will all go away if we just ignore her."

"But she still works at Preston-Brilon, right?"

She nodded. "Unfortunately."

"So does he have to see her every day? Are they on speaking terms?"

"She's been traveling a lot this month—and Jesse hasn't—so that's made things a little easier."

"Has Jesse said anything to her about—Sadie's claim?"

She sighed. "Seriously, can we change the subject?" She was growing uncomfortable with where this conversation was leading, plus, she'd promised Jesse. He'd given her the slimmest details about his confrontation with Michaela at work yesterday, saying only that she'd been frustratingly obtuse and hadn't admitted to anything at all. Yet for the first time, Jesse seemed worried that maybe Michaela had been involved after all in the incident with the girls disappearing from Danae's yard.

But Jesse had asked her not to say anything to her family. And she would honor that. They didn't need a dozen other opinions about how they should handle this. There were already too many disagreements about it—starting with her and Jesse.

The back door opened and Mom appeared with one of the twins in her arms. Corinne still had trouble telling them apart, especially in the waning evening light.

Landyn scooted out her chair. "Do I need to feed somebody?"

"Grace is still sleeping, but this one decided she was missing a party."

"That's my party girl." Landyn laughed.

"Can I have her, Mom?" Corinne rose and reached for the baby.

"It's not that I'm not willing to share, but your hubby asked me to tell you he's ready to go."

"Yeah, right. I'm not buying that one. Hand over the baby and nobody gets hurt." It was rare that Jesse was ready to end a Tuesday night before she was.

"I'll hand her over, but I'm not kidding about Jesse. He's rounding up the girls right now. He said they had swimming lessons tomorrow."

"Oh. Yeah . . . they do. Okay then." She patted her tiny niece's back. "Next time, sweetie. Aunt Corinne has first dibs." She gave her sisters what they'd called the stink eye when they were kids. "You hear that, aunties?"

Bree and Danae waved her off, laughing.

She kissed little Emma's cheek and started gathering up empty glasses and crumpled napkins from the table.

It was odd for Jesse to want to leave this early, but the girls did have swimming lessons in the morning. And she was exhausted. Mostly from trying to put on a "normal" face when their lives were anything but.

Jesse buckled Simone's car seat and went around to get in the driver's side. "You have everything?" he asked Corinne.

"Yes. I left the rest of the salad for Mom and—"

"Hey, guys."

They looked up to see Chase and Landyn picking their way across the gravel driveway. Landyn was barefoot and leaning heavily on her husband to navigate the rocky surface. Huckleberry tagged behind them, no doubt hoping for a ride in somebody's car.

"Hey there." Jesse shut the driver's side door and went around to meet them. "Did we forget something? I was just asking Corinne if she got everything . . ."

"No." Chase ducked his head briefly. "We just wanted to talk to you guys."

"Oh?" Jesse heard Corinne crunching on the gravel, coming around her side of the SUV. He wondered if she knew what this was about. Huck trotted over to her, and she took his large head in her hands and baby talked softly to him.

"We just wanted you guys to know we're praying for you," Chase said. "I know it's been a rough ride with everything that woman has tried to do."

Jesse put out his hand to shake his brother-in-law's, but Chase grasped his hand and pulled him into a quick hug.

"Thanks, man," Jesse said, clapping Chase on the back. "I appreciate that." He couldn't say more for the lump in his throat.

Jesse had always liked Landyn's husband, but the guy had really manned up once those babies came along.

"I know this has been hard on you guys," Landyn said. "We just wanted to encourage you about how our rough time kind of turned out to be one of the best things that ever happened to us."

Corinne's sister and her husband had almost split up just a few months after their wedding, unable to agree about their careers and where they would live. He didn't know all the details, but they seemed to have a strong marriage now, and they were doing a good job with their girls—who were adorable. Jesse had to admit, the twins kind of made him wish he and Corinne had another baby. Just one though. He didn't know how anybody survived twins. But Chase and Landyn seemed to have it down.

Corinne and her sister were hugging, and he and Chase stood there trying to look manly.

"Thanks, sis," Corinne said. "That really does help. We really do know that the hard times make us stronger, but it's good to hear it from you guys."

"Yeah," Jesse said. "You guys are setting a good example for us old folks."

They all laughed, but Jesse was serious about that, and told them, "I don't know if Corinne's told you, but we're talking about making some kind of scary changes."

He could tell by their curious expressions that they didn't know what he was talking about, but something about the timing and the mood of their exchange seemed right, so he filled them in. "Nothing's for sure," he said, looking to Corinne to be sure she wasn't feeling pressured. "Just things we're thinking about, so we'd appreciate it if you wouldn't say anything to anyone else until we've made some decisions."

"Well, I think you'd make an awesome teacher, Jesse," Landyn said.

"He would." Corinne hooked her arm through his and his heart warmed at her affirming words. Maybe she was adjusting to the idea more than she let on.

They talked for a few minutes before Corinne excused herself to check on the girls in the car. Huck got up to follow her, but she made him stay. He gave a whimper, but reluctantly plopped down on the gravel giving them all sad puppy-dog eyes.

Corinne came back from the car, smiling. "Sari's singing lullabies, and the other two are out like lights."

Jesse put an arm around her and the four of them stood in the driveway and talked for another thirty minutes. Chase and

Landyn told more of their story, how they'd been so at odds with each other after Chase quit his job and took a studio apartment in New York, chasing his dream of being an artist.

"Mind you, I'm not recommending my methods, Jesse," Chase said, laughing. "I had this woman pretty ticked off at me, and probably rightfully so."

"True." Landyn gazed up at her husband, looking anything but ticked off. "The thing was"—she looked pointedly at Corinne—"I discounted how important it was for Chase to be happy in his work, to be using the talents God gifted him with. And I know I'm not telling you anything you don't already know, Corinne, but—"

"Oh, you might be." Corinne reached out and touched her sister's forearm, smiling softly. Jesse let himself hope that she was softening.

They were both quiet on the drive home. The girls slept soundly in the backseat, but still, Jesse hesitated to ask Corinne what she was thinking about. Too often recently she seemed irritated by his questions about how she was doing or what she was thinking. As if it was none of his business. But she'd warmed to him tonight in a way she hadn't for many months.

When they got home, they worked together getting the girls in their beds, then they went down into the kitchen. He opened the fridge, looking for something to snack on.

"Do you want some ice cream?"

"Oh, man"—he patted his belly—"I shouldn't, but that does sound good."

She scooped two small bowls full, and he took them to the kitchen table. On the way past the bar counter, Corinne grabbed her laptop.

"Checking e-mail?"

"No, making a list." She poked her forefinger at his chest. "With you."

"A list?"

"What would it take, Jesse— What *will* it take to get this show on the road?"

"What show are we talking about?" But he thought he knew. And he was pumped.

∘═╤═∘

Corinne couldn't help but smile watching Jesse study her, an enigmatic smile growing on his face.

"Are you serious?"

"As a heart attack," she said.

"I know you're not one hundred percent on board, Corinne, but I can't thank you enough for making an effort to be enthusiastic about it."

"That's just it, babe. I'm truly not having to make an effort. I can't believe I'm saying this, but I'm actually kind of excited. It helped a lot, talking to Chase and Landyn tonight." She didn't tell him that most of her excitement was because she felt like she finally had her husband back. She still had plenty of qualms about what their future would look like, but a woman didn't have to speak every thought that crossed her mind. Mom had taught her that.

"Kind of funny, you getting advice from your baby sister."

She grinned. "Yes, it is. And good advice, at that."

Wrinkling her nose, she poised her fingers over the keyboard. "So what's the first thing we'd need to do?"

He shrugged. "Put our house on the market, I guess."

She gulped. That was going to be the hardest of all. Harder even than putting Simone in daycare and taking an outside job. Partly—okay, *mostly*—her reasons were pure selfishness. She loved their home and it was where her family had made most of their memories. They'd brought Simone home from the hospital to this house. She felt spoiled and petty thinking it, but she had trouble imaging herself in a "lesser" house.

157

She scolded herself. She had no right to think she *deserved* any of the good things they had. Especially when those things had come by the sweat of Jesse's brow, not her own.

Oh, he would have argued that. He would have said she made it possible for him to do his job well by having a sanctuary to come home to, *blah blah blah*. But the truth was, it *was* his hard work that had provided this wealth for them. Why shouldn't Jesse have the right to change careers, especially when he'd made it possible for her to stay home with the girls all these years?

She thought again of Landyn and how well things were working out for her and Chase. But Landyn had made even bigger sacrifices for her husband. Difficult ones. If spoiled Landyn could muster the courage to make a major change in her life, surely *she* could do this too. It's not like Jesse was asking her to work in the coal mines or put their children in an orphanage while he went golfing.

Willing it to be genuine, she mustered a smile and pushed up her sleeves. "Okay . . ." She typed the words at the top of the page: SELL THE HOUSE. "Next?"

Jesse grabbed her hand across the table. "I love you for this, Corinne. I hope you know that. I know it isn't easy. You're my hero and—"

"Don't go all mushy on me." She pulled her hand away and put it back on the keyboard. "Okay, what's next?"

"Trade in the Nissan."

She typed the words, even as she mourned her beloved Pathfinder. "Okay. Next?"

"Enroll in classes."

She typed it out. "Next?"

"Sell the kids."

She started typing: SELL THE K— "Hey, wait a minute!"

He burst out laughing.

"Let's keep at least one of them," she deadpanned.

That made Jesse laugh more, and she couldn't help but join in. It lifted her spirits just to see a glimpse of the husband she remembered from BMC—Before Michaela Creeve.

With the ice broken, for the next hour they itemized and prioritized the list—*their* list. When they were finished, Corinne felt like they were warriors storming a hill. Together. And with a game plan. One she printed out before they went to bed.

So she could read it over in the morning and start getting used to the idea of a big change coming their way.

19

Jesse stroked the razor over his jaw and looked down at Sadie's reflection in the mirror. She watched him intently from the doorway. Smiling through a cloud of shaving cream, he flicked a spot of the menthol lather onto her nose.

"Daddy!" she squealed. But she wiped the spot onto her cheek and came to stand beside him. "Can you shave my face?"

"Girls don't shave."

"Uh-huh. Yes they do. Mama shaves her legs. And her pits." She giggled.

"I stand corrected. Girls don't shave their faces though. Unless you're a bearded lady."

"What's that?"

"Never mind." He transferred a finger full of shaving cream onto her cheek then "shaved" it off with the wrong side of the razor.

That delighted his middle daughter. Which delighted him.

He finished shaving, dried his face, and scooped Sadie over his shoulder. "Ready for breakfast, squirt?"

"I'm not a squirt."

"You look like a squirt to me." He turned his head and blew a raspberry on her exposed tummy.

She giggled and squirmed on his shoulder all the way to the kitchen. He deposited her in her chair at the table in the breakfast nook where the other girls were already eating.

"Put me on your shoulder, Daddy!" Sari stood on her chair and begged for a turn. Jesse obliged, then came back for Simone who was doing her best to escape the high chair.

Corinne came down the stairs, and he almost bumped into her.

"What on earth is going on down here?" But her stern tone didn't fit the smile she wore.

"Just a little three-ring circus for your morning entertainment." He kissed his wife's forehead and trotted over to put Simone back in the high chair.

"I know who it is," Sadie hollered.

"Who *who* is, sweetie?"

"The three rings. In the circus. It's us, isn't it?" Sadie pointed between her sisters, counting off *one, two, three.*

Jesse laughed. "That's exactly right. I live in a three-ring circus. Make that four." He winked at Corinne over his daughters' heads, then went to put a slice of wheat bread in the toaster.

"You're awfully chipper this morning," she said.

"And with good reason."

"Oh?" She looked rather pleased with herself.

"Good reason, *indeed.*" Memories of their lovemaking last night buoyed his spirits further. He went to wrap her in a hug.

"I feel like we finally have our lives back," she whispered.

"That's funny, since our lives are about to kick into chaos. I hope you know what you've signed on to, baby."

But he had to admit that his heart had felt lighter by a thousand pounds ever since he and Corinne had talked last Tuesday night and she'd agreed to start the process right away of getting things set up for him to go back to school in the fall.

Thankfully, there wasn't much to do to get it ready to sell. The hard part would be just keeping it clean to show. He knew it hadn't been an easy thing for her to think of letting the house go, and sadly, most of the work would fall on her. He loved her for it and had tried to show his appreciation by helping with the girls, the meals, the dishes.

He'd promised her he wouldn't give notice at work for at least another month—in case Frank fired him on the spot when he did—and that if possible, he wouldn't quit working until a week before school started in the fall. Still, just knowing he had a quit date had lightened a burden he hadn't realized had grown so overwhelmingly heavy.

On Friday, the Realtor had come to evaluate the house and get it ready to list, and already they had someone coming to look at it today. Things were moving faster than he'd ever imagined they could. They would have an open house the following Sunday, and hopefully, before the end of the summer, they'd have a buyer. He'd already scoured the online real-estate sites, looking for a house that would suit them.

He hadn't told Corinne, but for what they needed to spend, they were definitely going back a step—or two. Or five. Not to mention they'd probably need to sell some of their furniture because "going back a step" meant downsizing too. He wondered if Corinne had made that discovery yet.

Baby steps. He wouldn't mention it yet. And he'd do some research on For Sale by Owner properties. They might be able to get a little nicer house for the money that way. He prayed hard—for Corinne's sake—that they could find something that wasn't too bad.

"Girls, quit goofing off and eat. We need to get this house cleaned up before the Realtor gets here."

"It's Daddy's fault!" Sari said in her best tattletale voice. "He's the one that got us all winded up."

"Daddy," Corinne said sternly, poking him in the chest with her index finger, "please settle down and quit bothering my girls."

The girls giggled and Sadie stood on her chair again, propping her hands on her hips. "We're *his* girls too."

Corinne started to protest, but he disentangled himself from her arms. "I've got this." He went around to the table, feeling Corinne's eyes on him while he got Sadie to sit down, then cleared off the Hello Kitty plates and Disneyland juice cups. He caught a sigh before it escaped. This would be as close as they'd get to Disneyland for a while.

⊙━◆━⊙

"Sadie! What did I tell you about leaving toys out?" Growling under her breath, Corinne snatched up the pink tub the little ponies went in. "We have to keep the house clean because someone is coming to look at it today."

"Then what're we supposed to do all day?" Sadie sulked and Simone toddled over to give her a pat on the back.

Feeling instantly sorry for her harsh words, Corinne went to give Sadie a hug. "I'm sorry, sweetie. I didn't mean to sound so angry."

She'd known it wouldn't be easy to do what Jesse was asking of her—least of all selling the house—but she hadn't expected how frustrating it would be to try to keep a house spotless while three little girls were in residence. But it wasn't fair to take it out on her daughters either. Though Mom had assured her they'd take the move in stride, they were a little bewildered about the changes that were happening so quickly in their lives.

Still, it was all worth it to have her Jesse back. She smiled to herself, thinking about how happy he'd been this morning before he left for work. She'd almost forgotten that side of her husband.

"What's so funny, Mommy?"

Corinne shook off her daydreams to find Sari looking up at her with curious eyes.

"I was just thinking about your daddy."

"How's come he was whistlin' at breakfast?"

164

The puzzled look on her daughter's face cracked her up. "He was, wasn't he?" She wrapped Sari in a hug. "He was whistling his heart out," she said, more to herself.

"No!" Sadie yelled. "Daddy can't take his heart out! He would be dead!"

"It's just an expression, sweetie." Laughing harder, she knelt beside Sadie and tried to explain. "Now help me get these toys picked up and then maybe we'll call Gram and see if she and Poppa are home."

Sari's eyes lit up and she clapped her hands. "Hear that, Simone? We get to go to Poppa and Gram's!"

"*After* we pick up toys," Corinne reminded them.

She'd dreaded this day, opening their home to someone who had the power to take it away from them. But it had been a very long time since Jesse had whistled at breakfast. She supposed she could find it within herself to live in a dilapidated cottage with the man she'd awakened beside this morning.

⊙══✦══⊙

Corinne could tell that her mom wasn't thrilled about them coming out. It hurt her feelings a little to be unwanted guests at her own parents' home, but at the same time she understood— more than she had before. Mom had to keep the inn spotless and ready for guests the same way Corinne was trying to keep their home spotless and ready for buyers.

She made a mental note to give her mother more warning next time—and to not plan to hang out at the inn every time they showed the house. Now that the weather was nice, she could take the girls to the park or the swimming pool. She already resented that these last few weeks in her home would be spent making a concerted effort to stay out of their home.

"So," her mother whispered. "How are the girls handling everything?"

She shrugged. "I'm not sure they really grasp what's going on. We didn't want to make a big deal of it in case things fall through."

"Fall through? Are you reconsidering?"

"No. I just mean, in case we can't get our price. This is the first—"

A ringtone sounded from her purse in the foyer. "Sorry . . ." She jumped up and crossed the room to fish out her phone. "Hello?"

"Corinne, this is Betty Heigel. Are you sitting down?"

"Um, yes." She reached behind her and slid onto the old church pew in the entry hall. "Why?"

"I have an offer on your home."

"What? Already?" She eyed her mother, who didn't try to hide her curiosity. "Is it . . . a good one?"

"It's as close to full price as you're going to get this early in the game. And no contingencies, there shouldn't be a problem with the loan. This may be the fastest I've ever sold a house."

"Oh, no," she whispered.

"Corinne? Are you okay?"

"Yes. Sorry. I just . . . I can hardly believe it went that fast. I guess I need to go home and start packing." A sick feeling settled in the pit of her stomach.

She looked up to meet her mother's gaze. "We may have sold our house," she mouthed.

Mom's eyebrows lifted.

"Betty, I need to call Jesse and let him know. Do we still have the open house now?"

"Yes, I think so. There's no reason to think this will fall through. They seem like serious buyers, but it won't hurt to have another bidder in our pockets. Who knows, you may be able to get full price. There's just one thing . . ."

"Oh?" Corinne didn't like the hesitation in the Realtor's voice.

"They need to be in the house in three weeks. The wife is pregnant and they want to be settled before the baby comes."

"Three weeks? I don't think there's any way—"

"We may be able to negotiate a moving fee or some other kind of help. You don't want to throw away a buyer on account of a few days."

"But—what would we do in the meantime? I don't think there's any way we could find a house and close on it and still get everything packed and—" She didn't even know what else to say.

"Talk to Jesse. I'll get back with you tonight. Meanwhile, I'll see what I can find out from the buyers. Maybe they're more flexible than they let on."

"I sure hope so." She couldn't hold back the groan that came.

"Hey, don't let it get you down. This is good news, Corinne. My other clients would trade you places in a heartbeat."

"I know. I'm sorry. I just didn't expect it to go this fast. I'll talk to Jesse and we'll wait for your call tonight."

She hung up, feeling numb. "Well, that's the end of that." She burst into tears.

"Corinne? What's wrong?" Mom hurried over and sat beside her on the bench.

When she could speak again, she tried to explain.

"It will all work out, honey. I have no doubt."

"But what are we supposed to do in the meantime?"

"You'll find something. Even if you have to rent for a few months while you house hunt."

The back door opened and her dad hollered, "Audrey? Where are you guys?"

"In here," Mom called.

He came into the foyer and looked between them. "What's going on?"

"Their house sold."

Dad looked to her. "Really? Already?"

"It must have been to the first people she showed it to." Corinne composed herself and told her dad the details she knew. "I don't think there's any way we can be out of there in three weeks."

"Sure you can. You've got lots of able-bodied family members who can help you get moved."

"Yes, but to *where*, Dad? We've been looking and there's nothing out there right now."

"Nothing?"

"Well, nothing we want to invest in."

"Have you looked at rentals?"

She shook her head. She hadn't even wanted to think about that possibility. Three little girls in an apartment? Or a small house? And rent wasn't cheap in this college town. Landlords knew they could rent a place out to four or more students and make far more than they could renting to one family. She felt close to tears again.

"Don't let it get to you, honey. Everything will work out. And you know Mom and I are here for you."

"Da-ad." It always made her cry harder when her father went all sweet and soft.

"Listen," he said, patting her back. "If worse comes to worse, you guys can stay here with us for a while."

"Grant!" Mom hissed. She turned to give Corinne an apologetic look for her unguarded reaction. "We . . . we'll work something out, I'm sure."

"Don't worry, Mom, we're not going to invade you. We'll take our house off the market if it comes to that."

"Are you sure you don't want to do that anyway?" Her mother looked hesitant, as if there was more she wanted to say.

"What do you mean?"

"I just wonder if there's some way you could keep the house. You guys have worked so hard— Never mind . . . it's none of my business. I'm sure you haven't made this decision lightly."

"Unfortunately, every penny of our savings is wrapped up in that house. Selling it is the only way Jesse could afford to go back to school. And I know that's the right thing to do."

"You guys are young," Dad said. "You'll have plenty of time to save up for another house someday."

She didn't remind him that they'd be living on a teacher's salary once Jesse graduated. She could go back to work once the girls were all in school, but she'd begun to accept that they would likely never again live in a house as nice as their current one. She still had trouble even imagining the day they'd move out of their house. She couldn't let herself think about it too long or she'd be a basket case.

Still, hard as it was to let the house go, she wouldn't trade the happy husband she'd been living with these last few days for the nicest house in Cape Girardeau. She just hoped Jesse stayed happy, because this was going to be hard.

She rose with a sigh. "I guess I'd better get home and tell Jesse the news."

"You didn't call him?" Mom said.

She shook her head. "He's in meetings all afternoon, and I don't want to just leave a message."

"Well, yes, you'd better go then." Mom stood and gathered up their iced tea glasses.

"You'd better go home and start packing, is what you'd better do," her dad said.

"Where are you going?" Sari appeared from around the corner.

"Nowhere, sweetie." Corinne cast a glance at her parents, hoping they got the signal. She didn't want to tell the girls any sooner than they had to.

Sari tipped her head. "Then how's come Poppa said you have to pack?"

"I'll explain it when we get home, sweetie. Right now we need to get your sisters rounded up." She and Jesse hadn't tried to hide the fact that they were putting their house on the market, but she wasn't sure even Sari understood the implications of that.

But neither had she and Jesse wanted to make a big deal about the changes that were coming, since no one knew for sure how it would all work out or how long it would take. She bent to speak to Sari. "Go on, now. Daddy's going to wonder what happened to us."

"Nothin' happened to us."

"I know. But Daddy doesn't know that. Now run and tell Sadie and Simone to start picking up toys."

When Sari was out of earshot, her dad turned to her. "Not to tell you guys what to do, but I wouldn't take the first offer you get. There are bound to be others interested. No need to sell yourselves short."

"I'll pass that advice along to Jesse."

"Well, I'm sure you two can make your own decisions. That's just my two cents."

"Thanks, Dad. I'd better run."

"See you Tuesday night?"

"If we're not packing."

Mom frowned. "Things surely won't go that fast. Besides, you've got to eat no matter what. You may as well come where the food is."

"I'll let you know."

"By the way, do you know what you're going to do about babysitting—once school starts? You'll be working, right?" Mom's attempt at casual was all too transparent.

"I will. As soon as I can find something. But I haven't figured out the babysitting yet."

"Maybe I can ask some of my friends and see if they know of anyone."

"Don't worry, Mom, I'm not going to ask you to keep the girls. I wouldn't want to drive out here every day anyway."

"I'm sorry, honey, but as much as I'd like to help, I just couldn't make a habit of it. Not with the inn to run."

Never mind Mom had kept the twins for Landyn *twice* recently.

As if she'd read her mind, Mom said, "And I know I've kept the twins quite a bit, but I kept your girls when they were little, too. It didn't seem fair not to do that for Landyn just because we have the inn. But—well, I just can't do it as often as I used to."

Dad cleared his throat and fidgeted with the table runner. "We'd do it in an emergency, of course."

"I know. And I wouldn't ask unless it was an emergency."

"Landyn was working on some advertising fliers for me, too. That was one reason I offered to help with the twins."

Yes, and you were probably paying her for the work too. Corinne hated the sarcastic thoughts that kept zinging through her mind. It was totally understandable that Mom would help out with the twins the way she'd helped when each of their daughters were small. It just hit her wrong to have her mom preempt a request she hadn't even planned to make.

She loved her mother with all her heart, but sometimes Mom got on her last nerve always trying to read her mind and give advice unasked. This whole thing was hard enough without having to fear that her parents disapproved of the decisions she and Jesse were making. She knew they were worried about her, but still . . .

She gathered up her things and got the girls in the car, trying not to let her parents see that she was upset. Mom was impossible to fool, but if she let on, she didn't say anything, for which Corinne was grateful. She didn't need complications in any more of her relationships.

20

Jesse's car was in the garage when Corinne pulled in twenty minutes later. She hadn't been able to talk to him at work—a scenario that always brought unwanted thoughts of Michaela Creeve. But she pushed those away now, eager for a chance to tell him the news about the offer on their house. But not in front of the girls.

He came from the house to help her unload the girls.

"Thanks, babe," she said. "How was your day? Did you get the mail?"

"You're welcome. My day was good. And yes, I got the mail."

She rolled her eyes, but couldn't help but laugh, too. "I sound like Sadie, don't I?" They'd been working on getting the chatterbox to wait for an answer to one question before she asked a dozen more.

"Well, I didn't want to accuse you of acting like a four-year-old, but . . ."

The girls jabbered like quarreling squirrels, and Corinne knew she wouldn't be able to get a word in edgewise, let alone tell Jesse about Betty's call, without the girls asking a thousand questions.

When they got in the house, Sari started to take off her shoes.

Corinne stopped her. "I want you girls to go play outside so I can talk to Daddy. We'll call you in when supper is on the table."

"But I'm hungry now," Sadie whined.

Corinne foraged in the fridge and came up with a bag of baby carrots. "Here. You can take these out with you for an appetizer."

"What's an appetizer?" Sari asked.

"I'll tell you later. Now go. I can't get a word in edgewise with you magpies jabbering."

"What's a magpie?" Sadie said.

"Go. I'll tell you later."

"But—"

"Sadie! Do what your mother said."

Pouting, Sadie followed her sister out the back door, arguing about who got to be in charge of the carrots.

Jesse closed the door behind them and turned to her. "What's up?"

"Betty Heigel called while I was at my parents. She has an offer on the house."

His jaw dropped. "Are you serious? A good one?"

She gave him the details while they started supper together.

Jesse buttered six slices of wheat bread and laid them on the griddle in quick succession. She came along behind layering cheese on the bread and he put on the "lids," as the girls called the second slice of buttered bread.

"Do you want bacon on yours?"

"Sure. That sounds good."

She went to the fridge and came back with a box of pre-cooked bacon.

He waited for her to place the strips on two of the sandwiches. "So? How are you feeling about things?" He touched a finger gently to her nose, a tenderness in his voice that touched her deeply. "Now that it's really happening . . ."

"It makes me sad, but . . . Maybe this is God's way of saying we're doing the right thing?" She hadn't intended it to come out as a question. And wished it hadn't when Jesse looked so hopeful.

"Do you really think so? I wish it were that easy. I don't want to make a mistake on this, Corinne."

"I know. But . . . even if it was a mistake, it wouldn't be a life and death one." She wanted so badly to believe that. And yet, thinking about leaving this house, she just wanted things to go back to the way they'd been before Michaela Creeve had put everything in their lives off-kilter.

Jesse flipped a sandwich over. "We'd better get those girls fed. We can talk about this more after they're in bed."

"Okay. Where'd you put the mail?" It wasn't in its usual drop spot on the island.

"Oh . . . Sorry. I think I only made it as far as the laundry room. Look on top of the dryer. You got a couple of letters, too."

"Really?" The mail was usually such a dud these days. They'd gotten past the years of college friends' engagement parties and weddings. And birth announcements all seemed to come via e-mail now. "You have everything under control?"

"Yes, but hurry. And holler at the girls to come in first, will you?"

She did that, then hurried to the laundry room. She riffled through the slim stack of credit card offers and coupons. With her luck, what Jesse thought was a personal letter was probably some gimmicky sales promotion. Or maybe a home sales party.

But there were two letters. The smaller envelope bore the return address of a couple from church. That would be a thank-you for a baby shower gift. The other envelope had a Cape Girardeau postmark. Odd. It was addressed by hand—only to her—but in block letters, in childlike printing. Probably a birthday party invitation for one of the girls. But why would they have addressed it only to her?

She turned the envelope over. There was no return address. She opened the flap to find a smaller envelope within the outer one. It was rather late in the season for a graduation announcement. But who did they know that was getting married?

She slid the second envelope out and unsealed it. A plain white folded card was inside. She opened it and a piece of ribbon slipped to the floor. Lime green ribbon. Her breath caught. She left the ribbon on the floor and read the message in the card.

Just thought you might have been missing this. May she wear it in good health.

21

Jesse stared at the green ribbon in Corinne's hand and anger boiled up inside him. "Let me see that." He reached for the envelope she was holding and turned it over in his hand, then read the cryptic unsigned note on the card. The printed block letters looked as if they had been purposely written to disguise the sender's handwriting.

"It had to be *her*, Jesse. No one else could have known about this! Sadie was telling the truth." Panic made her voice thin and taut.

But Corinne was right. Michaela was the only person who could have done this. And even though it still made him sick to think about the whole mess with her becoming public, between this and the pink blanket he'd seen in Michaela's vehicle, he was completely convinced that this crossed the line from stalking to threatening. "I'm taking this to Frank."

"Jesse . . . I think this has gone way beyond that. We need to call the police. I'm afraid to let our daughters play in our own backyard!" She glanced outside again.

The girls' voices carried through the open window, but he saw fear in Corinne's eyes. And felt it himself. He didn't want to think Michaela would actually harm another person, but this woman was disturbed. Seriously—mentally—disturbed.

"I don't know if we have enough proof that they would do anything about it, but—"

"What more proof do they need?" She snatched the ribbon from his hand and waved it in front of his face. "I want a restraining order on her. I want her out of my life, Jesse! *Our* lives . . . This is ridiculous!"

"Babe . . ." He tried to put an arm around her, but she shrugged him off.

He took a step back, scrambling to think what they should do. "Let's get the girls inside and feed them some supper. If you'll do that, I'll call the police and see what our next step should be."

That seemed to pacify Corinne. She went to call the girls in, and he went back to his office and searched for a phone number to call the Cape Girardeau police. He dialed the first number from the confusing list on the city website and was quickly rerouted.

"This isn't exactly an emergency . . . at least I don't believe it is, but I think we need to report an . . . incident." He explained what had happened with the missive containing Simone's hair ribbon. But as he answered the female dispatcher's questions, the story seemed far-fetched and convoluted to his own ears. "This woman has accused me of harassment in the past."

"I can send an officer to your home right away if you think that's needed."

"No." His refusal came out with more force than he'd intended. "Maybe it would be better for me . . . my wife and me . . . to come to your office tomorrow. I don't want to upset our daughters by having the police here." That was true, but more importantly, he did not want the neighbors to see a police car in front of their home. Especially when they were trying to sell it.

"That's your decision," the dispatcher said. "But if you think your family could be in danger, I wouldn't hesitate to talk to an officer about it."

"Thank you. We'll probably come in tomorrow. Do we need . . . an appointment?"

She told him the address and department, and who they should ask for.

He hung up the phone and sat at his desk in stunned silence. How had it gotten to this? Could he have avoided this disaster if he'd never spoken to Michaela? *If he'd never flirted with her.* The thought stopped him short. He'd truly not intended the mild flirtation to lead to anything. But he suddenly saw more clearly now. He had enjoyed her attention. And if he were honest, he'd encouraged it. Never in a way that anyone could have labeled "harassment" or even inappropriate—by the world's standards anyway.

But he didn't live by the world's standards. At least he claimed he didn't.

He put his head in his hands. "God . . . Forgive me. I've been trying so hard to look innocent in this situation. To be innocent. But I know I have to take some of the blame. For egging Michaela on. For not putting a stop to things sooner. I confess, God . . . I enjoyed her attention. It made me feel good. But I never meant for it to—" *Cut it out, Pennington. No more excuses.* He had to start being completely honest. With himself. And with Corinne.

But then, Corinne already knew. She'd tried to warn him. And yes, Michaela was unstable, maybe even mentally ill. But that didn't make his actions any less wrong. Maybe it made them worse! Not that he'd recognized her instability before she accused him. Still, he knew in his heart that his attitude had not been right. Not from the beginning.

It had stroked his ego to have Michaela attracted to him. He'd never admitted that. Not to himself or to Corinne. And trying to pretend he was merely a victim kept his family at risk. It was time to man up and take this bull by the horns.

⊙━✦━⊙

Corinne sat cross-legged on their bed, waiting for Jesse to quit pacing and tell her what was going on. The longer he paced, the more worried she became.

Finally he stopped and sat on the edge of the love seat in the window alcove, elbows on his knees, head in his hands.

"Jesse, what is it? You're scaring me."

"I'm sorry. I don't mean to scare you. There's just something I . . . need to tell you."

Her blood turned cold. There was only one thing she could think of that would cause him the kind of anguish she saw on his face right now. And she couldn't bring herself to put it into words. But that didn't stop the images from forming in her mind. Images of her husband with that woman. Of them—

"Corinne, I feel like I need to come clean." He looked up and met her eyes, but she couldn't find the reassurance she was looking for there.

"About . . . *her?*" The cold in her veins turned to ice. But the tears on her cheeks were warm.

"Yes, but—" He started shaking his head. "Don't cry, babe. It's . . . it's not what you must be thinking. At least not what that look on your face says."

For the space of another breath, she let herself hope. Jesse rose from the love seat and went to his knees at the end of the bed where she sat. He reached for her hands and enfolded them in his, kissing her fingertips. "This feels embarrassing and awkward. I just need to confess that . . . I let Michaela's attention go to my head. I liked the way it made me feel to have someone admire me the way"—he closed his eyes—"the way she seemed to. I should have nipped it in the bud. I should have run as far as I could run from her, but even though she has no basis for her accusations—*none*—I did probably encourage her just enough to keep her flirting with me. I'm so sorry, babe."

"Jesse." Relief warmed her, wrung her out. "What man wouldn't like that kind of attention? I'm not saying it was right, but . . . I understand."

"If I hadn't been so foolish, so immature . . . If I hadn't all but put out a welcome sign to her, maybe we wouldn't be where we are right now. And I want you to know I understand what you said about me needing to be cautious when I'm teaching. I blew you off, but I see now what can happen from a seemingly harmless flirtation. Please forgive me, Corinne."

"Of course I forgive you. I'm just so glad that's all it was. That you didn't—" Her voice broke.

"No. Of course not. I would never do that to you. To our girls. You can trust me, Corinne. I've learned a very important lesson here. I just hope I can get us out of this mess."

She started to speak.

But he held up a hand. "That's another thing I think God showed me: I was so afraid of this coming out publicly and . . . humiliating me. But maybe I need to be humiliated." Again he hung his head. "I let my pride thwart my better judgment—even when it could have meant putting you and the girls in danger. I'm so sorry."

She loosed her fingers from his and took his face in her hands. "I love you, Jesse. It'll be okay. We'll get through this."

"I think we need to go to the police."

She swallowed hard. "Yes. I agree."

"I would go myself, but I think it's important they hear firsthand the things you experienced—the day she talked to you in the grocery store, and the things Sadie said." He raked a hand through his hair. "I feel bad that we doubted her."

"I know. Do you think she'll have to talk to the police?"

"I don't know. I hope not. I'd just as soon the kids not be involved at all."

"Unfortunately, Michaela has already involved them."

He nodded. "The dispatcher said the police would come to our home if we preferred."

"I think that would be good. We can let the girls watch a movie or something. But if they want to talk to Sadie or the other two, they'll be here."

"Yes, and it won't hurt for them to be aware of our house when they patrol."

She sighed. "You know the neighbors will talk."

"I know. But I don't think we have a choice." He stood and offered her his hands.

Feeling better than she had in a very long time, she let Jesse pull her up into his embrace.

"Dear God," he whispered, "help us to do the right thing. Please get us through this without our girls getting hurt."

He tightened his arms around her, then started to pull away, but she felt compelled to add her prayer to his. "I confess, God, I've felt . . . *hatred* toward Michaela, but something must have hurt her deeply sometime in her life to cause her to inflict this much pain on us. We don't know why any of this has happened, but please"—she swallowed hard—"give her healing for whatever has made her this way."

Jesse drew back and looked at her. "You're an amazing woman, do you know that?"

"No, I'm not. But—I'm trying to be . . . understanding. What she's done isn't normal. There must be something in her life that has caused her to go off the deep end. And whatever it is can't be good."

"I'm not sure I can be so generous, but . . . I'll try. Let's go make that call, shall we?"

She nodded, feeling relieved and terrified at the same time. What were they about to set in motion?

22

To Jesse's great relief, the officer who arrived at their front door the next morning was attired in plain clothes, and the sedan parked in their driveway was unmarked.

Looking pale, her voice thready, Corinne invited the man into the living room. At the last minute, they'd enlisted Danae to watch the girls for an hour. If the officer wanted to speak to Sadie, they could arrange it for another time.

The more Jesse and Corinne had "rehearsed" what they knew to tell the police, the more Jesse wondered if they'd be taken seriously. Almost everything was "alleged" or conjecture on their part.

Still, he wouldn't take chances where his daughters were concerned.

The officer introduced himself as Lt. Jerome Harrald. He looked to be about their age, with a military bearing and haircut.

Jesse led the way through the entry hall.

"Would you like something to drink?" Corinne asked when they reached the living room.

"No, thank you. I just finished coffee. But if you'd like to get something, feel free."

They both declined and sat down beside each other on the sofa across from the occasional chair the officer had chosen.

"So, I understand someone has been giving you trouble?" he said. He slipped an iPad from the briefcase he carried. "You don't mind if I take notes while we talk?"

"Of course not," they said in unison.

"And if you'd like to file a complaint against this person, we can take care of that as well."

They both nodded their agreement, and Jesse felt a frisson of excitement—or maybe relief was a better term. He felt like he was finally doing what he should have done long ago to keep his family safe.

"So why don't you start from the beginning and tell me what has been going on, what your concerns are, and what you hope to accomplish by involving us."

Jesse was a little surprised by that last part. What *did* they hope to accomplish? To be relieved of the threat that Michaela might continue to frighten or harm Corinne or their daughters. That was all. But what would it take to insure that? Even if they were able to get a restraining order against Michaela, could she ever be trusted to abide by it? Her actions had become increasingly odd and threatening, indicating just how unstable she must be.

He and Corinne took turns recounting the events, beginning with the day Jesse had been called into Frank's office and informed about Michaela's accusation of sexual harassment.

"Were charges actually filed against you?"

"No. According to my boss, it was just a 'warning.' He said she'd have to file the papers she gave him with the State Department of Labor before it was official."

"And to your knowledge has she done that?"

"No. At least no one has told me if she has."

He nodded and turned to Corinne. "And you say she has been stalking you since this occurred?"

"It feels like stalking. I don't know what the legal definition is."

He brought the iPad to life, opened a program, and scrolled through several pages. "To meet the criteria of stalking in this state, we would have to prove that she purposefully and through her course of conduct, harassed or followed you with the intent of harassing you. Could you say with confidence that was her intent? And did she actually follow you?"

Corinne sighed. "I don't know how I could prove it. I suppose anyone watching would have said she was just making small talk with me—and the girls. She spoke to them also. If you knew the situation, I think you would have seen how she was . . . *toying* with me, for lack of a better word. But what woman would make an effort to have a conversation with the wife of the man she's accused of harassing her? And I couldn't prove it, but I don't think it was accidental that she 'ran into me' in the grocery store. I think she followed me. And then followed me to my sister's afterward."

"But you didn't see her?"

"No," Corinne admitted.

"Again, evidence—proof—is the issue." Lt. Harrald typed quickly on the small keyboard attached to the iPad cover. "Now, you said she picked up the two younger girls at your sister's home and took them for a ride? Did you witness this?"

"No," Corinne said. "I discovered them missing from my sister's backyard where they'd been playing. The yard is fenced. But the only entrance is through a side yard. She could have parked in the street and let herself into the yard. Since we'd just talked with her at the grocery store maybe an hour before that, the girls would have remembered her. In fact, our middle daughter—Sadie— insists that's why she went with Michaela. Because I'd talked to her, so she wasn't technically a stranger." Corinne laughed weakly.

"Well, if this woman did, in fact, pick up the children in her car without your permission, that would definitely reach the level of endangering the welfare of a child, second degree, probably, depending on the age of the child. How old did you say your daughters are?"

When they told him—Jesse even jumped up and retrieved a recent photo of the girls from the end table—Lt. Harrald seemed taken aback.

"This one looks about the same age as my son. And they were playing outdoors by themselves at your sister's?"

"Yes, but my sisters and I were just inside. We could see the girls from the windows of the room where we were visiting. That's how I knew they were missing. I looked up to check on them again, and they were gone. For all we know Michaela Creeve had just abducted them moments before."

Jesse could feel Corinne's defenses flaring. This was what he'd feared—that the blame would be turned back to him, because of Michaela's charges of harassment. He opened his mouth to pick up Corinne's defense, but then thought better of it. It might only make them look guilty if they protested too much.

"Again," Lt. Harrald said, "without witnesses and evidence, we have no proof that Ms. Creeve did what you're accusing her of. We would need to prove beyond a reasonable doubt that she committed . . ." He scrolled again on the iPad and read, "*acts of criminal negligence, in a manner that creates substantial risk to the life, body, or health of a child less than*— Oh, well, this says less than seventeen years, which your girls certainly fall within that criteria. But again, we'd have to prove the act was committed."

"But what about the ribbon she sent?" Corinne sounded on the brink of panic.

Jesse was feeling the same. "She is the only one who could have known our daughter—Simone—was wearing a green ribbon that day. And that the ribbon had gone missing. Our other daughter, Sadie, told us that Michaela took a ribbon from Simone's hair in the car."

"And you're sure it's the same ribbon she allegedly mailed to you?"

Jesse didn't like the way he kept labeling everything alleged, though he guessed it was necessary for an officer of the law to train himself to speak—and think—that way.

"If it's not the same ribbon, it's identical," Corinne said. "Same style, length, exact same color. It even still had wrinkles and creases in it from being tied in her hair."

"Why do you think she would mail the ribbon to you? It was addressed just to you, Mrs. Pennington, is that correct? Could I see the letter?"

Corinne rose and went after the card, handing it to Lt. Harrald when she returned. "I think she was just . . . taunting me. I think she's mentally unstable. To the point of being dangerous. Could you get fingerprints off of this?"

He examined the envelope and its contents. "If this were a homicide there might be methods that could lift at least partial prints. But"—he waved the envelope—"this doesn't constitute a threat. No matter what you believe it to be, to a judge it looks like a greeting from a well-wisher."

Jesse had the brief note memorized: *Just thought you might have been missing this. May she wear it in good health.* And Lt. Harrald was right. Without any other proof, Michaela's note didn't sound in the least threatening.

"I'm sorry," the officer said. "We simply don't have the resources, and given the lack of evidence for criminal intent, it's not likely we'd pursue it at this point. Is there anything else that could serve as evidence? Or a witness, perhaps? Maybe some of your sister's neighbors saw something the day Ms. Creeve allegedly took the girls?"

"No," Jesse said. "We canvassed the neighborhood after we found the girls—hoping for that very thing. But most of the neighbors were at work when it happened, and the one elderly woman who thought she'd seen them, had too many details wrong to be credible."

Lt. Harrald typed something on the iPad keyboard, and Corinne threw Jesse a look that said "do something!"

Jesse turned to the officer. "If we tried to get some sort of . . . I don't know, restraining order or something, would we risk getting in trouble for falsely accusing her—if it turns out we can't prove she did it?"

"A judge would have to issue a restraining order after making the determination that it was necessary. But you could certainly file a complaint without risking any consequences of false accusations. Even if there isn't enough evidence to reach the level of 'beyond a reasonable doubt' for court conviction, you still have the right to file, and your accusations would not be considered false because you believe them to be true. But again, we need proof before we can take any substantive action. You have to realize that by requesting a restraining order, you're asking the court to limit Ms. Creeve's freedom. We don't take that lightly."

Jesse sighed and bit his tongue. It seemed like her actions had already limited their freedom. "So where do we go from here? We really do feel this woman is a threat. And her actions have escalated—or at least they've been ongoing. I don't want my wife to have to look over her shoulder every time she goes to the grocery store or takes our daughters to story hour at the library."

"I certainly understand your concerns, Mr. Pennington. What I could do is interview Ms. Creeve to see if we can find any merit to your complaint."

"But . . . she'll just lie about it the way she did to us," Corinne said.

"We might be able to get her to be more forthcoming. People usually are when they're talking with law enforcement."

Jesse was dubious, but he didn't say anything.

"But if you talk to her, she'll know we contacted the police. That might just set her off and make her do something worse." Corinne twisted the hem of her shirt. She'd practically shredded the fabric since Lt. Harrald arrived.

Jesse's own nerves were equally frayed. They seemed to be in a lose/lose situation. "So we couldn't get a restraining order on her in the meantime? To keep her away from our children?"

"We can direct you to the court that deals with orders of protection. You would complete an affidavit of the allegations, and then it would be up to the judge to make a determination as to the necessity for an immediate ex parte order of protection."

"Ex parte? I'm not sure what that is?"

"It just means it would be a protection of you, without giving Ms. Creeve an opportunity to present evidence to the contrary of your charges."

"And do you think a judge would do that?" Corinne asked.

The officer frowned. "Frankly, I don't see that you have enough evidence that she's the one who did this." He held up a hand. "I'm not saying I doubt what you've told me, but a judge is going to require proof."

"Then what do you suggest we do?"

"I'd continue to be cautious where you and your daughters are concerned. Be very aware of your surroundings at all times, be on the lookout for her following you or attempting to interact with you in any way." He pointed out the front window. "I notice you have your house on the market?"

"Yes. We may actually have a buyer," Jesse said.

"Are you selling because of Ms. Creeve?"

Jesse and Corinne spoke at the exact same instant, except he said no and Corinne said yes.

She looked embarrassed and started to say something.

Jesse stepped in to explain. "It's indirectly because of this whole thing with her . . . Michaela. I felt I needed to leave the company. I've been wanting to go back to school. So that's why we're selling."

Lt. Harrald looked at Corinne as if waiting for her to confirm. "Yes. It's indirectly because of her. It makes it hard . . . this all happening at once."

"I'm sure that's true. Well, you might want to let the Realtor know what's going on. In case she tries to get in the house under the guise of being an interested buyer."

Corinne gave a little gasp.

"Is it possible that's already happened?" Lt. Harrald asked.

"I don't think so. The offer came from the first people who looked at the house—the only people—and it's a family."

"That's good. So it will be going off the market?"

"Once we've accepted the offer," Jesse said.

"It might be a good idea to show the Realtor Ms. Creeve's photo."

He nodded, adding that to his ever-growing to-do list.

"And as much as you'd like to avoid it," the officer continued, "you should probably warn your daughters about this woman as well. And keep your phone close at hand any time you're out."

Corinne looked hopeful. "To take photos? Would that qualify as the proof we need?"

The officer smiled. "Well, yes, possibly. What I meant was to have your phone ready in case you needed to call the police. And certainly *do* call us again if anything further happens, or if you think of anything you forgot to tell me." He reached in his pocket and withdrew a business card. "My direct number is here. Meanwhile, we can still file the affidavit, and at the very least, the judge would order a hearing to determine if a full order of protection is warranted."

"Would we have to go to court if we did that?" Jesse asked.

"They wouldn't make Sadie testify, would they?" Corinne's forehead seemed to have developed a permanent crease.

"At that hearing, you would be allowed to state your case fully for the judge. And the respondent—Ms. Creeve—would also be given an opportunity to present her side. Her defense. I don't know about your daughter. That would be up to the judge. You'd want to involve your attorney if it came to that."

They didn't have an attorney. Preston-Brilon retained an attorney, but since Michaela was employed there, too, it would surely create a conflict of interest for either of them to use the company's lawyer. Besides, except for the fact that Jesse had met Michaela at Preston-Brilon, and Michaela had filed the initial complaint against him after a business trip, this no longer had anything to do with the company or Jesse and Michaela's working relationship. It was personal now. "So there's really nothing else we can do?"

"Not unless you can think of something that would actually serve as evidence of her stalking."

And that was exactly the problem. Michaela Creeve had denied everything, had seemingly calculated ways to *not* leave any trails. And that fact, more than anything, made Jesse's blood run cold.

23

Wednesday morning, Corinne decided not to take the girls to swimming lessons. She and Jesse had wiggled out of Tuesday night family dinner last night for the second time in six weeks. And Dad would be keeping track. She'd dreaded making that call, knowing they'd have to explain why eventually. She was already feeling like a prisoner in her own home, and it didn't help that Jesse hadn't argued with her when she told him she was staying home. Thankfully, the girls didn't ask about swimming, but they'd probably remember when nap time rolled around.

Sari and Sadie were playing in the sandbox with Simone, oblivious to the drama that was being played out on their account. She would give anything to keep them innocent, to not ever have to explain this whole pathetic ordeal to them. But she supposed they'd eventually have to say something—even if it was years from now.

It was easy to keep these things from Jesse's mother. But they'd decided they wouldn't tell Corinne's parents about the new developments just yet. Especially about talking to the police officer yesterday. Of course, they'd have to spill all the first time they left the girls with Mom and Dad. Although Corinne wasn't sure she could ever leave the girls out of her sight again. She was just glad school was out and she didn't have to worry about someone snatching Sari out of her classroom.

Maybe it was a good thing they were moving. Maybe they should be looking for houses out of state.

But their lives were already in chaos with Jesse planning to quit his job, the house on the market, and the prospective buyers due to come back and look at the house a second time this afternoon. She might be sorry later, but she found herself praying that the buyers would change their minds. Or at least that by some miracle they wouldn't want to take possession for a few months.

She listened again for the girls in the yard, then went to look out the window, not quite trusting even the new locks Jesse had put on the gates. They still hadn't talked to the girls about Michaela, other than a generic "you don't go with strangers no matter how nice they seem" conversation. For now, they'd opted to keep the girls with them at all times and be ever watchful for anything remotely suspicious. It broke her heart watching her daughters play together, while pondering how early in life children had to lose their innocence just to stay safe—thanks to people like Michaela Creeve.

The doorbell interrupted her thoughts, even while it illustrated them. Adrenaline shot through her veins, and she hurried to peer out the peephole, wishing they'd sprung for the security camera the architect had wanted them to install.

Relief went through her, seeing her sister standing there. She unlocked the deadbolt and opened the door. "Danae. Hi. Come in."

She couldn't quite read Danae's expression, but her sister rarely stopped by without a reason. "Are you off today?"

"No, just going in later this morning." Danae worked part-time for an accountant. "How are you doing?"

It was clear by her tone and expression that she wasn't asking lightly. And even though Corinne was sick of the subject, it suddenly sounded good to have someone to talk things over with. "We're hanging in there. I feel like I'm in limbo. Not just the whole mess with the Wicked Witch of the West, but everything's kind of hitting at once. Jesse's job, selling the house—"

"That's actually what I wanted to talk to you about."

"Oh?" She closed and locked the door behind Danae. "Come on in. There's still some coffee." She led the way to the kitchen.

She poured coffee for Danae and herself, and took a chair at the kitchen table where she could see the girls in the yard without getting up.

Danae sat down across from her, seeming far too intent on the coffee in her mug.

She looked at her sister expectantly. "So, what's up?"

Danae took a deep breath. But she was smiling, so it couldn't be too bad. "I don't know how you'll feel about this, but it might actually solve a problem for you."

"What's that?"

"Dallas and I are thinking about buying your house."

"Our house?"

"You know I've always loved it. Dallas too. I don't know what the current buyers' offer is, but we could pay your asking price. If the other offer isn't too much over that, we'd like to buy it. And we'd be willing to let you guys stay here for a couple of months . . . That's what I meant about it solving a problem for you."

"Wow." She was truly stunned. She hadn't even known Dallas and Danae were in the market for a house. They'd always said they'd wait until— "Wait a minute— Danae! You're not pregnant, are you?"

"No." The heavy sigh her sister breathed told the truth. "I wish that was the reason. We really didn't plan to look until we had a baby on the way, but when your house came up for sale, we just couldn't quit thinking about it. It'll be a little bit of a stretch and we might have to dip into our baby savings, but we decided to go for it. At least that way when we do get pregnant, the house part will be out of the way. And I love the way you have the girls' rooms fixed up, so I wouldn't even have to change that."

She smiled. "Well, unless you have a boy."

Danae laughed into her coffee cup. "After your girls, and now Landyn's twins, I can't even imagine a boy in this family."

"Don't let Dad hear you say that. I think he's counting on Link to come through with at least one boy to carry on the Whitman name."

Danae was silent, and Corinne knew by the faraway look in her eyes that they were both thinking of Tim. That their brother had never had the chance to give his father a grandson.

"So," Danae said finally, "would you consider selling to Dallas and me?"

"Of course. I mean, that would be great. I never thought about you guys wanting it . . ." She couldn't quite identify the emotions that were bombarding her right now.

"You're sure it wouldn't bother you—to have your house still in the family?"

"No. No, actually that might make it easier. At least we'd know it would be taken care of." But even as she spoke the words, she wasn't so sure they were true. It was one thing to be giving up their house, but quite another to think of her sister taking it over. Still, she couldn't deny that it was an answer to their prayers. It would buy them the time they needed to find another place. And it would keep them from having to show the house to anyone else, which would close one more avenue Michaela might employ to get to her and the girls.

"We actually wondered if . . ." Danae hesitated, as if she wasn't sure she should voice whatever it was she'd started to say.

"What?"

"Dallas wondered if you guys would be interested in buying our house. Kind of a swap—well, except for the money. I mean . . . Oh . . . That didn't come out right." Her cheeks flushed.

Corinne chose to ignore it. She knew Danae hadn't meant anything by her words. Still, it stung to be reminded that she was moving down in the world. "Wow," she said. "I hadn't even thought of that possibility."

"I know our house is kind of small—from what you're used to. The girls would have to share a room but you know how big that second bedroom is. And I don't know yet what we'd have to ask for it. We're still working out the details. But I wanted to see if that was even a possibility for you guys."

"Well, it's your decision. About buying our house, I mean. It's a free country." That came out harsher than she'd intended.

"I know, Corinne, but we wouldn't do it if we weren't a hundred percent sure you and Jesse were okay with it. Whether you bought our house or not."

"Let me talk to Jesse about all this. It . . . you kind of took me by surprise."

They finished their coffee and made small talk. Then Danae went out to say hello to the girls before heading for work.

Corinne made sure the doors were locked before going to the backyard. She sat on the lovely covered stone patio and watched the girls play, trying to imagine what it might be like in a few months when she would be a visitor in her own home—well, *former* home.

She wasn't sure she liked this twist. Yes, it would solve a big problem for them, but how would she feel having Dallas and Danae living here? Having her sister take over her home, her neighbors, her life? No, worse than that. *Exchanging* lives with Danae and Dallas. Not that there was anything wrong with the Brooks's home. Danae had it fixed up cute, and the backyard was wonderful. The girls would be ecstatic to inherit the playhouse. But Corinne would always connect that yard to the day Sadie and Simone had gone missing.

She bit her lip. If she was honest, what bothered her even more than the memories she had of that day was embarrassing to admit, even to herself, but . . . The Brooks's home was a starter house. The type newlyweds bought. And yes, Dallas and Danae had fixed it up, made lots of improvements, but still . . . And the neighborhood. She'd just never thought she'd have to go back . . . down to that.

Why was she having such a hard time getting past the economic implications of this move? People would understand. College wasn't cheap. But it would be different if he was going back for a post-grad degree. Something that would advance his career. Get them ahead.

She admired teachers greatly. It wasn't that. Jesse was choosing an honorable profession. And there was no question in her mind that he was gifted greatly as a teacher. But they were never going to be buying a house in Silverthorne Woods or Dalhousie like she'd dared to dream. She felt guilty that it was so hard to let a dream like that die. Especially when God had already granted her deepest dream—getting to stay home with her girls. So many of her friends had to choose between that and having a nice house. She'd been blessed. And truly, she could have been happy in this house for the rest of their lives. But to go back to a little starter home? That felt on the verge of humiliating.

And Danae's offer to buy their house only emphasized the feeling of being a charity case. It would be different if they were selling their home to move up. Or even if they were willingly selling it. But they weren't. At least *she* wasn't. She'd only agreed to do so for Jesse's sake. But it wasn't what she really wanted. And the closer they got to this actually happening, the more she realized how sad the decision made her.

But as she'd told her sister, it was a free country. They had no good reason to prevent Danae and Dallas from buying their home. Good grief, it was probably an answer to prayer. Certainly Jesse's.

Still, something didn't sit right with her about it. No matter. She'd best get used to it.

She remembered when Landyn and Chase had first moved back from New York, they'd had no money, no place to live, and babies on the way. She'd felt sorry for them, but she'd never thought about how difficult it must be for them to be dependent on everyone else. But then, they'd been newlyweds, which made it excusable. She and Jesse were far from that. They should have their lives and careers established by now. They should be on their way up. They *had* been on their way up, until Michaela Creeve entered the picture.

Corinne had never hated anyone before. But these feelings of . . . *rage* was the only way to describe it, and she hated the way it had changed her.

Now, the way things were going, she—the oldest Whitman offspring—was going to be the lowest of them all on the ladder of success. She may have been a lowly stay-at-home mom before all this, but she'd been that by choice, by design. And her husband's success had afforded her a certain status that—she wasn't ashamed to admit—she'd enjoyed.

And now, to her shame, her main goal, when she considered a job search next fall, was finding something where she wouldn't run into her more successful friends. Yet, the only reason she allowed herself to worry about that was because it kept her from thinking about the day she would drop Simone off at some impersonal daycare center.

She swallowed the lump in her throat and forced her thoughts to something that wouldn't ruin her makeup. This wasn't going to be easy.

24

You going to China next week, Pennington?" Larry Waymire blew across the cup of coffee he'd just poured. The fragrant steam reminded Jesse of why he'd braved coming down to the break room. Now he was sorry.

He shrugged and reached for a foam cup. "If I am, I haven't been informed yet. Why?"

"You're probably off the hook then. Lucky dog." He frowned. "Wayne and I just got the great news. That hotel industry show you and Wayne did last year. He's not real thrilled about having to go two years running. He got food poisoning last time. Remember that? He like to have died."

It didn't take a psychology degree to detect the resentment directed at him. "Man, I'm sorry. I don't know how I've managed to dodge the bullet these last few weeks."

"Yeah, well, we fly out Sunday night. The two of us and Michaela. My missus is not a very happy camper."

He wondered if Larry's wife was merely upset about Larry being gone—or about the fact that Michaela would be traveling with him. For the first time it struck him that he may not have been the only one Michaela had targeted. Surely Frank would have said something if that were the case. But he didn't dare ask.

Larry cocked his head. "You talk to that chick much when you're on the road?"

"Michaela?" Jesse felt heat rise to his face. "Not much."

Larry shook his head. "That girl's got issues. I mean she's nice enough, but she's got a screw or two lose, if you know what I mean."

"I guess I don't." He really wanted to change the subject, and yet he was curious what Larry was getting at.

"Well, who can blame her for being a little . . . *off.* I knew her dad. Buck, we called him. I guess that was his real name. He worked here back in the seventies. Hit the sauce a little too hard and got fired. But I think maybe he still has some connections with the higher-ups, which is probably how she got hired on. Anyway, her husband dumped her, like two years into the marriage . . . took pretty much everything in the divorce. Went back to New York or somewhere back East, wherever he was from."

"I didn't even know she'd been married."

"Oh, yeah. Kind of surprised she's never remarried, really. She's not exactly hard on the eyes, if you know what I mean. Just a little different."

Jesse was feeling antsy at the conversation. It seemed odd that as much as Michaela talked, he'd never heard her even hint at any of the stuff Larry was telling. She never talked about herself, unless it was to say what restaurant she'd eaten at or where she liked to shop. Anyway, if she'd ever mentioned anything more personal, he'd missed it. And he'd never bothered asking either. Not that he was trying to get to know her. "I'd better get back to my desk. You guys have a good trip."

"Yeah, well, your turn's coming, Pennington. You can't get the lucky breaks forever."

He forced a laugh. "Don't worry, I'm sure I'll make up for lost time once the fall season kicks in. Who knows what Frank's got up his sleeve." His words felt disingenuous—because they *were.* But he couldn't very well tell Larry that he suspected that Frank—despite his words to the contrary—had let him off the hook for this trip because of Michaela. Whether by design or not, he appreciated the fact that his boss hadn't scheduled him to travel with Michaela and had sent her on the road, insuring they had as little time in the office together as possible. He'd managed to avoid her since her little stunt with mailing Simone's hair ribbon to Corinne.

Or maybe Michaela was avoiding him? That seemed more likely, since it seemed she usually went out of her way to run into him if she wanted to. Maybe that fact was evidence of her guilt. Either way, if she was guilty, she'd gone to great lengths to see to it that they couldn't level any accusations without opening a gigantic can of worms.

Thankfully, he was just biding his time here until he could give his notice. He'd do that a month from now. And in six weeks school would start. In fact, as of today, July 1, he could start telling himself, *just gut it out till next month, Pennington. You can do that.*

"So, do you think Frank is going to drop Ferreman?"

Jesse was grateful for the change of subject, but he couldn't speculate about the distributor Larry had named. He made an excuse and hurried from the break room.

When he got back up to his office, Frank Preston was there, leaning on Jesse's desk, pretending to study a sales chart that Jesse knew for a fact the man had memorized.

"Frank. Hi. Sorry . . . I hope you haven't been waiting long." He held up his coffee cup as if to explain where he was, then checked his watch. "We didn't have an appointment, I hope?"

"No. No, and I just got here. Do you have a minute?"

"Sure." He indicated the chair in front of his desk, then spotted the stack of files he'd piled there this morning. He whisked them onto the bookcase. "Have a seat."

Frank sat, and Jesse went around to his desk chair and settled in, curious about the reason for his boss's visit. Maybe Michaela had finally gone through with her threat and filed an official complaint. He realized that what had once struck terror in him would now feel a little like relief. He'd talked briefly with Jim Houser, an attorney at their church, who'd put his mind somewhat at ease. Jim reminded Jesse that he had a right to defend himself against any charges, and had suggested Jesse could even try to beat Michaela to the punch and file his own harassment charges against her. What she'd done was equally discriminatory according to the definitions of the law.

But neither he nor Corinne wanted to go that route if they didn't have to. That would guarantee a messy, public trial, and no guarantee they'd win. Unless things escalated, they weren't willing to take such a drastic step.

It had given Corinne some comfort just to know they had Jim Houser in their pocket if they needed an attorney. But it seemed that their best hope was to wait it out and pray that things quietly went away, and that ultimately the statute of limitations—one hundred eighty days—ran out before Michaela changed her mind about filing. That would happen around Thanksgiving. And boy, would they have a lot to be thankful for this year if they made it that far.

Frank glanced over his shoulder into the hallway. "Mind if I shut the door?"

"No. Sure."

Frank pushed the door closed, sat forward on the chair, and without preamble said, "I have an offer to make you." He eyed Jesse as if he should know what this was about—and be responding.

"An offer?"

"This whole thing with Michaela Creeve is complicating things. I've managed to keep her on the road and keep you in the office, but—"

"And I appreciate that, Frank. I really do."

"Yeah, well, don't thank me too soon. I can't orchestrate things around you two forever."

Jesse held up a hand. "I know. I realize that." He should tell Frank about his plans now. How could he not? He'd been given the perfect opening. But they were counting on this last six weeks of pay to get through the summer. If Frank let him go on the spot—which he very well might—it would mean Corinne would have to find work immediately. Him too, and they hadn't lined up daycare. Not to mention the move. As it was, if they took Dallas and Danae up on their offer, the move was all going to fall on Corinne.

"Here's what I propose," Frank said, sitting straighter. "I can't offer you a promotion—a raise, I mean—but we can move you to the marketing department, keep your salary where it is. You wouldn't have to travel but maybe once a year, and Michaela would have no reason to be in that building." He stopped and studied Jesse, as if trying to gauge how he was taking the news.

Jesse was sure his face told nothing, except maybe that you could have blown him over with a Dustbuster. If only Frank had made this offer a year ago, they might not be where they were right now.

And yet, except for the whole mess with Michaela, he was more thankful to be where he was than he could say. The dream of going back to school had always been a pipe dream. He'd accepted that he'd discovered this dream of teaching too late in life. After Corinne and the girls came along. And they were his first responsibility.

And then it struck him. Maybe that's what this was all about. Maybe God was trying to show him that. And this was how he was providing. He should have been grateful, but the thought made him sick with disappointment. And yet, he knew it would make Corinne equally giddy with relief.

He looked up and realized Frank was waiting for a response.

"I . . . wasn't expecting this. I'm sorry this whole thing—with Michaela—has caused so much trouble."

Frank waved off his apology, which Jesse had only reiterated to buy him some time.

"Can I talk this over with Corinne and get back to you?"

His boss looked surprised. "Sure. I thought you'd be relieved. About the change. This is a lateral move, Jesse, if that's what you're worried about. It won't hurt your chances of promotion in the future. I can assure you of that."

"I am grateful. I don't mean to sound otherwise. I just . . . want to make sure."

"That's fine. But you need to know that if you decide to stay in sales, you will go back to a traveling schedule, and I simply cannot mess with juggling things to keep you and her apart."

"I understand. I . . . wouldn't expect you to."

"Well, I'll get out of your hair then." Frank rose, reluctantly, Jesse thought. "If you could let me know by Monday, I'd appreciate it."

"Sure. I'll make a decision before then."

Frank left the door open behind him, but Jesse got up and closed it again. He didn't know how to process this turn of events. If not for the fact that he and Corinne had a whole new set of plans in motion, he would have felt Frank's news was a huge relief. An answer to prayer even. And maybe it was. He hoped not though. Because he was more excited about their "Plan B" than he'd felt about anything in his life for a long while.

He flirted with the idea of not telling Corinne about Frank's offer at all. But after everything they'd been through, if he'd learned anything at all, it was that honesty was paramount in marriage. Even when it was hard.

And telling Corinne would be hard. Because he didn't want to get her hopes up. He sensed she was having big-time second thoughts about the plans they'd set in motion. And he felt pretty sure this news would put her back to square one.

25

Go put your shoes in your closet, sweetie."

"But I want to wear them." Sadie held the new sandals to her flat little chest as if they were a beloved kitten.

"No, remember, Mommy told you they're just for Sunday school."

"But—"

"Sadie." Corinne gave a little growl. Why did this child have to test the smallest request? "Please just do as you're told. Daddy will be home in a few minutes, and I need help with supper."

Bingo. That did the trick. The two little girls ran back to their bedrooms, but Sari ran around to the kitchen island. "I'll help you make the salad, okay, Mommy?"

"That would be great, sweetie. How about you tear up the lettuce and I'll chop the veggies?"

"But first I hafta wash my hands, right?"

"Exactly. First rule of the kitchen." She kissed the top of her daughter's head, her hair still warm from the sun.

"I want a apron."

"An apron," she corrected. "Alrighty, aprons it is."

She looped the neck strap of Jesse's freshly washed grilling apron over her own head and quickly tied the strings in back, then fit one of her mom's old half aprons around Sari's chest. The five-year-old hopped up on the step stool in front of the kitchen sink, and side-by-side, they washed their hands in the deep sink.

"You were a real trouper this afternoon," Corinne told her. "I'm very proud of the way you cooperated and didn't complain while we shopped for your sisters."

"But *I'll* get new shoes next time, right?"

"Well, maybe not the very next time. But soon. Before school starts. There should be some back-to-school sales starting soon." She'd always shopped sales, but never had she been so conscious of how expensive things were. She might have to start shopping consignment stores and garage sales to keep these three in clothes. But she would not skimp on their shoes. Still, almost eighty bucks for two tiny pairs? She frowned.

"What's wrong, Mommy?"

"Why?"

"You were going like this—" Sari demonstrated with a deep-furrowed forehead.

Corinne laughed. "I was just thinking about how much the girls' shoes cost . . . Open the fridge for me, would you?"

Sari hopped off the stool and went to open the door. "Is thirty-nine ninety-nine a lot?"

She curbed a grin. "Yes it *is* a lot. It's like twelve allowances."

She heard Sadie playing school with Simone and decided to let them play while she had some one-on-one time with her oldest— who was growing up faster than she could fathom.

Corinne wrestled a head of lettuce from the crisper and handed it to Sari, then made a sling of her own apron and loaded it with salad veggies. She deposited them on the island cutting board and moved the step stool over for Sari.

They worked side by side for a few minutes, filling the large pottery bowl with crisp greens, bright yellow sweet peppers, and tomatoes from Dad's garden.

"Mommy?"

"What, sweetie?"

"What's a trouper?"

Corinne laughed. "It's just an expression. It means you did a great job and you were brave and strong and *amazing!*" She opened her mouth to explain further but realized she wasn't actually sure where the expression came from. It didn't matter. Sari was beaming, and Corinne's heart overflowed with love for this daughter of hers.

Listening for the little girls' voices upstairs, and satisfied they were still playing happily, she gathered up the vegetable peels and scraps. "Want to help me butter the French bread next?"

Sari nodded eagerly.

Corinne opened a loaf of bakery bread to slice to go with ham and scalloped potatoes Mom had sent home with them Tuesday night. The house would smell heavenly when Jesse got home.

If she tried, she could almost imagine that nothing had changed. Or ever would. That they were still the happy little family who'd moved into this house three years ago.

For this one evening, she would just enjoy her girls and pretend Michaela Creeve had never happened.

At the grind of the garage door going up, Sari's eyes sparkled. "Daddy's home!" She jumped down off the step stool and ran to the mudroom.

"Hey, punkin!"

Corinne washed her hands quickly and went to greet Jesse.

He put Sari down and gave Corinne a kiss, then looked behind her expectantly. "Where are the other two?"

"They're upstairs playing school."

"Ah." He set his briefcase on a bench and loosened his tie. "What's for supper? It sure smells good."

"I helped make supper, Daddy."

"You did? Which part did you make?"

"The salad."

"I bet that'll be the best part, too."

"Uh-huh. And I helped Mommy butter the bread."

"So we're having bread and salad?"

He was teasing, but Corinne thought he was slightly preoccupied too. She wondered if something had happened at work. Supposedly Michaela was on the road this week, but then, that's what they'd thought the day the girls disappeared. And with that thought, the idyllic afternoon she'd had with the girls dissipated like a vapor.

Supper was the rowdy event it usually was at the Pennington's house. Jesse played with the girls while she loaded the dishwasher. Then she gave Simone her bath while Jesse got the older girls to bed.

She pulled the room-darkening curtains in Simone's nursery and settled into the rocking chair with her. She heard Jesse administering last-minute drinks of water down the hall and tried to imagine how all this would work if all three girls were in one room. Well, people did it and made it work. Her friend Beth's five boys shared two bedrooms—small ones, too. Three small girls sharing one room was the kind of "problem" she should thank God for and never speak of again.

Simone grew heavy in her arms and Corinne rose slowly from the rocker, testing if the toddler was in a sound enough sleep to put down. Simone stirred and stretched but settled right back to sleep. Corinne put her in bed and covered her with a light blanket. She smoothed a strand of wispy hair from her baby's face and stood beside the crib in the dim room, watching the blanket rise and fall with Simone's drowsy breaths.

They were blessed. No matter what had happened or what the future held, she and Jesse had so much to be grateful for.

A shaft of light fell across the carpet and she looked toward the door to see Jesse slip in. "She asleep?" he whispered.

She nodded.

He came to stand beside her, putting an arm around her shoulders and drawing her close. "I think she's the cutest one, don't you?"

"Shh. Don't you dare wake her up," she mouthed. But she couldn't help but smile. It was a running joke that Jesse declared each of their daughters cuter, sweeter, brighter than the others—depending on which girl he was admiring. She'd finally told him they'd best not have any more kids lest the world be unable to handle the level of cuteness, sweetness, brightness that was likely to result.

She leaned her head on his shoulder and savored the moment. There was peace in their house, and that wasn't something to be taken lightly.

"If it's cooled off, let's go sit out on the terrace," he said, still whispering.

"Okay. Let me start a load of laundry first."

They tiptoed out into the hall. She looked in on each of the other girls and gathered the dirty laundry from their floors. Sari was still awake, looking at a book, but Sadie was out like a drunken sailor. She pulled the door shut and was surprised Jesse was still there.

"Anything I can do to help?"

"No, it won't take me but a minute to get this going." She held up the small pile of mostly pink clothes.

"Okay. I'll be outside. You want anything to drink?"

"Some ice water, maybe." She tilted her head and studied him. "You're being awfully accommodating."

He looked sheepish. "There's something I want to talk to you about."

She held her breath for a second. "Should I be worried?"

He hesitated a moment too long. "Not worried. But things may have just gotten more complicated."

She sagged.

But he smiled and patted her back. "It's not bad, I promise. Just . . . complicated."

⚬━✦━⚬

Corinne blew out a breath and stretched her shapely legs out in front of her, and Jesse watched with renewed appreciation.

Even with a frown creasing her forehead, she looked beautiful. Her hair was pulled loosely back from her face the way he liked it, and she'd gotten some sun this week, giving her skin a rosy glow.

She regarded him through hooded eyes. "So what are you thinking? Frank's offer doesn't change your mind, does it?"

"No. But I thought it might change yours."

"What do you mean?"

"Well, it would kind of solve all our problems if I took the position he's talking about."

She gave him a look he could only label as disgust. "It doesn't solve *your* problem, Jesse. Unless the position Frank is offering you is a teaching job."

He shrugged. "No, of course it's not. But I could do it, babe. I would."

"Do you think you should take it?"

"I don't have a clue. I—" He hesitated, knowing he might be giving Corinne ammunition that he didn't really want used against him. But he'd determined to be straightforward and one hundred percent honest with her—and let the chips fall where they would. "I hate to say this, but it almost seems like this could be God's way of pointing out a direction."

"Do you really think that?"

He crossed an ankle over his knee and worried a loose thread on his sandal. "I honestly don't have a clue what to think, Corinne. It's sure not something I'm gung ho to do. But I could do the job. I wouldn't be miserable in marketing. I pretty much know the position."

She bit her lower lip. "Well, I'd be lying if I said I didn't like the idea of keeping a steady paycheck, staying in this house, and you not traveling anymore. Not to mention in a completely different building than the Wicked Witch of the West."

He grinned at the name she'd taken to calling Michaela. "But?"

"But what?"

He shrugged. "You sounded like there was more to that thought."

"There is." But she stayed silent, looking out to the yard where fireflies flitted just above the manicured grass.

"Corinne, I just want you to know that if you want me to take this offer, I am willing to do it. All you have to do is say the word."

She turned to him and what he saw on her face was . . . peace. He hadn't seen that in her countenance for a long time.

So that was his answer. *God, help me to accept this and change gears.*

"Don't tempt me, Jesse."

He cocked his head. "What do you mean?"

"I'm tempted to just 'say the word' . . . whatever it takes to get things back the way they were before this whole thing started. But—I know we can't go back. And . . ." She bit her lip, and though it was hard to tell in the dusky light, he thought there were tears in her eyes.

When she spoke again, her voice quivered. "I want you to be happy. Ever since we've started planning toward you going back to school, you've been . . . different. In a good way. I don't want you to think it's easy for me to say this." She giggled. "I want to be able to throw this back in your face someday if I need to."

He laughed, but the deep disappointment he'd felt earlier lifted, and he let himself hope. "But?" he prompted again.

"But I want you to be able to dream too. You—" Her voice broke again. "You've made it possible for me to have my dream all these years. To stay home with the girls, and to have all this besides." She swept her arms out, encompassing the house and grounds. "I think it's your turn. And I'm willing to do whatever it takes to make your dreams come true too."

"I could be a little patient. Wait a few years. Even a couple. Just until Simone is in school."

She shook her head and curled her legs up under her, angling her body toward him. "No. I think it's time now. I don't know how we'll figure everything out, but I do know that we already agreed about you going back to school. And we were both happy with it."

"Are you sure you were happy?"

She looked like a kid with her hand in the cookie jar. "I'll *get* happy. I've already mourned what I'll be losing, and that's a big step. If we wait, there'll just be something else stopping us. There's never a perfect time for change. Sometimes you just have to do it."

He nodded, loving the certainty in her voice and feeling more relief than he wanted to admit. "There's only one problem. Kind of a big one . . ."

She frowned. "What's that?"

"I need to let Frank know. By Monday. And it wouldn't seem right not to tell him then that I'm leaving. There's a chance—possibly a good chance—that he'll let me go right then. And even if he lets me stay on for another month, I might have to travel during that time. With Michaela."

Corinne shook her head vehemently. "If that happens, I'd say quit right then."

"I have some vacation pay coming, but it would really strap us for me to quit now. Until we've sold the house—"

"Then let's just do it, Jesse. We have an offer from Danae and Dallas. Let's just get it over with."

He couldn't tell if her tone was determined or angry. "Are you speaking out of frustration or . . . conviction?"

"Probably a little of both. But honestly, I think the anticipation is worse than things will actually be. I don't know how we'll figure everything out, but I do know that we'd already reached an agreement we both could live with. I don't think Frank's offer changes that. Our agreement wasn't about money or even . . . Michaela. Those were just things that figured into the decision. The important thing is that you're not happy at Preston-Brilon. You feel gifted—called—to teach. That should be the more important thing."

"I don't know what to say."

"Just say, 'thank you, my darling wife.' "

He laughed and leaned to kiss her. "Thank you, my darling wife. I hope you know I mean that. And don't forget that once I start teaching, I'll have summers off to fix up a house or teach summer school, or whatever, to make a little money. And I'd probably never have to travel again. That means more time with you and the girls and—"

"Let's just do it," she said again. "Let's go for it."

"Wow. This is not how I thought this conversation was going to go."

She reached across the arms of their chairs and grabbed his hand. "Let's get some stuff on paper before I change my mind."

He went to her then and pulled her up into his arms. "Have I ever mentioned how much I love you?"

"You just love me because you got your way," she teased.

But he wasn't in a teasing mood. "No, Corinne. I love you because you are an amazing woman. I mean it. And I don't tell you often enough. And I know this isn't easy for you. I'm sorry for that. I truly am."

She pulled back and looked at him. "Don't apologize again. I feel bad that you didn't think you could be honest with me. Not just about . . . Michaela, but about your dreams of teaching. Let's promise that we'll talk about this stuff. That we won't ever be afraid to tell each other the truth. About everything."

"Okay. Then you want to know the truth?"

She gave him a suspicious look. "I guess . . ."

He grinned. "I do sort of love you because I got my way."

"I knew it." She swatted his arm, but she cracked up too. And for the first time, Jesse thought they just might get through this year in one piece.

26

Corinne settled in at the end of a row near the back of the sanctuary, fanning herself against the oppressive July heat and humidity that even the air conditioning couldn't combat. She looked over her shoulder, searching for Jesse. He usually got caught visiting in the hall after Sunday school and often didn't slip in to second service until halfway through the worship songs. But Pastor Flynn was making his way to the podium to begin his sermon and still no Jesse.

By the time she'd dropped the girls off in their respective classes, the sanctuary was nearly full, and she'd had to sit a few rows behind their usual spot, but surely Jesse would see her.

She'd skipped church more often than not this summer. Between everything that had happened with Michaela Creeve, and then getting ready for a possible move, it had just seemed simpler most mornings to stay home. Jesse had taken Sadie and Sari with him to Sunday school most of those mornings, and Corinne had enjoyed having some one-on-one time with Simone, too. But she knew Jesse frowned on her skipping, and she knew how easy it could become a habit to skip.

She didn't like sitting through worship alone. Jesse knew that, and after more than one discussion about it in the car on the way home from church, he truly had made an effort to find her and sit with her as soon as possible after the service started. But like he'd told her, "I feel like part of my commitment to teach Sunday school is being there for the kids afterward."

Somebody must have had a crisis this morning. Of course, the term "crisis" was relative for seventh and eighth graders.

Ten minutes into the sermon, still no Jesse. She fished her phone from her purse and texted him, knowing it was useless, since he turned his phone off in the parking lot and sometimes "forgot" to turn it back on until Sunday afternoon.

Maybe not seeing her in their usual spot, he'd sat somewhere else. She started scanning the chairs one row at a time looking for him. The church had two center aisles and she could just barely see the far section, but they'd never sat there in all the years they'd attended Community Christian.

She caught Beth Hodge's eye in the center aisle, and they exchanged a smile across the aisle and a look that said "it's been too long! We need to do lunch." She made a mental note to call Beth next week.

Corinne turned to face the front again. But just as she did, she glimpsed another face, two rows behind Beth. A familiar face . . . In the space of a breath—though it felt like much longer as realization hit her like a tsunami—

Michaela Creeve! The blonde hair, the petite stature. The bling.

Corinne's heart catapulted to her throat.

She looked back again, not even trying to be discreet. But at that very same moment, the song leader invited everyone to stand and sing.

Corinne was first out of her seat, trying to get a better view. But by then, people in the row between them had stood too, blocking her view.

She tried again to position herself for another glimpse She'd only had the one face-to-face encounter with Michaela—that day in the grocery store—so she couldn't be absolutely certain it was her she'd seen. Still, if it wasn't her, it was her twin.

Where *was* Jesse?

Had he seen Michaela and opted not to come in to the sanctuary? Did that woman have no shame? Now she wanted them to believe she'd suddenly gotten religion and just happened to choose Community Christian?

Her breath caught. The girls! She gathered her purse and Bible from the seat she'd been saving for Jesse, then rose and slipped into the aisle. When she got to the back of the church, she took a deep breath and turned to look at the center seating section. Several teenage boys sat right behind where she thought she'd seen Michaela. Two of them were tall, and she couldn't see over them.

She walked slowly across the back of the church, trying to get a better angle. She nodded to a couple of the greeters who were still stationed by the door, and one of them, Greg somebody, motioned her over. She didn't want to lose sight of the spot where she thought she'd seen Michaela, but she didn't want to be rude either.

"Are you looking for your husband?" Greg whispered.

"Yes. Have you seen him?"

He motioned toward the foyer. "He was talking to a couple of the middle schoolers when the service started. They were pretty deep in conversation."

"Thanks," she whispered back. "He's probably still out there."

An elongated triangle of light fell across the carpet, and she turned back toward the stage in time to see a side door on the far end swing shut. She tried again, unsuccessfully, to spot Michaela in the center section, but didn't see so much as a blond head.

Thinking only of her daughters now, she hurried past Greg to the double doors at the rear of the sanctuary, turning one more time to see if she could spot that woman. Maybe she'd been imagining things. Ever since Lt. Harrald had told them it would be almost impossible to get a restraining order on Michaela with no more evidence than they had, Corinne had tried to let the whole thing go and simply trust God to protect them. And except for the occasional nightmare, or an overly protective reaction if one of the girls disappeared from sight for a second too long, she'd been successful.

She always breathed a sigh of relief when Jesse could assure her that Michaela was traveling out of state. He knew their sales meetings and trade show schedule well enough to reassure Corrine when it was probable that Michaela was on the road. She'd let that comfort her—despite the fact that Michaela was supposedly traveling the day she'd confronted Corinne and the girls at Schnucks. But this was Sunday, and the sales team usually got back into town Saturday afternoon at the latest. It *could* have been her she saw.

She pushed through the doors into an empty hallway. She looked left toward the pre-school and elementary rooms, then right in the direction of Jesse's classroom. The door she'd seen closing a moment earlier led directly into the corridor where the nursery and children's classrooms were. Walking faster and faster until she was almost sprinting, she turned the corner to see that hallway empty too. Mildly relieved, she jogged past walls plastered with children's colorful drawings and crepe paper craft projects until she arrived at the two-year-old's nursery.

The upper half of the Dutch door was open and Corinne immediately spotted Simone, toddling around to the miniature slippery slide, the ID sticker on her back, hanging by one sticky corner.

One of the teachers, a young college girl, came to the door. "Do you need to pick someone up?"

"Yes. Simone Pennington." She pointed to the slides. "I'm going to pick up my older daughters across the hall, but I'll be right back to get her." She started to turn, but felt compelled to tell the teacher, "Don't let anyone else pick her up. I'll be right back."

The teacher gave her an odd look, but nodded. "Yes, ma'am. Of course."

She went down two doors and across the hall into the four- and five-year-olds' classroom. There were at least thirty children in the large room, playing at various stations or eating snacks at the tiny round tables in one corner. She saw Sadie immediately, playing with a puzzle at a table with three little boys. But she didn't see Sari anywhere.

One of the teachers looked up from a table and noticed her, and Sadie saw her at the same time.

"Mommy! Come look at the puzzle we're doing."

"Just a minute, sweetie. Where's Sari?"

"I dunno. Come look. Hurry."

Ignoring her daughter, she asked the teacher, "Where is Sari?"

The teacher looked around. "She was here just a minute ago." She slid out of the miniature chair she'd been sitting in and turned a one-eighty, looking around the room.

Panic pressed at Corinne's throat, and she turned to race down the hall in search of her eldest when the door to the restroom opened. Sari emerged, and her face lit up when she saw Corinne.

Weak with relief and feeling queasy, Corinne was grateful for the support of the door jamb. "Go tell Sadie it's time to go, Sari."

"Already? But we didn't get our snack yet."

"We did snacks in shifts," the teacher explained, giving Corinne an odd look. "But I can get them something to take home with them if you like."

"We don't . . . have time." Corinne turned to Sari. "Please tell Sadie. Right now."

Thankfully Sadie didn't throw her usual fit, and practically dragging her daughters back up the hall to the nursery, she went to retrieve Simone.

She was almost surprised to see Simone still there. "Did anyone else try to pick her up?"

The teacher looked puzzled. "No. But church won't be over for another ten minutes."

"I know. We . . . need to leave a little early today."

"How's come, Mommy?"

"Sari, shh. I'll explain later. Let's go find Daddy."

Corinne carried Simone and urged the other two to keep up as she went past the sanctuary and down the opposite hall to Jesse's classroom. She was tempted to stop and look into the sanctuary one more time, but the girls would cause a commotion. And besides, she was desperate to talk to Jesse.

He was seated on one of the grungy sofas in the courtyard area in the center of the youth classrooms, in rapt conversation with a scrawny teen boy and a woman who looked like she could be the boy's mother.

Sadie ran to him, and he looked up to meet her eyes. He glanced at his watch. "Wow. Is church out already?" He gave the woman an apologetic smile. "I kind of lost track of time. We'll talk more next week if you like."

He shook hands with the teen and motioned toward his classroom. "I need to gather up my stuff. Wait right here."

He was back in a few seconds, receiving the girls' hugs and taking Simone from Corinne's arms. "Sorry I stood you up, babe. Was church good?"

"Actually, it's not quite over yet."

"Oh?" He studied her. "What's wrong? Why'd you leave early?"

She nodded pointedly toward the girls. "I'll tell you later. Can we go?"

With the girls settled in the backseat and an exception made for watching a movie on the car's DVD player, even though it wasn't a "long trip," Corinne told him what had happened.

"But you're not sure it was her?"

"I'm ninety-nine percent sure."

"Was she sitting with someone?"

"I couldn't tell. And like I said, I never could spot her again after that first time."

"It was probably just someone who looked like her."

She could tell he was a little peeved at her. "Well, I wasn't going to take a chance. You don't think I should have waited till after church to see if the girls were still in the nursery, do you?"

He gave her a look. "No. Of course not. I'm sorry. You did the right thing. Whether it was her or not."

"It was her, Jesse. Somehow, I know it was."

"Well, then, I guess we should be glad she's going to church. She needs all the help she can get."

She tossed the look right back at him. "I don't think that's funny."

He checked the road and his rearview mirror before turning to her. "I wasn't trying to be funny, but we can't live our lives looking over our shoulders. If it was her, and if she'd wanted to do something this morning, she would have. We can't dictate where she goes to church, or where she does her grocery shopping. It's just something we're going to have to live with. And besides, you know how careful they are with security at church. They are not going to let someone walk in and take one of the girls. But if it would make you feel better, we could let them know about our situation so they'd be extra cautious." He reached across the console for her hand. "It's not worth ruining our lives over, Corinne. Is it? Do you want me to contact Lt. Harrald again?"

She blew out a frustrated sigh. "What could he do? She's so deviously sneaky about everything . . . There's no way we can prove what she's doing."

"Then we're just going to have to deal with it. It'll be okay." He squeezed her hand.

But she couldn't reply. She knew Jesse was right, and even though he felt sure Michaela would never do anything to actually harm them, still, they couldn't know that for sure. It filled her with rage to think that woman might show up at church again. At any event they ever attended, they might discover she was there, too. As long as it was a public place and she didn't bother them, she was perfectly within her legal rights. But even if she wasn't there with the intent of harassing them, it felt like an assault nevertheless. It didn't seem right.

It was enough to make a person want to move across the country. But then, there was nothing stopping Michaela Creeve from following them *anywhere* they might go.

Jesse pointed through the windshield at the Burger King. "Do you want to stop for burgers? So you don't have to cook?"

She nodded. "That would be good. Don't order me anything though. I'm not hungry."

He gave her the same look he gave the girls when they were being brats.

"I'll be fine," she said. "But I'm really not hungry. I don't feel well."

It was the truth. This whole thing made her literally sick to her stomach.

27

So what do you think?" Jesse squeezed Corinne's hand under the table. So hard it hurt.

Dallas Brooks looked at Danae as if making sure they were on the same page. Apparently he saw agreement in her face because he turned to them with a big smile. "We're game if you are."

"Okay! Let's do this."

Corinne wanted to kick Jesse under the table for being just a tad too excited about trading off their beautiful home for the little two-bedroom cottage where they were sitting at the eat-in kitchen—because there was no formal dining room. But even now, she could hear the girls' chattering and giggling, their voices carrying through the open windows as they played in Aunt Danae's playhouse in the backyard. A playhouse that might soon belong to them.

Her sister's house looked especially pretty tonight, and soft jazz played from somewhere in the kitchen, adding to the ambiance. It was obvious Danae had gone to extra pains with the house before they got here. Not that Corinne would fault her if she had. Danae knew this was hard for her, and even though they were sisters, this was a business deal for both of them.

Jesse took the reins now, steering them to the most difficult part of the conversation. "I think you guys know what we were asking for our house. We have a little room to wiggle, but not much. But we don't know where you're wanting to come in on your house."

Dallas jumped up and retrieved a file folder from the rolltop desk in the corner of the living room—the space he used for his office. Corinne cringed inwardly. Well, it was convenient. She had to give him that. She tried—unsuccessfully—to mentally arrange their living room furniture in this space. Oh well. They'd talked about selling some of it anyway. Extra cash was the name of the game right now. She swallowed hard. This wasn't going to be easy. But she was determined not to be a big baby about it.

"Why don't we move to the living room."

"Let me check on the girls," Jesse said. He stooped to look out the dining room windows.

"Do you see them?" Corinne asked, working to keep her voice level. She couldn't help feeling vulnerable when the girls weren't in sight.

"They're fine."

"You see all three of them?"

"Yes, babe. They're right out here. One, two, three."

"Did Danae tell you we put locks on the side gates? They're both locked. I checked before you guys got here."

"I hadn't told her yet," Danae said, looking a little sheepish.

"Thanks, you guys." She knew Danae hadn't said anything because she didn't want to remind her of that day the girls had gone missing. As if she could ever forget. But it did help to know the gates were locked.

Dallas led the way, and when they were settled, he opened the folder and spread it on the coffee table in front of the sofa where Corinne and Jesse sat. "I've talked to a Realtor friend and printed out some comparable homes in this neighborhood. I also know this is close to what our neighbors to the west of us paid for their home about"—he looked to Danae—"two years ago, wasn't it, honey?"

"Probably closer to three."

"Anyway, we have a little wiggle room, too. We're not going to be able to put as much down on your house as you guys did, but this house is paid for, so that helps."

Corinne was surprised to learn that Dallas and Danae didn't have a mortgage on their home. She assumed since they'd been socking so much money into their "baby fund" that paying off the house had gone on the back burner.

"So . . . How do you want to do this?" Jesse shifted in his seat the way he did when he was feeling socially uncomfortable.

Corinne spoke up. "What if we each write our offer on a piece of paper and work forward from there?"

"Sounds good to me," her sister said. "Everybody?"

Nods all around, and Danae went to the kitchen and came back with slips of paper and pens. She gave a nervous laugh. "Is this legal, you think?"

Dallas shrugged. "Sure. We're doing two FSBOs. We can do anything we want at this point."

He pronounced the acronym "fizz-bo," which Corinne would not have understood before her recent real estate research.

In the car on the way here, she'd asked Jesse to pray with her that nothing that happened tonight would endanger their friendship with her sister and brother-in-law. So far, so good, but this part could get sticky.

"Do we need to go talk amongst ourselves," Dallas joked. "Or are we ready to write down some numbers?"

Jesse looked at Corinne. "I think we're ready. You guys?"

"Do the wives need to sequester themselves in a soundproof booth?" Danae asked, smiling.

Corinne laughed. "It does kind of feel like that time we tried to play The Newlywed Game at Mom and Dad's."

The guys both groaned, and the sisters exchanged conspiratorial looks. She and Danae had orchestrated the game. And it had been a blast. At least the women all thought so. The guys, not so much.

With the ice broken, they settled in to work out the business deal. Exchanging slips of paper, Danae hurried to explain theirs. "We're offering you guys full price, but we'd like to negotiate for some of the furniture if that's okay."

"Sure." Corinne swallowed—more like a gulp. "Do you have certain things in mind?"

"Kind of," her sister said. "But if you'd rather, we'd be happy to just wait until you've decided what you plan to sell, and then we'll talk about those pieces."

"That might be better," Jesse said.

Corinne could have kissed him.

He looked at the slip of paper Dallas had written on and handed it to Corinne. "Is this right?"

Their asking price was almost thirty thousand dollars less than she and Jesse had been anticipating. "Did you guys take into account all the updates you've done to the house?"

"We did." Dallas stroked his chin. "It's a great neighborhood and we love it here, but it hasn't kept its value very well."

"Partly because too many of these houses get rented out to college kids. Or at least the basements or attic apartments do."

"But you guys have said before that it doesn't get too rowdy?"

"No," they said in unison.

"We've had a couple of times where we could hear a party going on up the street, but it never got too out of control."

"The only problem you'll have in our neighborhood is the HOA patrol," Jesse said.

Danae's forehead wrinkled. "What's that?"

"Don't pay any attention to him," Corinne told her sister. "He's just being facetious. There are a couple of people on our home-owners association board with too much time on their hands."

"There's one old lady who walks the streets with a ruler, measuring to be sure nobody's grass gets over four inches tall."

"Seriously?" Dallas looked doubtful.

"Oh, she does not, Jesse." Corinne elbowed Jesse and turned to Dallas. "They're pretty strict about the covenants, but not that strict."

"I'm telling you, Corinne, I have seen her with a ruler."

She smirked. "Maybe so, but it wasn't to measure the grass. Don't listen to him, guys."

"Yeah, man," Dallas said. "Are you trying to change our minds about that full-price offer?"

"No way!" Jesse held up a hand. "We're all over that offer. In fact, I just happen to have a contract out in the car." He started to rise, but Corinne pulled him back down, laughing.

When the room quieted, Jesse picked up the slip of paper with the Brooks's price on it. "Guys, this is a really nice offer. You're sure it's not an act of charity? Because we really don't need you to—"

Dallas halted him with an upraised hand. "We feel like it's a fair price. I seriously don't think we could get any more than that if we put it on the market."

"You're sure?"

"And besides," Danae said, "you guys are giving us a nice deal too, with the furniture and all."

Jesse winked at Corinne before turning to Danae. "Have you taken a good look at our furniture lately?"

"Renegotiate, renegotiate," Danae said, laughing.

Corinne watched her sister and their husbands joking with each other and seemingly in competition for who could be the nicest to whom, who could bless the other guy more. It warmed her heart. She'd never considered that expression before, but there truly was a warmth in the region of her heart. No matter what happened, she would always remember that about this evening.

Dallas got up and offered to refill drink glasses, and Jesse went to check on the girls again. With the kitchen right around the corner from the living room, Corinne could hear ice clinking into glasses and tea being poured. This—*coziness*—would take some getting used to.

Jesse returned smiling. "I think we may actually be getting a better deal than we thought."

"Why's that?" Danae said.

"Because I think those girls would be plenty happy to just move into the playhouse permanently. Corinne and I can have the whole house to ourselves."

The whole house. Yeah, all fourteen hundred square feet of it. But the playhouse would soften the blow for the girls, that was for sure.

When Dallas returned with refills, he remained standing. An uncharacteristic gentleness came to his voice. "I've gotta say, guys, this has to be the most fun business deal I've ever done."

"Well, sure, you're the one getting the big house out of the deal," Jesse said.

"I'm also the one writing the big check."

Jesse beamed. "Touché, brother. Touché."

Dallas held out his iced tea glass. "A toast. To trading spaces."

"You're toasting a TV show?" Corinne said.

"Cute," her sister said wryly. But she raised her glass.

Corinne and Jesse did likewise, and they clinked glasses all around to murmurs of "cheers."

Dusk came on quickly, and while Jesse and Dallas came up with a plan for who would take care of each aspect of their real estate trade, she went out to round up the girls. The evening had gone better than she could have hoped. And like she'd told Jesse, the actual doing was far easier than the dreading of it.

Later, in the kitchen, while the girls colored at the table, Corinne helped Danae put glasses in the dishwasher.

"Are you okay if we tell the family Tuesday night?" she asked her sister. "Do we dare wait that long?" Most of the Whitmans had been together last week to celebrate the Fourth of July, so they'd skipped a Tuesday family dinner.

"I'd rather not do it like a big . . ." Danae frowned. "Like a big *secret* announcement."

"What do you mean?"

"Because if we make a big deal of announcing it, the first thing everybody will think is that I'm pregnant." Danae looked at the floor. "And I'm definitely not. I started my period this morning."

"Oh, Danae. I'm so sorry." She reached for her sister and gave her a hug. "I know it's got to be so hard to be disappointed month after month."

Her sister shrugged out of her embrace. "I'm getting used to it."

"Your turn will come, Danae. I know it will. And I'm sorry for being so thoughtless. I hadn't even considered that the family might take it that way. We'll just tell people privately as they get there. Sound okay?"

Danae nodded. She glanced over at the girls and lowered her voice. "I know this whole house swap isn't easy for you, Corinne. Please don't feel like you have to pretend you're excited about moving into our house."

"No, I'm not—"

"I think you guys will be really happy here. Dallas and I have been. And, if it's any consolation, it's helped a lot to keep my mind off our baby woes having your house to get excited about. And to dream about filling it with babies."

"Aww." A lump came to her throat. "That helps a lot, sis. And don't misunderstand. I love your house. It'll just be kind of hard to downsize."

"Well, it won't be for long. I wouldn't be surprised if you were back in your neighborhood in a few short years. Just think, we might end up being next-door neighbors."

Corinne was touched. She hadn't thought about how this move—and their house—might be a much-needed blessing to Danae while she and Dallas were going through a hard time.

But she didn't tell her sister that there was no use hoping they'd someday be next-door neighbors. She and Jesse had done the math. Unless they won the lottery—unlikely since they never bought a ticket—they would never again live in a house as nice as the one they were moving out of.

Corinne finished buckling the girls into their car seats and climbed into the passenger seat beside Jesse. She was eager to hear his thoughts about the evening with Dallas and Danae, but given the way he was whistling under his breath, she was pretty sure she could guess how he felt.

The girls were asleep in the backseat practically as soon as they pulled out of the Brooks's driveway. Their driveway. At least it soon would be.

"So what do you think?" she asked, once they were on the main road.

"What do you think?"

"I asked you first."

"Well, for starters, I can't believe their asking price. I almost fell out of my chair." He shook his head. "It almost feels like we'd be cheating them."

"Maybe we should offer a little over their asking price."

"Even if we did, do you realize what this means, Corinne?"

She shook her head, not understanding.

"Babe! You won't have to work. At that price, and with what they're paying for our house, we will own that house free and clear. We'll have no mortgage payment. Zero. And with such a small house, we'll have lower utility bills, lower taxes. I really won't have to make much to pay the bills. And Dallas even gave me a lead on a job. We may have to dip into savings for anything extra, but we'll be sitting pretty good."

"Are you sure?"

"I'm positive. You saw the numbers. I mean, we'll still have to be careful with our money. But we do that anyway. And I know there are probably things you want to do to the house. But you can absolutely stay home if you want to."

"Wow. How did I miss that? But—maybe you should be the one who doesn't take a job. You could carry more hours that way." She wished she hadn't opened her big mouth, because she was really liking the idea of not having to find a job. Of getting to be home with Simone for another few years.

"I'd feel better if you were home with the girls," he said. "And if we don't have to pay for daycare—and a work wardrobe and gas for your car—we're that much more ahead. And you're creative, and paint is cheap; we're moving some nice furniture. The house will look a lot better—and more like ours—once we move our things in. What do you think?"

"Oh, Jesse. That would be like a dream come true."

He laughed and reached across the console to squeeze her knee. "Listen to you. This is a little different song than you were singing a few weeks ago. And are you calling that little cottage we're moving into a dream come true?"

She wrinkled her nose. "The jury's still out on that one. I may be wishing I could get a job just to cure my claustrophobia."

"The house is pretty small, isn't it?" He winced. "I never realized."

"I know. You start looking at it with different eyes when it's going to be yours."

"That red wall in the kitchen will have to go." He made a gagging sound.

"Seriously? I kind of like it. Our dishes would look really good against that shade of red."

"You really think the hutch will fit on that wall?"

"Oh, sure." She made a face. "At least I think so."

He took both hands off the steering wheel and held them up in surrender. "Hey, I bow to your superior knowledge. Honestly, I know you'll make the place look great. All I ask is that I have a quiet corner somewhere where I can study."

"A quiet corner? In that house? Dream on, baby. But hey, I know the perfect place."

"Oh yeah?"

"It's called the public library."

He rolled his eyes. "I guess I could always go sit in the car in the garage and study."

"That's not a half-bad idea. Why didn't I think of that?" She grinned up at him, then turned serious again, in full brainstorming mode. "I think we could fit that smaller desk in a corner of the master bedroom for you. That room is actually a little bigger than I remembered. Or maybe you could use the playhouse for an office?"

"Do you think for one minute the girls would allow that?"

"Good point."

"How do you think they'll react when we tell them?"

She grinned. "Probably a whole lot better than I did."

"We'll figure it all out." He looked at her in the dim light of the car. "It's just for a while, babe. Just until I can get through school and get a teaching position."

"No, Jesse. It's not just for a while. It's a big change. And it's forever. For the rest of our lives. And—I'm okay with that."

And she was. Or she would be. Hard as it might be, she would be okay. *They* would be okay.

28

Audrey sat at the dining room table, her favorite place in the house because it afforded her a panoramic view of most of the inn's first floor—this beautifully transformed home she'd dreamed of and longed for all the years she and Grant had spent raising their children here. Of course, back then the carpets were worn— never mind ugly—and the woodwork was dark and scuffed. But there had been so much joy inside these walls. And she'd wasted entirely too much time wishing for something she couldn't have at that time.

She wondered, if God had afforded her a future glimpse of this life she and Grant were living now, would she have been more content and less fretful for what she didn't have in the early years of their marriage? She sighed. Probably not. After fifty-eight years in this skin, she knew herself well enough to know that God tended to have to repeat life's lessons before she finally got them.

The clock in the upstairs hall chimed four o'clock. Two large pans of lasagna were in the oven—and filling the house with an irresistible aroma—and she had almost two hours before the kids started arriving for their weekly Tuesday gathering.

Tonight would probably be the last time everyone was together for a few weeks given the big "trading spaces" escapade that was going on between her two eldest daughters. They would both be busy getting settled, and since Grant—bless his heart—had offered to let Corinne's family stay at the inn for a week while they did some painting at their new home, which was Dallas and Danae's old home.

Thankfully they hadn't booked all the rooms for the intended week, which ordinarily would have been a bad thing, but now she would keep Landyn's room and the room Tim and Link had shared as boys open. And she would hope the guests in the rooms they *had* booked wouldn't mind having three little girls running about the inn. She would be so glad when everyone got settled in their new places and the upheavals they'd each been through were resolved.

This running an inn and trying to be the quintessential grandma at the same time was not working out like she'd envisioned. She hated how often she felt torn between her new career and her family—most of whom were supposed to be grown and independent, but apparently some of them had yet to get the memo.

She did love their Tuesday night family dinners, but as she recalled, one of the reasons Grant had instituted the tradition was so the kids would have a set time to visit the inn—and would make themselves scarce the rest of the week.

Instead, it seemed she was babysitting somebody's kids every time she turned around. Landyn and Corinne were both thoughtful to not ask her too often, but she didn't think they considered that even if they asked only twice a month, the other one likely also asked twice—or more—and that meant at least one day every week taken up with babysitting. And it wasn't just the time she had the little girls but the time spent cleaning up after they left, too. And all that on top of cleaning up after Tuesday nights. Grant always helped her, but his idea of "that's good enough" was very different from hers.

She sighed. Grandchildren—especially granddaughters—were something she'd dreamed of while she planned the Chicory Inn in her imagination. She didn't want to miss a blessing. And her time with those five little girls was a blessing of the highest degree. But her daughters forgot that she also had a job these days. And the inn had turned into a full-time job and then some.

She couldn't remember the last time she'd had time to sit for more than five minutes and just enjoy the inn. And when she had time to sit, it was usually because the inn wasn't booked, so then what could have been a rest turned into a worry fest.

Oh, Lord, help me to live in the moment. Forgive my ungrateful attitude.

She'd thought she would have grown up by now, but she remembered praying that same prayer almost daily when the kids were all living at home.

For some reason, she'd been thinking of those days often lately. Probably because of Corinne and Jesse's upcoming move. She'd never seen her eldest daughter in such a tizzy. And as frazzled as Corinne was, Jesse was equally at ease and absolutely flying at the prospect of going back to school. It didn't help Corinne that Danae was so excited for the move. Audrey was thankful her second-born had come out of the funk she'd been in for most of her childless marriage. Unfortunately, Danae's delight was the reason for Corinne's distress.

Audrey sighed. She feared both of her daughters were in for rude awakenings.

She heard Grant come in through the garage. He was always like a kid at Christmas on Tuesdays. She took a breath and willed herself to put her worries aside. No use spoiling her sweet husband's favorite day of the week.

"There you are." Grant appeared around the corner. "You're not expecting guests, are you?"

"No. Why?"

"Somebody just pulled in. The car had Missouri tags, but I didn't get a look at the county."

"Oh, dear. Well, nobody called. And if it's a walk-in, will you please tell them we're not open tonight?"

He turned on his heel and headed through the front foyer.

She jumped up and hurried after him.

He stopped short and turned to her. "I'll take care of it. You go sit."

She gave him a wry smile. "I'd feel better coming with you. I don't trust you to 'just say no.'"

He chuckled and started to make some retort, but as he opened the front door, they saw a cream-colored sedan heading down the driveway toward Chicory Lane, going fast enough to kick up dust. Grant winked at her. "Guess they heard you coming."

Audrey frowned. "Did they drive all the way in?" It wasn't unusual to have people get lost on the labyrinth of county roads and use the entrance to the inn's driveway as a turnaround, but it appeared this car had come all the way up the long drive.

Grant frowned. "They did. That's strange."

"Well, good riddance," Audrey said. She glanced across the lawn as the sedan turned onto the lane and disappeared over the hill. "Is everything ready for tonight?"

"I've got things set up for yard games." Grant wiped his brow with his shirt sleeve. "I just hope it cools off a little before we go out."

"It's July, my love. Cool is a relative term. But I think you and I are the only ones who mind so much. Shall we eat inside though?"

"No, let's tough it out in the shade. The trumpet vine keeps things pretty cool under the pergola. We can set up a fan if there's no breeze. Don't you have a hunk of ice in the deep freeze? We can blow the fan across that. Should keep things tolerable."

"Okay. I think the girls are both bringing homemade ice cream, so that'll help too." At the mention of her daughters, her thoughts picked up where they'd left off before Grant came in, and she instantly resumed worry mode.

"Yep, ice cream ought to do the trick. But right now I need a glass of sweet tea." Grant gave her a kiss, but when he pulled away, he studied her, and his expression told her she hadn't managed to smooth the worry lines from her forehead in time.

"What's wrong?"

"Nothing."

"Oh, no you don't. None of that. Tell me what's bothering you."

She sighed. "I'm just thinking about our girls. I hope they're not headed for a falling out."

"Corinne and Danae? Why would they be?"

That man could be so dense sometimes. "Because Corinne is giving up everything she loves and Danae is taking it out from under her."

"Well, that's a whale of a way to look at it."

"I'm not saying that's Danae's intent, but that's how Corinne probably sees it. And I'm afraid Danae is just trying to fill her empty arms with that beautiful big house. I hope she realizes there won't be babies in those bedrooms when they sign the contract."

"I don't think our girls are that petty, Audrey. Give them a little credit."

"I know. And even if they were, they'd eventually work it out. Just let a mother worry a little, will you?"

He raised his eyebrows. "If you feel good about that, you go right ahead."

That made her smile. As she knew was his intent.

She rose, pushed her chair in, and went to check on the lasagna, patting her sweet husband's cheek as she went by.

She'd get a better feel for things after she saw the girls together tonight.

29

Well, I think that's it." Corinne blew her bangs off her forehead and surveyed the mountain of moving boxes in front of her.

Landyn, with a wiggly four-month-old on each hip, shook her head. "That's a lot of stuff, sis."

"I know. I feel a giant garage sale coming on." She felt a good cry coming on too.

"Don't forget, I called dibs to go through stuff first."

"Don't worry. I told Danae and Bree I'd have all you guys over as soon as we get moved in. You can have at it."

"Maybe you should have the garage sale here?" Landyn looked a little shell shocked.

Corinne laughed. "Bite your tongue, sister. I am *not* lugging all that stuff back here."

"Any bets on whether the overflow will fit in that garage at Danae's?"

She growled at her sister. "You are not being very helpful."

"Just being realistic." Landyn laughed, but she must have sensed the panic welling up in Corinne, because she hiked the babies up on her hips and gave her most winsome smile. "We'll help you guys. It will all turn out just fine. And believe me, I know how you feel. You never saw Chase's studio apartment in New York, but I about freaked when I first saw it. It was about the size of your master bedroom closet."

"You mean Danae's master bedroom closet. My new closet is the size of a postage stamp."

"Before you know it, this will all be over and everybody will be settled in and back to normal." She moved close and gave Corinne as much of a hug as she could manage with a fifteen-pound baby in each arm.

Corinne put down the box she was carrying and wrapped her arms around the three of them. "Thanks for coming by to offer moral support. I mean it. It really helped."

"You'll be fine. And you can always visit Danae if you get homesick for this house."

She shook her head. "It wouldn't be the same." Not at all the same. And now she wondered if she'd ever feel comfortable visiting the sister she loved. Had they made a gigantic mistake?

"I hate to leave you in this jungle," Landyn said, heading to the corner of the garage where she'd stashed the diaper bags and other baby paraphernalia. "But Chase will be home by the time I get there."

Corinne glanced at the clock on her phone. "Yeah, Jesse'll be home in a few minutes too. Hopefully with pizza."

She heard the faint ringing of the phone from inside the house. "I'd better get that. Thanks again, sis." She ran inside and caught the phone mid-ring. "Hello?"

Silence. But she could have sworn someone was on the other end.

"Hello? This is Corinne. Hello?"

And then the line went unmistakably dead. She felt sure someone had been on the line. It was the second time this week she'd gotten a hang-up call. Of course, her mind immediately went to Michaela Creeve. But when she'd told Jesse about the first call, he reminded her that it could be someone trying to reach Dallas or Danae. Both couples had decided to use the move as an opportunity to get rid of their landlines and go to cell phones only, but they'd agreed to leave the landline phones connected until they were both moved in so the various workers coming and going from their houses and everyone helping with the moves would have access to a phone if needed.

She wondered if Danae had gotten similar calls at their house. She wanted to ask her sister but decided she'd rather not know. Because if she found out Danae *hadn't* gotten any hang-up calls, she would definitely suspect it was Michaela.

She listened to the silence for another moment before putting the cordless phone back in its charger. She took comfort in the fact that this number would be disconnected in a few days. And after today, Jesse would no longer have his company phone, so that was yet another connection to Michaela Creeve that would be severed.

Corinne could scarcely believe how quickly everything had unfolded. Jesse would pull in the driveway for good tonight. Today had been his last day at Preston-Brilon. They were grateful the company had allowed him to stay on a full month after he'd given his notice.

But a week from tomorrow would be their first day of living in a much smaller house. On a much smaller salary.

Over the past two weeks—in the unbearable heat and humidity of a Missouri August—they'd boxed up their belongings and moved everything into two bays of the three-car garage. And Landyn was right. Even with leaving behind the furniture Dallas and Danae wanted, there was no way even half of their things would fit into the "new" house.

Mom had the girls overnight tonight, and she and Jesse would finish cleaning and getting the house emptied. In the morning, the movers would bring Dallas and Danae's things, and she and Jesse would go over and start painting, and then they'd see how much of their stuff they could fit into Dallas and Danae's house. No, *their* house. She was finding it a challenge to let go of the old and embrace the new.

Thankfully, Mom and Dad were letting them sleep at the inn during the transition. It would be a long week. Admittedly worse for her parents than for her and Jesse and the girls.

If there was one good thing about all this, it was that Jesse was no longer a part of Preston-Brilon, which meant the Wicked Witch of the West no longer had any power over them. Without mentioning it to Jesse—because he had his plate full with getting enrolled for school and taking care of the move—Corinne had done some checking to see if Michaela still had the right to file sexual harassment charges after Jesse left the company.

From what Jim Houser, their attorney friend from church, said, the statute of limitations would expire one hundred and eighty days from the last time Jesse had traveled to Chicago with Michaela. November 19, according to Corinne's count. After that, it would be much more difficult for Michaela Creeve to file charges.

But until then, she was afraid she'd be holding her breath every waking moment.

Audrey carried the heavy platter to the table, then thought better of it. They could eat buffet style. Having five extra at the table every night for the last three days had been fun. But apparently three days was her limit, because it was starting to feel more like work.

Grant seemed to thrive on having his granddaughters there, tagging after him all over the property like ducklings after their mother. And it did warm her heart to look out the window and see them tagging behind, asking questions and making Grant laugh.

If she hadn't been so busy keeping their laundry done and food on the table—and of course, worrying about how they were going to make up the loss of having mostly empty guest rooms this entire week—she might have enjoyed it more.

She kept reminding herself that it was only temporary and they would be gone by this time next week, and she'd probably miss their incessant chattering. Of course, they'd be back on Tuesday night. And every Tuesday after that, Lord willing.

She heard Grant and the girls come in through the back door, and hushed whispers coming from the mud room. They were up to something. No doubt something Grant had schemed.

"Supper's just about ready," she hollered down the hallway.

That set off a cacophony of stage whispers before they paraded into the kitchen wearing smug smiles, Grant bringing up the rear, with his hands behind his back.

"You girls need to get washed up for supper," she said, pretending she didn't see that Grant was concealing something behind his back. Probably a bouquet of wildflowers from down by the creek.

But they ignored her and marched up the staircase as if on an important mission. She dried her hands and went to the bottom of the stairs. "What are you guys doing up there?"

"You'll see, Gram!" Sari said, while the other girls giggled.

"Yeah," Sadie echoed. "You'll see, Gram."

"Can I come up?"

A muffled commotion followed and Grant hollered down, "Not quite yet."

"Almost, Gram. Just a couple more minutes," Sari said, sounding much older than her not-quite-six years.

A hammer pounded three sharp raps, and it was all she could do not to march up there and see what they were destroying. But she resisted, hoping her faith in her husband wasn't misplaced. You never knew when it came to those girls who had him wrapped around their pinkies.

"Okay, Gram! You can come up now! You can come up!"

There was much jumping and stomping and squealing as she ascended the stairway, bracing herself for whatever it was that had them all so excited.

When she reached the top of the stairs, they all beamed at her—Grant widest beam of all—and pointed to a newly installed sign over the door to Landyn's old room, where the Pennington family was sleeping.

Painted on an old piece of board that looked like a leftover from Chase and Landyn's rustic loft restoration, the sign read: *Reserved for Friends and Family.*

"Poppa says we have a *permament* reservation now," Sadie said with a bob of her pointy little chin.

"Don't worry, Gram," Grant said with a wink. "It's not a *permament* fixture. It can be easily uninstalled should we ever actually manage to get paying guests here."

She grinned. "That's good to know, Poppa." She inspected the sign for the girls' sake.

"Do you like it, Gram?" Sadie asked, eyes eager.

Audrey bent to scoop Simone into her arms. "I love it, girls! And I'm so glad you have a reserved room here."

She put a hand over her heart, emotion catching her unaware. Those three had a spot reserved right there, too.

30

"Jesse, have you seen Simone's nightgown?" Corinne rifled through the diaper bag for a third time with no success.

"The orange one?" His voice came from the cavern of the closet where he was searching for something in his own duffle bag.

"No, that's Sadie's. Simone doesn't even own an orange nightgown. The one I'm looking for is yellow with little white flowers." This living out of suitcases and sleeping every night with three little girls scattered on the floor around them was for the birds.

"Well, I sure don't know where it is." His tone said, "And why are you bothering me with it?"

Tempers had been short all day, and it didn't help matters any that Dad had checked a walk-in guest into the room at the other end of the hall after supper. Mom had cornered Jesse and begged him to keep the girls quiet tonight, which did not sit well with him.

"Does she know what she's asking?" Jesse said once they were alone. "And why didn't she tell you? Now if they're noisy, it's all on me."

"Oh, she didn't mean that. You know Mom. She just gets frazzled when they have guests."

"You mean she's frazzled six days a week?"

Corinne ignored that. He was just looking for a fight.

At least the room where the man was staying had a private bath, unlike theirs. They'd be traipsing across the hall a dozen times before the night was over, getting drinks and going potty and brushing teeth—all times three.

Poppa had taken Sari and Sadie into Langhorne to the swimming pool this afternoon, so hopefully they were worn out enough that they'd go right to sleep. Simone, on the other hand, had taken an extra-long nap, so her batteries were fully charged. She was likely to be burning the midnight oil. And there was no keeping her quiet if she didn't want to be.

A minute later, still hearing Jesse muttering and digging in the closet, Corinne asked, "What are you looking for?"

"My last nerve."

She didn't find that very funny given the circumstances. "If you'll tell me what you're looking for, maybe I can help you find it."

"I'm fine. You worry about the girls. I think I can get myself ready for bed."

"You're just a regular barrel of laughs tonight, aren't you?"

He ignored her.

For the last four days, the two of them had painted at the old house, which was really the new house, and hauled more furniture back to the new house, which was really the old house, because they simply didn't have room for it. She and Jesse had started calling the two homes "the big house" and "the little house" in their conversations, just to be clear which home they were referring to. She didn't want to add to the confusion, but in her mind she'd begun to switch the labels to "the nice house" and "the tiny house."

They'd accomplished a great deal and Corinne was feeling better about how the house would work for them, but they were all exhausted to the point of extreme crabbiness, and it seemed to be catching, since even her formerly good-natured mother had been cranky. Of course, Mom'd had three little girls underfoot for most of the week, so Corinne understood why she was crabby.

It was time for everyone to move back to their own homes. She'd talked to Danae a couple of times, and it sounded like they were already almost settled in the big house. Corinne knew she'd eventually have to go over and ooh and aah over what her sister had done with the house, but she was grateful the painting and moving had given her a good excuse to stay away so far.

"Hey, babe, will you do toothbrushing duty tonight so I can go help Mom get stuff laid out for breakfast tomorrow?"

No reply.

She tried again. "Jesse?"

"I heard you. Yeah, go ahead. I'm on it." He emerged from the closet. "Come on girls. Everybody follow me."

He seemed more himself, and the girls were giggling, so she went down to help her mother lay out breakfast makings for the inn's lone guest, a Mr. Fordham from St. Louis, who Mom seemed convinced was a "secret shopper" that would be evaluating the inn for some mystery publication.

Corinne doubted he was that, but she did feel guilty that her parents had essentially shut down the inn for the whole week on her and Jesse's account.

Corinne came back up to read bedtime stories to the girls, and heard Mom and Dad talking to the inn's guest in the kitchen below. He was a talkative fellow, and she had to admit that some of the questions he asked made her wonder if her mother was right about him being there to review the inn. If so, they had nothing to worry about. Mom was being her charming self, and the scent of her famous Apple Cinnamon Crisp—served with a big scoop of cinnamon ice cream, if Dad had anything to say about it—wafted up the stairs.

It was after nine o'clock when the girls finally settled down and went to sleep. Jesse had an early class and fell asleep before the girls. Corinne decided to make herself scarce, and instead of going downstairs as she had the last few nights, she curled up in bed with a couple of magazines.

She must have fallen asleep sitting up, because the next thing she knew, Simone was standing at the foot of the bed crying. The alarm clock on the nightstand said one forty-five. Jesse stirred beside her in that way that told Corinne he was awake but playing possum so she would handle the kids. She'd never minded that little game when he worked and she was home with the kids. She didn't feel quite as magnanimous about it tonight. But Jesse did have class in the morning.

She threw the covers back and eased her legs over the side of the bed. "Sweetie, shh. It's okay. Go back to sleep."

"Mama!" Simone cried louder, and Corinne knew she wasn't likely going back to sleep on her own.

Sighing, she got up and started toward the end of the bed. "Ouch!" Stupid bed frame. Pain zinged from her big toe to her ankle.

"What?" Jesse sat straight up in bed. "What's going on?"

"Go back to sleep. I just stubbed my toe." She moaned and wondered if she'd broken it.

Simone cried louder.

"Can you hush her up?"

"Jesse, what do you think I'm trying to do?"

He mumbled something she couldn't understand. Which was probably for the best.

Simone toddled to the corner, crying ever louder.

"Sweetie. Mama's right here. Come here." Feeling her way across the dark room, she tripped on Sadie and stumbled. She caught herself on the mattress, but not before her knee hit the floor with a thud. Thank goodness, Dad hadn't opted to put the inn's guest in the room below them. Hopefully he was a sound sleeper.

Determined to avoid turning on the light and waking the other girls, she felt her way to where she heard Simone crying. She picked her up and one whiff told her that a dirty diaper was the culprit for waking her youngest. "Oh, baby girl. That's a stinky one. Come here. Let's go get you changed."

Where had she put the diaper bag? She felt along the edge of the wall where she thought it was but to no avail. Combing the wall for the closet light switch, she finally found it. But she guessed wrong and turned on the overhead light. Like it had been choreographed, Jesse and both the older girls stirred and moaned.

"Babe . . ." Jesse squinted up at her. "Can you please turn that off."

"I'm trying to find the diapers," she hissed.

He mumbled something that sounded like, "Well, *I'm* trying to sleep."

She gave him the benefit of the doubt, certain he would never be so rude and insensitive. Yeah, right.

She turned on the closet light and switched off the room light, but opened the closet door wider just for spite. Unfortunately, a simple diaper change was not going to do the trick. This was going to require a bath and a full change of clothes, which might be just the trick to calm Simone down anyway.

She gathered clean pajamas and a diaper, flipped off the light, and started across the hall to the bathroom.

"Mommy? Where are you going?"

"Go back to sleep, Sadie. I'm just going to change Simone."

"I wanna come too."

"No, it's the middle of the night. I'll be back before you know it. I just need to get your sister bathed and changed. You go back to sleep."

"She gets a bath? In the whirly bathtub?"

"Go to sleep, Sadie."

"But I never got a bath. No fair!" Sadie burst into tears.

"Corinne?" Jesse sat up in bed. "I really do have class in the morning."

"I know, I'm sorry. Why don't you go sleep on the sofa in the basement. It's cooler down there anyway."

Without a word, he slid out of bed and headed downstairs.

Corinne gave in to Sadie just to keep her quiet, and the three of them went across the hall to the bathroom shared by the two rooms on the second level. She closed the door and turned on the water, doing her best to keep the girls quiet while she undressed them and lifted them into the tub. She turned to find their towels and ran smack into a man's bare chest.

By the time she realized it was Jesse, it was too late to take back the blood curdling scream.

"Where does your mom keep extra blankets? It's cold down there."

"You scared me half to death." She knelt beside the tub and lathered a washcloth. "Look in the closet in our room. I think I saw some blankets on the top shelf."

Jesse padded out. And Sari padded in. "How's come everybody left me alone," she whined.

"You were sleeping."

"No I wasn't. I was awake the whole time." She looked over Corinne's shoulder to where her sisters were swimming in ten inches of water. "Can I take a bath too?"

Corinne blew her bangs out of her eyes. "Oh, sure. Why not."

Two minutes later all three of the girls were wide awake, splashing each other and squealing as they tried to escape Corinne's washcloth—a game that was more suited to eight p.m. baths than two a.m. washups.

Apparently her mother thought so too. Mom knocked on the door and stuck her head in. "What's going on?"

"Simone had a stinky diaper."

"Are you about finished? Because Dad and I can hear you clear upstairs."

"Sorry. We're almost done." She pulled the plug. "Girls, quiet down and get out so I can get you—"

Woof! Huck charged into the room, knocking Simone to the floor on his way to the tub.

Mom gasped. "Who let him out?"

Sari and Sadie squealed with delight as the big Lab dipped his huge head between them in the tub and lapped at their soapy bathwater. Meanwhile, Simone let out a delayed wail and sat naked on the cold tile, sobbing.

Corinne wrapped a towel around her and picked her up. "Where *was* Huck?"

"Dad put him in the basement for the night." She lowered her voice to a stage whisper. "Our guest is apparently allergic to dog dander."

"Uh-oh. Jesse went down there to sleep. He must have let Huck out."

"Why? Are you two fighting?"

She shot her mother a look. "No! It was too noisy in our room and he has class in the morning."

"It is morning." Mom tied her robe around her waist and turned to open the door. She gave a little gasp and jumped back.

"What is going on in here?"

"Hi, Dad." Corinne gave a little wave and rose with the swaddled toddler on one hip. She deposited Simone in his arms. "Can you get this one ready for bed please?"

"You'd all better quiet down," Mom said. "The walls were literally shaking when I came down."

A pounding sound came from the hallway outside the bath, and an angry voice boomed. "Is anyone there?"

Mom gasped again. "Oh, no! It's Mr. Fordham! Shh! Everybody hush!" She gave her reflection a quick inspection, made a gagging sound, then rolled her eyes and opened the door.

Corinne couldn't quite make out the conversation that ensued, but there were raised voices, the masculine one using words like "ridiculous" and "outrage" and "never again." And the feminine one starting with "sorry" and "apologize" but quickly escalating to "don't give a rat's rear end" and "wouldn't be welcome here anyway."

Dad met Corinne's glance and cringed, hiding his face in Simone's soggy towel.

Corinne stood there with her jaw hanging open.

Half an hour later, Mr. Fordham had checked out, without paying, and Corinne sat at the kitchen table with her parents—and Jesse, who'd been jarred awake when Dad confined Huckleberry to the basement again, long enough for the angry guest to make his getaway.

The girls were asleep—or at least quiet—piled into Jesse and Corinne's bed, and Huck lay contentedly under the kitchen table.

Mom blew out a breath. "Shall I put a pot of coffee on?"

Jesse stretched. "Not for me. I think I'm going to try to get an hour or two of shut-eye before I have to leave."

"I'll come with you." Corinne rose, then sat down again, frowning. "I'm so sorry, Mom and Dad."

Jesse took up the apology. "We should . . . at least pay you for the guy's room."

"Nonsense," Dad said, winking. "Someday your kids will do something like this to you, and then we'll be even."

They all laughed, but Corinne felt terrible. "But you lost the one paying guest you've had all week because of us. I bet you'll be so glad to see us go."

She felt near tears but did *not* want to lose it in front of her parents.

Dad patted her hand. "Honey, this is all temporary. Just a few short days from now, you'll be back in a place of your own, and yeah, sure, there'll be adjustments there, too. But give it a few weeks, and everything will start to right itself again."

"That's right," her mom said. "You'll be settled in your new home, Jesse will be settled in school, the girls will start to sense that their world is stable again . . ."

Dad gave a little chuckle. "Well, at least until the next time it tilts on its axis." He pushed his chair back from the table. "I don't know about you guys, but I'm going to bed."

Mom went through the house turning out lights, and Corinne and Jesse climbed to the second floor. The girls were curled like spoons in the queen-size bed, and she and Jesse worked to put together a makeshift bed from the sleeping bags the girls had been lying on.

She could hear her parents' low murmurs in the kitchen below them just like it had been when she was a little girl.

Jesse pulled her head onto his shoulder, and they lay that way until she thought his breaths had evened.

His voice startled her. "That was quite a night, wasn't it."

She giggled. "Did you hear my mom ream that guy out?"

"Your *mom*?"

She gave him an instant replay of the exchange in the hallway, embellishing the parts she couldn't hear for Jesse's benefit. His chest shook with laughter beneath her head, which only made her laugh harder.

"Shh!" He felt for her lips in the dark and covered her mouth with two fingers. "You'll wake the girls!" He rolled on his side and exchanged his fingers for his lips.

She recognized this timeless prelude, sensed his kiss grow serious, but she couldn't help it. She burst out laughing, still remembering the look on Dad's face when Mom was out in the hall chewing out that man.

Jesse tickled her. "What's so funny?"

"This whole night. Our whole lives."

He laughed with her, and the harder they tried not to, the harder they laughed.

"Hey!" Dad's voice came from the bottom of the stairs. "Put a sock in it up there!"

That sent them into convulsions.

⊙━✦━⊙

"Sari, can you buckle yourself?" Corinne flopped the heavy curtains onto the passenger seat and jabbed the keys into the ignition. The tears came then, so hard she could barely see to drive. Thank goodness she'd managed to make it to the car before she broke down.

It was so hard seeing her sister living in "her" house. She got that Danae would have traded her places in a heartbeat to have the three little girls in Corinne's rearview mirror, and would probably have been happy living in a dump if that's what it took to have babies of her own. But still . . .

And why had her sister felt the need to repaint the kitchen and change the curtains? Danae had always complimented her taste, but apparently she hadn't liked it as well as she pretended. Corinne would never tell her sister, but she thought the new curtains she'd chosen made the whole room look a little old-fashioned—and smaller. Of course, the rooms in that house could afford to look smaller. She'd had to bite her tongue more this last month than in her entire life. And she didn't like that feeling.

She took the right fork of the divided entrance to their former neighborhood and flipped on her blinker. Danae had offered to give back the keeping room curtains from the big house, and Corinne was eager to see if they would work in the dining room of the little house.

She really was trying to make an attitude adjustment. But it was hard! Counting her blessings helped. For one, Jesse had never been happier. He loved his classes and didn't even seem to mind the hours he put in at the college where he worked in the field house thirty hours a week for a friend of Dallas's. His checks just covered the monthly bills, and already they'd had to take out of savings for a couple of things for the house. But they weren't destitute.

At least not yet.

The girls were still enamored with *their* house, which was what they called the playhouse Dallas had built. Her brother-in-law was already planning a bigger, better playhouse at the big house, and she knew she'd have to get prayed up before she could *ooh* and *aah* convincingly over that one.

Turning onto their street, Corinne counted another blessing. The older neighborhood was tidy and friendly. Her daughters had made new friends with a family two houses down, and Corinne was surprised, but charmed, when the girls' mother had brought over a plate of cookies the second day after they'd started moving in.

She and Jesse had started sitting on the front porch in the cool of evening, and she surprised herself by how much she enjoyed visiting with neighbors walking by. They'd barely known their neighbors in the other house, given the distance between acreages. She'd thought she liked it that way, enjoyed the privacy, but she was counting this new neighborhood camaraderie in the blessing column.

She pulled into the driveway, hoping Jesse hadn't beaten her home. She wanted to get the dining room curtains switched out and surprise him. He'd actually been disappointed to discover she'd promised to leave their curtains for Danae.

"How's come you're not goin' in the garage, Mommy?" Sari asked.

"Don't you remember? There's too much junk in there."

Despite selling several more pieces to Dallas and Danae, and what they got rid of at the garage sale, the garage was still full of furniture and decorative items that would never fit in this house. If she sold them, it meant she'd given up hope of ever getting out of this house and into a larger one.

But renting a storage unit for them didn't make sense either. That would just be one more bill, and who knew if they'd really ever need any of those things again.

She blew out a sigh, put the Pathfinder in park, and turned off the ignition. She was exhausted just thinking about everything else they had to do before they were really moved in. It took all her energy just to keep her daughters fed and clothed and clean. There was little left over to work on the house, and she couldn't expect much help from Jesse. If he wasn't working, he was in school or studying for a class. To make matters worse, she felt like she was coming down with something.

She unbuckled the car seats and doled out grocery bags. "If you girls can carry in the groceries, Mommy can get these curtains put up before Daddy gets home."

An argument ensued over who got to carry what. Corinne herded Sadie and Simone inside and hollered for Sari to close the door behind her.

They worked together putting groceries away, and then Corinne sent the girls back to their room to play so she could spread things out in the dining room and get the curtains hung. The girls' shared bedroom was turning out to be a bonus. The girls had become best of friends in just these few weeks, and Corinne couldn't help but think that even though she and her sisters had complained about it, the bedroom they'd shared as children may have been part of the reason they were so close now.

The frilly navy drapes Danae had left with the house came down easily, and Corinne quickly hung the colorful floral panels in their place. She stood back to see the effect and smiled. The whole room looked bigger and brighter—and more like home.

Jesse had won the "the red wall has to go" argument, and they'd painted the whole dining room and kitchen a barely there shade of aqua. She scooted the white-painted hutch a few feet to the left and brought a tall floor lamp from their bedroom to place beside it. The glow it cast, even in daylight, was homey and inviting. Best of all, the whole arrangement looked like her. Like them. Not like Dallas and Danae's house.

She hauled a few moving boxes that were still stacked in one corner out to the garage, which opened up the room even more. Then she traded out some dishes between the cupboard and the hutch. The new arrangement brought out the corals and greens in the curtains and pulled everything together.

One thing led to another, and by the time Jesse pulled in the driveway, she had the room looking like something from her favorite cottage decor blog. She looked at the clock on the stove.

She'd only been working for a little over an hour. At this rate, she could have the whole house "tweaked" in a day. Of course, that wasn't realistic, but things didn't seem quite as daunting as they had before.

And best of all, she had a garage full of furniture and decor to "shop" from.

She heard Jesse's car on the drive—a warning she'd never gotten at the big house—and she ran to the kitchen window to watch him come up the walk with that lightness she hadn't seen in his step since they were dating.

She waited eagerly for him to come in through the front door.

He rounded the corner, and his reaction was exactly what she was hoping for. He stopped short, drew back, and let out a low "Whoa! Somebody's been busy."

She clapped like a giddy school girl. "What do you think? Honestly."

"Babe, it looks great! It looks . . . bigger."

"I know! Doesn't it? And so much brighter."

Hearing Jesse's voice, the girls ran from their room and attacked him, climbing him like a tree in the middle of the living room.

When he whirled around with Sari on his shoulders, she gasped and pointed at the dining room. "Hey! It looks like our house! Our other house, I mean."

"It does, doesn't it?" Jesse scooped her up. "Mommy did a good job, didn't she?"

"Uh-huh." Sari nodded. "I like this house the bestest."

"Do you really?" Corinne tilted her head, curious. "Why?"

Sari shrugged. "I dunno. I just do. When's supper?"

She ran back to the bedroom without waiting for an answer, subject changed. But the look Jesse gave Corinne was pure triumph.

She shook a finger playfully at him. "Never mind we can't fit even half of our stuff in here. Never mind the girls are shoehorned into that bedroom like sardines. Never mind we can't get one car in the garage, let alone two."

But he wasn't offering sympathy today. "You look like you're adjusting okay."

She didn't have an answer for that. Because the truth was, she was adjusting. She'd agreed to make a sacrifice, and well, it wouldn't really be a sacrifice if it was all roses and sunshine, now would it?

31

Corinne slipped her sunglasses off the top of her head and put them on before backing out of the driveway. Though September was half over, recent rains had seen to it that the carpet roses remained in full bloom and the trees forming a canopy over their street still wore the full spectrum of greens. She had to smile. *Their.* She'd begun to think of it as *their* street. Without even wrinkling her nose.

They'd been in the house for just over a month now. The chaos of the move had finally subsided, and life had taken on a comforting, crisis-free rhythm.

She was headed out to the inn, sans kids, and was looking forward to a day helping Mom and Landyn get ready for a teachers event the inn had been rented out for—a celebration luncheon for staff at a local Christian school. Mom was going all out with decorations and a new menu.

Thankfully, Jesse didn't have classes today and had volunteered to watch the girls for the day. Well, maybe volunteered was too strong a word. But he hadn't complained too loudly either.

The route to the inn was so familiar that the SUV almost went on autopilot as she wove through their quiet neighborhood. Heading out of town on Highway K, she relished the quiet inside the car. She glanced at the clock on the dashboard. She'd gotten a later start than she intended and sent a quick text to Landyn through her car's hands-free system. She was grateful every day that she hadn't had to give up her beloved Pathfinder.

Well, not yet anyway. They still had a few years of poverty-level living to go. She immediately checked the thought. Applying the word "poverty" to any part of her life was tantamount to sacrilege. They were blessed. In so many ways. How strange that she'd had to "move down" in the world to recognize that.

She rounded a curve on the gently winding highway and saw a vehicle stopped on the side of the road ahead. She slowed and checked for oncoming traffic before moving to the left of the center line. But as she got closer, she saw a woman kneeling beside the car. She tapped the brakes and approached slowly.

The woman appeared to be attempting to change the tire, but dressed in a rather fancy white dress and layers of bracelets, she didn't exactly look up for the task. Corinne tried to see into the vehicle to determine if there was anyone with her. She could only imagine how frightened she'd be if she had the girls in the car and had to try to fix a flat. Emphasis on *try*.

Dad had taught them all how to change a tire when they were teens, and she'd had to relearn it in driver's ed, but that was many years and many brain cells ago, and the only thing she remembered about it was that the lug nuts required muscles. Probably more muscles than she had these days. Certainly more than the dainty young woman on the side of the road possessed.

She pulled over behind the vehicle, a sedan about the same color as hers. Checking for traffic, she started to get out of the car but decided it wasn't wise to leave her car running, so she turned off the engine, tucked her phone and keys into her jeans pocket and stepped from the car.

She walked toward the woman, who seemed not to have heard her approaching. She cleared her throat. "Do you need some help there?"

The woman started and looked up from the tire. She leaned on the crowbar end of the tire iron with one muddy hand and shielded her eyes from the sun with the other. "My tire went flat, and I can't even get the stupid hubcaps off."

Corinne reeled and took a clumsy step backward. She would have recognized that voice anywhere. *Michaela Creeve.*

For one terrifying moment, she wondered if this was all a setup, another stunt of this woman who'd made it her mission to disrupt their lives. She braced her knees, ready to turn and dash for her car if necessary. Yet she was afraid doing so might set Michaela off.

But Michaela stayed on her knees, eyes downcast. Was she on something? But when she looked up again, Corinne saw that tears had carved rivulets through the dust on her face. Tears that seemed genuine.

She didn't think Michaela had recognized her yet.

"Have you called anyone?" Corinne took another step backward, wanting to put as little distance between her and her means of escape as possible.

"No." Michaela threw down the tire iron and struggled to her feet. "I let my Triple A expire and I don't—" She gave a little gasp, and Corinne saw recognition come to her eyes. "You're—"

"I'm Corinne." She stood there, not knowing what else to say.

The young woman's head dropped. "Oh, God."

Corinne didn't think it was a prayer. But she was saying prayers of her own. Desperate ones. *What should I do, God? Do I need to get out of here? Do I need to call Jesse?*

Strangely, she felt no urgency to flee. "I'm not very mechanical, but can I help you? Is there someone you can call?"

"No," she said, a little too quickly. "There's . . . no one."

Corinne thought she heard despair in the response. Jesse had said someone at work told him Michaela's husband had left her. But she had no one? What would it feel like to be a person who truly had no one to call in a crisis? Was that why she'd attached herself to Jesse?

"I—I really don't know enough about it to try to change your tire, but let me call—" She'd been on the verge of saying "let me call Jesse" but something stopped her. Jesse would have had to bring the girls with him, and that seemed like a recipe for trouble.

"Let me call my dad," Corinne said more firmly. "He doesn't live far from here, and he can have it fixed in nothing flat." She realized her pun as soon as the word "flat" came out, but somehow this didn't seem the time to point it out and laugh about it.

Michaela seemed not to notice. "Why are you here? Why did you stop?" She almost looked as if she was afraid of Corinne.

If that were true . . . oh, how the tables had turned.

"I didn't know it was you. Not until you looked up. I'm sorry. But that's the truth. I just saw—someone who needed help. So I stopped."

"So why are you here now? Still."

Corinne shrugged. "You needed help." Oh, brother. Truer words . . .

Michaela narrowed her eyes. "You don't get how lucky you are, do you?"

"I'm sorry?" *Oh, God, please show me what to say, what to do. Please give me the right words.*

The woman brushed at a streak of dirt on the hem of her dress. "You have a whole list of people you can call, people who will come running for you."

"Just . . . let me call my dad, okay?" She scrolled for his number on her phone and pressed send, not waiting for Michaela's permission.

But she didn't argue. She leaned against the driver's side door of her car and traced the toe of her sandal in the fine gravel. "Is your dad going to hate me? Your whole family probably hates me."

Please pick up, Dad. Please. She started to play dumb. But it seemed she'd been given an opportunity for honesty. "No one is going to hate you, Michaela."

"I don't believe you."

"Well, it's true. We . . . we're not happy with the things you've done. You've made things very difficult for us. For all my family. I don't know what we did to deserve that."

"You—"

"Hello? Corinne?"

"Dad! Hi. Um . . . Hey, can you help me out?" Her voice sounded unnatural even in her own ears.

"What's up?"

Corinne could tell by the caution in his voice that he was curious, maybe even suspicious that something was off. "I'm stopped out here on Highway K, and there's . . . a woman here with a flat tire. She can't get the hubcaps off. Would you be able to come and help us out? We're probably about two miles out . . . maybe three." She looked around for a landmark. "You know where that old machine shed is? I think it used to be a body shop? I passed that a minute or two ago."

"I know the place. . . . Is everything okay, honey?"

"Yes. I . . . think so." She glanced at Michaela, who was watching her closely. "I'm not sure how far past the machine shed I am, but it's right by that outcropping where they blasted the road through, you know . . . just before you get to that school." She knew she was jabbering a mile a minute, but she couldn't seem to help herself. "That'd be great if you could come, Dad, and um . . . I'll wait here with Michaela."

"Corinne—" His pause told her he was putting two and two together. "Are you talking about that woman? Honey, are you okay?"

"Yes. I am. We'll wait here for you. Thanks, Dad." She pressed End, hoping she hadn't scared her dad. Or triggered something in Michaela. She truly didn't think she was in any danger. But neither did she want to take any chances.

Still, she hadn't wanted her dad to be shocked when he got here and realized who it was. She hoped he hadn't gotten the wrong message from her voice and called the police or something. She slipped her phone into her jeans pocket.

"Must be nice to have a family to call."

"I'm sorry you don't—" She didn't know how to finish the sentence. And that fact caused a stab of guilt. They'd been so focused on their fear and their . . . *fury* over the havoc Michaela Creeve had wreaked in their lives—and they'd *needed* to be, certainly—but she knew nothing about why this young woman was so broken, so damaged. A husband who'd left her . . . but there had to be more to it than that. "I'm sorry you're . . . alone."

Michaela narrowed her eyes. "Are you? Really?"

"I am. It's . . . it's very sad. And I'm sorry for that. No one should be all alone." She wanted to lecture Michaela with all the biting words she'd rehearsed, all the anger she'd hoped to someday have a chance to spew. But the words seemed strangely unavailable to her. And she knew God was answering her prayer for the *right* words.

Sometimes silence was the answer to a prayer for the right words. *Thank you for closing my mouth.* Perhaps there would be another day to say those things. But that day was not today.

She looked up the road, watching for her dad's Highlander. They were only five minutes from the inn, and she knew her father wouldn't waste any time getting here, but every minute seemed like an eternity.

The sun was hot overhead, and heat rose up from the surface of the highway as well. If it was anyone else, she would have suggested they wait in her car with the air conditioner running, but she was leery of getting into a vehicle with this woman. Instead, she motioned across the road where a couple of sprawling oaks offered shade. "Why don't we wait over there . . . get out of the sun."

Michaela looked across to the opposite ditch and shrugged, but she looked both ways, then crossed with Corinne.

Corinne imagined herself telling Jesse about this strange encounter. In her mind, she heard Jesse's first question. "What was she doing out there?"

Startled, she heard the question come from her own lips. "Where were you headed?"

Michaela moved deeper into the shade of the tallest oak tree. "Why do you want to know?"

"I'm sorry. I . . . didn't mean to pry. I was just making conversation."

"If you must know, I was going out to the Chicory Inn."

Her heart stuttered. Did Michaela know the inn belonged to her parents? Willing her voice not to give her away, she took a shallow breath. "Oh? That's a nice place."

"You do the PR for them, huh?" The sly look on her face sent a wave of nausea through Corinne.

"My parents run the inn." She forced a smile. She had no doubt Michaela already knew that, but she didn't want to tip her hand. "Are you . . . staying there tonight?" *Over my dead body.* She hoped that thought wasn't prophetic.

"No. Not staying. I just wanted to see it again. To see what a place like that looks like."

Again? Had Michaela been to the inn before? "A place like that?"

She shrugged. "Jesse always talked about it at work. Telling the guys how your family all gets together there. You don't get how lucky you are," she said again.

"I do get it, Michaela. I know I'm very privileged, very . . . blessed. I don't deserve anything I have. I know that." She was trying to say the things she suspected Michaela was thinking. But she meant every word.

"Kind of funny you're the one who came along."

"Came along?" She wasn't sure what that meant.

"On the road." Michaela waved a thin arm in the direction of the highway. "Just seems like an omen or something that I'm going out to see what it must be like to be you. And here you come. That's kind of odd, don't you think?"

Was she implying that Corinne had followed *her?* How did someone carry on a conversation with someone as emotionally disturbed as this woman had to be.

"I know you think I'm pathetic and—"

"No. Michaela . . . I don't." *But you're freaking me out a little, reading my mind like that.*

"You don't have to pretend. I know what you must think. I'd think the same if the tables were turned. But that's just it. They're not. The tables won't ever be turned. I'll always be the one who's on the outside looking in. I'll always be the one who can't have what she wants. And girls like you will always be the ones who get the good men, the good kids, the good parents."

"That's not true."

"Of course it is." She gave an eerie, humorless laugh.

It might have sent chills up Corinne's spine. But instead, it made her deeply sad.

"It's okay. I'm used to it." Michaela scrubbed her face with her hands, then looked at her hands in horror, as if she'd discovered blood there instead of dried mud. "I must look awful."

"I have some baby wipes in my car. If you want to wash up a little . . ."

Again, that strangled, self-deprecating laugh. "It's going to take more than a baby wipe to clean me up, honey."

"Michaela . . ." She swallowed hard. *Give me the words, God.* "You need help. You may not think anyone loves you, but . . . that's not true. God does. He loves you more than you can imagine." The words spilled out faster than she could think.

"Now you're sounding like that preacher at your church."

Corinne's breath caught. So it *was* her. "You . . . need to talk to someone. To get some help."

Michaela stared at her, defiance thick in the steel of her eyes and the jut of her chin. "It's so easy to say those words." Her voice sounded hollow. "So easy when somebody with real flesh and blood loves you. When you've got your daddy on his way to rescue you."

Even though threat seemed intended in that word—*rescue*—Corinne felt no fear. She closed her eyes. "I know. I know that. And I don't know what else to say to you, except that I'm sorry. I wish you could understand. I wish you would let yourself *feel* God's love for you."

An engine roared behind them, and she heard the beautiful toot of her dad's car horn. She waved at him.

"And there he is," Michaela said. "You go on. You're off the hook now."

"No. I'll stay. I need to learn how to change a tire. In case I'm ever in your shoes."

32

Corinne took a deep breath and waited for the crescendo of nausea to pass. And it would, later this afternoon. Only to return with morning's light. As it had for almost two weeks now. She reached for a tissue on the bathroom counter and wiped her mouth.

She gathered up the drugstore box and instructions from the counter, and looked one more time at the pink line on the test stick. At least she knew what was causing her strange queasiness now. She must have skipped her pill one too many times during that week they'd moved.

She braced both hands on the counter and leaned in to study her reflection. *Oh, my word. What have we done?* She thought she was going to cry, but what came out instead was a giggle. She was losing it. And if not now, she would eight months from now. Four kids in this tiny house? She laughed harder.

"What's so funny in there?"

Oh, Jesse . . . She had to tell him.

She took several deep breaths, ran a hand through her hair, and picked up the instrument of doom.

Jesse was propped up in bed studying for a test. What if he freaked out? This was so not in their plans. This was so not what they needed right now. Or ever.

"Jesse?" Biting her bottom lip, she held out the test stick.

"What's this?"

"Jesse . . ." She said his name softer this time, hoping it would somehow soften the blow.

He looked from her to the stick and back again, realization dawning in his eyes.

"Corinne?" A smile came, slowly. "Are you serious?"

"As a heart attack." Her lip quivered against her will.

"Well . . . Don't cry about it! Babe . . . This is great news. This is *awesome* news." He sounded like he really meant it. "Come here." He pulled her down beside him on the bed.

"You're not upset?"

"I'm . . ." He shook his head as if he were coming out of a trance. "I think I'm in shock."

"Welcome to the club."

"How long have you known?"

"About two minutes longer than you have. But . . . I was starting to suspect. Remember I told you I thought I was coming down with the flu?"

"But that was a long time ago."

"About three weeks ago."

"Holy cow. We're having a baby." He was absolutely beaming.

"You don't have to be quite so happy about it."

He frowned. "You're not?"

She sighed and hung her head. "Give me a little while to get used to the idea."

"Nine months be enough?"

"More like eight. Oh, Jesse . . ." She moaned. "I sold all the baby stuff in the garage sale!"

"Well, that was a dumb move, Pennington." He laughed.

And it was contagious. He pulled her close and they laughed the same way they had that night at the inn, which, now that she thought about it, was probably the night it had happened. Which made her laugh harder.

"What's so funny, everybody?"

They turned to see Sari standing in the doorway, rubbing her eyes.

Jesse raised his eyebrows at Corinne in a way that said, *Can we tell her?*

But she frowned and gave a discreet shake of her head. Eight months was a long time for a five-year-old to wait. Not to mention, five-year-olds had big mouths.

Danae. Oh, it would be so hard to tell her sister the news. And things were already a little strained between them. But it wasn't like she'd done it on purpose. Lord willing, maybe she and Danae would share a pregnancy.

"Oh!"

"What?" Jesse looked alarmed.

She must have groaned louder than she thought. "I sold all my matern—" She caught herself and looked pointedly at Sari. "My *special* clothes in the garage sale too."

He shrugged. "So you'll buy more."

"Are we goin' shopping?" Sadie stood in the doorway, looking as wide awake as Sari looked sleepy.

"Mama!" Simone peeked from behind her sister then made a dash for the bed and scrambled up to weasel her way between them.

"Monkey pile on Mommy!" Jesse said, pulling Sadie up on the bed.

Sari dove into the mess, the whole lot of them giggling and wiggling.

"You think this bed can take any more?" Jesse said, speaking code over their daughters' heads.

In that instance, a memory pushed its way into her mind. She must've been about Sari's age, because Landyn hadn't come along yet, but Danae and Link and sweet Tim were all there. And the "monkey pile" was on Dad—in Mom and Dad's big bed in the house she'd grown up in. Back when the inn was a creaky, chipped-paint, orange-shag-carpeted house where so much love had grown. And where there'd been plenty of room for Landyn when she came along. And plenty of love.

Her mind was far away in a place where she'd first learned what love and happiness were, but the background music for her memories was the laughter of her precious husband and her own three little girls—with a baby on the way.

Maybe the song was right: maybe love did grow best in little houses. Nothing would make her happier than if her daughters could grow up to share the kind of friendship she and her sisters had—spats and all.

"Hey, Mommy?" Jesse's hand was warm on her face. "You okay?"

She snuggled closer to him and let the chaos that was their daughters wash over her like a healing balm.

"Never been better, babe. Never been better."

Group Discussion Guide

1. In *Two Roads Home*, Jesse Pennington has to travel a great deal with his job. What are some of the hazards and temptations of traveling away from your family? If your family has ever had to deal with this, what are some things that helped you stay connected while one of you was on the road?

2. Do you think there was anything Jesse could have done to prevent the frustration and pain that Michaela Creeve inflicted on him and his family? What could Corinne have done to possibly circumvent the situation if she had known about it?

3. Corinne and Jesse chose to take a big step down in the economic realm. How did they each handle that change? Why do you think it was harder for Corinne than for Jesse? Discuss some of the adjustments both Corinne and Danae will go through with their switch in lifestyles.

4. How much do you think where you live and the kind of home you live in determines your lifestyle? Have you ever made a drastic change from one economic state to another? What surprised you about that change?

5. Though the Whitman sisters love and respect one another and are close friends, they sometimes get irritated with and sometimes feel envious of one another. Do you think sibling friendships are more difficult than friendships with people to whom you have no family connection? Why or why not?

6. Audrey had mixed feelings about having her children and grandchildren in and out of her house. Why was she torn between enjoying time with them and feeling as if it was a burden? Do you understand her seemingly conflicting feelings? Have you ever felt the same? How could she have reached a compromise that would have kept everyone content?

7. Have you ever had a person in your life who was manipulative or a borderline stalker/harasser like Michaela Creeve? How did you handle it? What do you think about the way Jesse and Corinne handled the issues with Michaela? Do you think Jesse and Corinne were forceful enough when it came to protecting their daughters and getting help from the police? How, if at all, would you have done things differently?

8. If you've read the first book in The Chicory Inn series, do you see any parallels between Chase and Landyn's issues in *Home to Chicory Lane*, and Jesse and Corinne's in *Two Roads Home*? How are the two marriages different? How are they similar? Is your marriage similar to that of your siblings or siblings-in-law? If it is different, how has that affected your relationship with extended family?

9. What do you think might happen to Michaela in the future? Is there hope for people like her? What responsibility, if any, do you think Corinne has in Michaela's life, especially concerning Michaela's future?

10. Jesse and Corinne received surprising news at the end of the book. Have you ever gotten similar news? What was your reaction? Did it take a while to get used to the idea?

11. Corinne was afraid of how the news would affect her sister. Have you ever experienced misplaced guilt when you knew that your good news would cause someone else pain or envy?

12. Which family member do you identify most with in the Chicory Inn series so far? Why? Who do you find most likable? Least likable?

Want to learn more about Deborah Raney
and check out other great fiction from
Abingdon Press?

Check out our website at
www.AbingdonFiction.com
to read interviews with your favorite authors,
find tips for starting a reading group,
and stay posted on what new titles are on the horizon.

We hope you enjoyed reading *Two Roads Home* and that you will continue to read Abingdon Press fiction books. Here are excerpts from book 1, *Home to Chicory Lane*, and the forthcoming book 3, *Another Way Home*.

1

So, *Mrs.* Whitman, is everything ready?" Grant stood under the archway dividing the formal dining room from the parlor, smiling that cat that swallowed the canary grin Audrey adored. And had for nearly thirty-five years.

She went to lean on the column opposite him. She loved this view of the house—no, the *inn*. She must remember to refer to it as such. This wonderful house where they'd raised their five kids and where she'd played as a little girl had finally become *The Chicory Inn*. The stately home just a mile outside of Langhorne, Missouri, had been built by her maternal grandparents on a wooded fifty acres with a clearwater creek running through it. Now it was her fifty-five hundred square-foot dream fulfilled. Or at least that was the plan.

Audrey gave her husband a tight smile. "I'm as ready as I'll ever be. I just know I'm forgetting something."

"Come here." He opened his arms to her.

She stepped into his embrace, desperately needing the strength of him.

"Everything looks wonderful, and anything you forgot can't be too important. Just look at the weather God supplied—sunshine, cool October breeze, and the trees are at their autumn peak. Even the chicory is still in bloom in the ditches. Made to order, I'd say."

She nodded, feeling as if she might burst into tears any minute.

Grant pulled her closer. "Can't you just enjoy this weekend? It's no fun if you're in knots the whole time."

"Were we crazy to invite the kids home for this?"

He kissed the top of her head. "We were crazy to *have* kids, never mind five of them. But hey, look how that turned out."

"I wish your mom could've been here."

He cleared his throat. "Trust me, it's better this way. Besides, you know she'll find a way to get in her two cents, even from the wilds of Oregon. What do you want to bet she'll call, just as guests are arriving, to make sure you didn't forget anything?"

She loved Grant's mother dearly, but the woman did have a way of trying to run the show—even when it wasn't her show to run. Grant was probably right. Cecelia—or CeeCee, as the kids called their grandmother—had timed her trip to visit Grant's brother perfectly.

Audrey's cell phone chimed, signaling a text message.

"See?" Grant gave her an I-told-you-so grin. "There she is."

She checked her phone. "Your mother barely knows how to make a call on a cell phone, let alone send a text. Oh, it's Link. He's running late." She texted a quick reply to their son.

"Link late? Well, there's a huge surprise."

She laughed, grateful for the distraction. Their son was notoriously tardy. But after she put her phone back in her pocket, Audrey turned serious. "Oh, Grant . . . What if this whole thing is a big fat flop?"

"And why, sweet woman, would it be a flop, when you've poured your heart and soul and passion into it for the last eight months?"

"And most of your retirement funds, don't forget." The thought made her positively queasy. It wasn't as if he could just return to his contractor job tomorrow and get back his 401K. "Not to mention a lot of sweat equity."

"And don't forget the blood and tears." He winked.

"And your blood *pressure*," she said with a look of warning. "How can you joke about this, Grant? What if we—"

"Shh." He tipped her chin and silenced her with a kiss.

She knew Grant had been relieved to get out of the rat race his job had become. In fact, his doctor had prescribed retirement along with the blood pressure meds he'd put Grant on last fall. The past year of renovations had been anything but relaxing, but things would settle down now that the remodel was finished. Maybe this was all a sort of blessing in disguise. She let that thought soothe her. For the moment anyway.

The doorbell rang.

"That'll be Corinne." She pushed away from him. "She promised to help me with the hors d'oeuvres."

"I don't see why we couldn't just have chips and salsa or pretzels or—"

"And don't forget your tie." Audrey scooped the despised *noose*, as Grant had dubbed it, off the end of the hall tree and tossed it at him.

He caught it and dangled it by two fingers as if it were a poisonous snake. "You're not really serious about that?"

"Serious as a heart attack."

Grant's grumbling faded behind her as she hurried to answer the door.

Their eldest daughter stood on the wraparound veranda with almost-two-year-old Simone propped on one hip.

"Corinne?" Audrey sagged. "I thought Jesse was going to watch the kids?"

"He is, but I think Simone's cutting teeth, and I didn't want Jesse to have to deal with that, too. You know how he gets when—" Corinne stopped mid-sentence and eyed her mother. "It'll be fine, Mom. Dad can watch Simone if we need him to."

"No, your dad has a whole list of things *he's* in charge of. I need him." She pushed down the resentment that threatened. "Never mind. You're right . . . it'll be fine." She reached for her youngest granddaughter and ushered Corinne into the foyer.

Corinne walked through to the parlor, her eyes widening. "Wow! It looks gorgeous, Mom. You've been busy."

"I just want everything to be perfect. Just this one time." She didn't have to look at her daughter to know Corinne was rolling her eyes.

"Just this once, huh?"

She ignored the sarcasm and tweaked little Simone's cheek. "Are those new toofers giving you trouble, sweetie?"

The baby gave her a snaggletoothed grin and wiped her turned-up nose on the shoulder of Audrey's apple green linen jacket.

"Simone!" Corinne's shrug didn't match the grimace she gave Audrey. "Well, at least it matches."

Audrey did not find that amusing.

Corinne swooped in with a tissue, which made Simone screech like a banshee. Which made Huckleberry come running, barking as if he'd just cornered a squirrel.

Great. Just great. "Can somebody please take this dog outside? How did he even get in here?" Audrey hated raising her voice to her family, but she knew too well that the playful Lab could undo in two minutes everything they'd spent a week preparing. "I want him outside until the last guest leaves."

"Come here, Huck," Corinne coaxed, stroking the sleek chocolate-colored coat. "You bad boy."

"It's okay. I'll take him out." Audrey handed the baby off to Corinne, put Huck outside, and came back to the sink. Grabbing a damp dishcloth from the basin, she scrubbed at her jacket, exchanging the toddler's snot stain for a dark wet spot. She prayed it would dry before the first guests started arriving.

The clock in the foyer struck eleven, and a frisson of panic went through her. They had less than two hours and so much still to do. She heard Link's voice at the front door. Maybe she could enlist him to watch Simone for a few minutes. Like his brother Tim, Link had always had a way with kids.

"Hey, Mom. Dad said to report in." Tall and rugged-looking like his father, Link appeared beneath the arch of the kitchen doorway. "Smells good in here." He gave Audrey a quick hug before snatching a bacon-wrapped canapé from a silver tray. He popped it in his mouth before Audrey could protest.

She placed herself between her son and the gleaming marble counter full of food. "There are snacks out in the garage for you kids, but I'm not joking; this stuff is off limits until we see how many people show."

"Got it, Mom. Off limits." In one smooth motion, Link gave her a half-salute and reached behind her for a sausage ball.

"Cut that out! Shoo! Out of my kitchen!"

"Place looks good, Ma."

Grant appeared in the doorway. "Reporting for duty."

Link shot his dad a conspiratorial grin but obediently backed into the entryway. Audrey wondered for the thousandth time why some sweet young girl hadn't snapped up this handsome son of hers. But that was a worry for another day.

"Hey guys," Audrey said, "can you bring in some folding chairs from the garage? Maybe just half a dozen or so. I don't want to set up more than we need."

"You'll need more than six." Grant sounded so sure the day would be a success. "Bring a dozen, Link."

She hoped he was right. But if not . . . Well, there would be no problem getting rid of all the food she'd made. The good ol' Whitman family reunion they'd planned for the rest of the weekend would take care of that. The thought brought a pang of longing with it. It was wonderful to have most of her family together, but it wouldn't be the same without Landyn and Chase.

And Tim. Nothing would ever be the same without Timothy.

⸺

Landyn Spencer craned her neck to check the Interstate traffic behind her in the rearview mirror, but all she could see was the U-Haul trailer she was pulling. The extended mirrors on the behemoth were smeared with a dozen hours of rain and dust.

New York was thirteen hours behind her, and with the sun finally coming up, she realized she was in familiar territory.

She'd left the city after ten last night, starting out on only four hours of sleep. She'd been watching the lit-up Empire State Building fade into the skyline in her rearview mirror, and not until she'd passed through the Lincoln Tunnel and come out on the New Jersey side had she finally allowed herself tears.

That was a mistake. She'd been crying ever since. But enough. She had to get hold of herself before she got home. She swiped at damp cheeks, took a deep breath, and steadied her gaze on the road in front of her. If her eyes got any more swollen, she'd have to pull the Honda over. And if she did that, chances were good the stupid thing wouldn't start again. Then she'd *really* be up the Hudson without a paddle. Besides, right now, she just wanted to put the past—and Chase Spencer—as far behind her as she could.

She still couldn't believe that her husband of six months had gone so far off the deep end. Without even discussing it with her, he'd let their great, albeit small, apartment on the Upper West Side go—sublet their *home* to a stranger—and rented a fleabag excuse for a studio apartment in Brooklyn. What was he thinking?

He *wasn't*. That was the problem. He'd let his art rep convince him that living in Bedford-Stuyvesant near some stupid gallery that was supposedly the next hot thing would jumpstart his career. The agent had told Chase the studio would pay for itself in a matter of months—and probably herald in world peace too.

Well, fine. Chase had made his choice. But they were newlyweds. *She* should have been his choice. Oh, he claimed he wasn't forcing her hand. But if she did what he wanted and followed him to Brooklyn, it meant an almost two-hour commute for her every day. They saw each other little enough as it was! Had he thought any of this through? No, he had not. And despite what Chase said, leaving Fineman and Justus, and a marketing position she loved, didn't leave her with many options. Especially not now . . .

The tears started again and she shook her head. She couldn't even let herself think about that right now.

She attempted to distract her maudlin thoughts with the stunning colors October had painted on either side of the Interstate. She thought she'd crossed over into Kentucky, though she didn't remember seeing a sign. If Chase were here, he'd no doubt be sketching the trees or shooting photos in a vain attempt to capture the vivid colors. Then he'd complain that the pictures didn't even come close, and she'd have to—

A horn blared behind her. She checked the mirror and then the speedometer. She was barely going fifty in the left-hand lane. Stupid cruise control had quit working again. Heart pounding, she accelerated and tried to whip back into the right lane only to have the trailer tug her over the line into the passing lane. She finally managed to maneuver to the proper lane, and she glared hard at the driver as he passed her.

It was a stupid, childish thing to do. She was the one in the wrong. But the guy had almost scared her into having a wreck. It would serve Chase right if she had an accident. She quickly checked the thought. He wasn't the only one she had to think about. Mom and Dad had already lost one child. Her throat tightened at the thought of her brother. If they had to go through that again, she wasn't sure they'd ever recover. Besides, Mom and Dad didn't know she was on her way home. If she had a wreck, no one would know why she was on a road all alone, miles from New York.

It did make her smile to think about what her parents' reaction would be when she pulled into the driveway. She hadn't seen Mom and Dad since her wedding in April, and it would be fun to surprise them. Suddenly she missed them the way she had that first summer she'd gone away to church camp and learned the meaning of "homesick."

But how could she tell them she was leaving Chase? After only six months of marriage. She could hear her dad now. "Landyn Rebekah Whitman," he'd say (somehow forgetting she was now a

Spencer), "you get in that car and you drive yourself right back to New York." He'd be mad at Chase, too, but she'd be the one who'd get the talking-to.

Well, they didn't know the details. And they wouldn't. Chase had fought hard to win her parents over, and she wasn't going to make him out to be the bad guy now—even though he was. One hundred percent, he was. It still made her furious.

No . . . worse than that. It broke her heart.

She was beginning to understand why her parents had been skeptical about Chase in the first place. He was letting this . . . *delusion* of getting rich and famous selling his art sidetrack him. Not that he wasn't good. He was. He had a ton of talent, but that didn't mean he could make a living at it. And their finances didn't exactly allow for risky investments right now.

Chase had landed a job in New York right out of college, working in the art department for a small local magazine. It was a job that used his art skills, and one with room to grow.

But then this nut job art rep had seen Chase's work and gotten him all wired with delusions of grandeur. In a way, she understood. Chase hadn't received much encouragement growing up. His dad left when he was five, and he'd been raised by a single mom who seemed to have a new boyfriend every other week. The minute Chase graduated high school, Mona Spencer had followed some guy out to California. She'd come back for their wedding on the arm of yet another flavor of the week, but Landyn didn't expect to see her again unless she and Chase took the initiative to make a trip out West someday.

Still, despite his rough childhood, and a couple of wild years in high school, Chase had defied the odds and turned into a good guy. A really good guy. Their youth pastor from Langhorne Community Fellowship took Chase under his wing, and by the time Landyn was old enough to date, he was toeing a pretty straight line. Well, except for that tattoo. Dad had come completely unglued when he heard Chase had gotten inked. She'd finally calmed him down by explaining that Chase's Celtic cross—on his collarbone, so it was hidden under most of his shirts—was a symbol of his faith and of the permanence of God's love for him. Landyn had always loved her husband's tat—one he'd designed himself. She'd even toyed with the idea of getting one to match. But so far the fear of her father's reaction and the lack of cash had prevented her—not to mention the disturbing image of herself as a grandma with a shriveled tat on her chest.

After Chase proposed, Mom and Dad insisted they go to counseling before getting married—more intensive than the required premarital counseling—with Pastor Simmons. And though she'd balked big-time at the suggestion, Chase had been willing. And when their sessions were over, she was certain Chase Spencer was ready to be the husband of her dreams—even if her parents weren't convinced.

Maybe she should have listened to them.

Because now he'd quit his job and all but forced her to quit hers. Forced her to run home to Missouri. Except she didn't have a home in Missouri anymore either. Her parents had turned their house into a bed-and-breakfast, and her room was now a guest room at the Chicory Inn. *Real original, Mom.* From what her sisters said—and from the photos Mom had e-mailed her of the finished renovation—Landyn wouldn't even recognize the place.

Sometime this week was the big open house for the inn, too. She'd told her parents she and Chase couldn't get away—which was true at the time. But now she had no choice. She'd stayed with a friend from work for three days, but if she'd stayed there one more day, she'd have had one less friend. So she'd loaded up what little furniture Chase didn't take with him, and she was headed back to Langhorne.

At least in Missouri she wouldn't be shelling out two thousand dollars a month in rent for some roach-infested studio. And she'd be a world away from New York. And him.

Please enjoy this excerpt from *Another Way Home.*

Chapter 1

Danae Brooks buttoned her shirt and slipped on her shoes, trying desperately not to get her hopes up. The dressing rooms in her doctor's office were more like something in an upscale spa—heavy fringed drapes curtained private alcoves decorated with framed art prints, and flameless candles flickered on tiny side tables. Soft strains of Mozart wafted through the building. Of course, for the fees her obstetrician charged—or rather, her "reproductive endocrinologist," as his nameplate declared—the luxuries felt well-deserved.

She gathered her purse and continued to the window at the nurse's station.

Marilyn—she was on a first-name basis with most of the nurses by now—looked up with a practiced smile. "You can go on down. Dr. Gwinn will be with you in just a minute."

Danae had quit trying to decipher the nurses' demeanor. So far, month after month, every smile, every quirk of an eyebrow, every wink, had meant the same thing: she wasn't pregnant. Again. Still.

She walked down the hall to the doctor's sparse office and was surprised to find him already sitting behind his desk. She forced herself not to get her hopes up, but she'd always had to wait for a consult before. Sometimes twenty minutes or more. Could it be . . . ?

"Come on in, Danae." He looked past her expectantly.

"Oh. Um . . . Dallas isn't with me today. He...couldn't get off work." Of course he could have if he'd really wanted to.

"I understand. No problem. Come on in and have a seat."

She took one of the duo of armchairs in front of his desk, feeling a bit adrift without Dallas beside her.

Dr. Gwinn scribbled something on the sheaf of papers in front of him, then slipped them into a folder before looking up at her. She knew immediately that there was no baby.

"Well..." He pulled a sheet of paper from the folder he'd just closed and slid it across the desk, pointing with his pen at an all too familiar graph. "Nothing has changed from last time. Your levels are still not quite where we'd like to see them, but we're getting there. I'm going to adjust the dosage just a bit. Nothing drastic, but you might notice an increase in the side effects you've experienced in the past."

"It hasn't been too bad."

He steepled his fingers in front of him and frowned. "That's good, but don't be surprised if the symptoms are a little more marked with this increase."

Dr. Gwinn wrapped up the consultation quickly and suggested she call his office if she experienced any problems on the new dosage.

For some reason, his warning encouraged her. Maybe this boost in meds would be the thing that finally worked. As quickly as the thought came, she tried to put her hope in check. Almost every week there was something that got her hopes up . . . only to have them dashed again.

But Dr. Gwinn sounded so hopeful this time. Of course, they'd all been hopeful. For more than three years now, a string of clinics had offered endless hope—and had happily accepted their checks for one fertility treatment after another. But despite test after test, a string of doctors in a string of clinics could not seem to find any reason she and Dallas could not have a baby together. "Unexplained infertility" was the frustrating diagnosis. They'd done just about everything but in vitro. Or adoption. And though Dallas was adamant they would not take that route, Danae was beginning to think it might be the answer. The only answer.

At the reception desk, Danae slid her debit card across the counter. Another three hundred dollars. She dreaded Dallas seeing the amount in the check register. She wasn't sure how long they could keep draining their bank account this way before her husband said, "Enough."

The woman handed her a receipt. "We'll see you in two weeks, Mrs. Brooks."

"Thank you." She forced a smile and sent up a prayer that next time she wouldn't have to endure the shots and medication—because she'd be pregnant. But it was getting harder and harder to be optimistic. And she wasn't sure how long she could hold up under repeated disappointment.

She shoved open the door as if shoving away the discouraging thoughts. Or trying to. The late September air finally held a hint of autumn, and she inhaled deeply. As she unlocked the car door, her phone chirped from her purse. Dallas's ring. She fished it out of the side pocket. "Hey, babe."

"Hey yourself. How'd it go?" The caution in his voice made her sad.

"Same ol' same ol'. But he upped my dosage a little."

An overlong pause. "It's not going to make you bonkers like the last time they did that, is it?"

"No." She hadn't meant to sound so irritated. She'd kind of forgotten the incident Dallas referred to—like the worst PMS in the history of the world according to her husband. Which was funny given she'd never really experienced PMS, so how would he know? It was probably an apt description though. "That wasn't even the same drug I'm on now, Dallas. And even if it was, everything went back to normal as soon as they cut my dosage back again. Remember?"

"I know . . . I know." His tone said he was tiptoeing lightly, trying not to start something—and trying too hard to make up for not coming with her to today's appointment. "So, do you want me to pick up something for supper on my way home?"

"No, I'm making something." No sense adding expensive take-out to the financial "discussion" that was likely to happen after he saw the checkbook. "Maybe scalloped potatoes? It actually feels like fall out here today." She held up a hand, as if he could see her testing the crisp air.

"I need to go, Danae. We'll talk tonight, okay? But you did remember I'm going to the gym with Drew after work, right? Can I invite him to eat with us?"

"Dallas—" She gave a little growl. "It's Tuesday. You know we're going to my folks tonight."

"Oh, yeah. . . . Sorry, I forgot."

"Did you think we were only having scalloped potatoes for supper?"

"I didn't think about it. Sorry. Well, I'll invite Drew another night then. We can—" A familiar click on the line—the office call waiting signal—clipped his words. "Hey, I've got to take this. See you tonight."

"Sure." She spoke into the silence, feeling dismissed. Sometimes she thought Dallas preferred his brother's company to hers.

She climbed into the car and buckled up, imagining the day when she'd be buckling a precious baby into a car seat first. *Please, God. Please.* After three years, this shorthand had become the extent of her prayers.

Pulling out of the parking lot, she was tempted to come up with an excuse to get out of going to the inn tonight. She'd almost come to dread these weekly family dinners for fear of all the questions about their quest to have a baby. But the truth was, her family had grown weary of the subject and had mostly quit asking. Maybe that was just as well.

She rarely volunteered information to her parents and her sisters now that it had become obvious they'd run out of encouraging things to say month after month.

For the first year after they'd started seeking medical treatment, Dallas hadn't even wanted to tell anyone. But she convinced him that she needed someone else to confide in. Once tests had confirmed that the fault was hers alone, and that Dallas was fully capable of fathering a child, he had been more willing to talk with friends and family about their issues. But she sensed he was losing interest in the whole subject as well.

She turned toward home instead. *Home.* It still felt a little odd to turn into the new neighborhood. The divided, stone entrance was an elegant introduction to the upscale development. She and Dallas had traded houses with her sister in August—almost two months ago now—and she still felt like she was going to visit Corinne and Jesse whenever she pulled into the driveway. They'd traded houses, and she and Dallas had traded a paid-off mortgage for a house payment. They'd put a nice down payment on the house and they could afford it, but it had definitely made things a little tighter than they were used to. And made writing checks for the fertility treatments even more painful.

She pulled into the garage and pressed the remote to lower the door. She loved this house and was slowly getting her own touches added to the decor. The trade of homes had been a real blessing to Corinne and Jesse at a time when they needed to downsize quickly, and Danae had no regrets. She and Dallas had been looking for a house big enough for the family they hoped to have, and this place was perfect.

Corinne had given up a lot to make it possible for Jesse to go back to school and get a teaching degree. Danae felt for her sister. She couldn't imagine Dallas suddenly deciding to switch careers after almost a decade of marriage—and three kids. And now Corinne's family of five was crammed into the little two-bedroom house she and Dallas had owned. And yet, they seemed happy. She sensed it was still hard for Corinne to see someone else in the house that had once been her dream home, and it had strained the sisters' relationship, but Danae thought time would take care of that. Hopefully Jesse would have a teaching job in a couple of years and things would get back to normal for all of them.

And hopefully, *hopefully*, she and Dallas would have a baby by then. Because if they didn't, she wasn't sure she could go on believing in a loving, caring, *fair* God.

It was only nine-thirty when the last of the kids pulled out of the driveway, the taillights of the minivan casting a red glow on the new sign Grant Whitman had just erected in front of the Chicory Inn. Watching the vehicle disappear down Chicory Lane, he patted the head of the chocolate Labrador panting at his side and inhaled the crisp night air.

He caught the scent of woodsmoke from their nearest neighbor's chimney half a mile up the lane. Tonight was probably the last time the weather would allow them to eat outdoors, although Audrey usually managed to talk him into one last wiener roast before they stored away the lawn furniture and put the gardens to bed for the winter.

He sighed. "Come on, Huck. Let's call it a day." He bent to scoop up the last of the stray paper cups that had blown off the tables and caught in the corners of the vine-covered pergola. The trumpet vine enveloping the structure was beginning to turn a rainbow of autumn colors.

Grant had instituted these Tuesday family dinners more than a year ago, and he still wasn't sure whether the kids truly enjoyed them or merely tolerated them. The evenings had gone well throughout the summer, but already, now that Jesse and Corinne's oldest was in school—and Jesse too—Grant saw the handwriting on the wall. Now there would be early bedtimes to worry about, and at least during the school year, his kids would understandably want to cut the evenings short.

Chase and Landyn's twins were starting to be a handful, too, now that they were semi-mobile. He smiled, thinking of little

Emma and Grace. The babies were growing faster than he could keep up with. Born nearly bald, they'd both quickly turned into carbon copies of their curly-headed mother. And speaking of growing . . .

Landyn had done some growing up since the twins were born. Watching his daughter with the babies tonight, Grant had been so proud of her. She'd turned into a devoted, conscientious mother. He suspected a lot of people thought Landyn was his favorite because she was the baby of their family. But like any father, he had a soft spot in his heart for each of his daughters—and for his daughter-in-law, Bree.

And the truth was, that soft spot was reserved for whichever daughter was hurting. And right now, it was Danae who clutched at his sympathies. Their second child—"my second favorite daughter" he always teased her—Danae was the one with the tender heart. And so pretty he'd wanted to lock her up and throw away the key when she turned ten.

Danae was pretty still. She wore her distinctive pale blonde hair shorter now, but always sleek and stylish. But it just about killed him to see the premature lines creasing her forehead, the spark gone from her lively blue eyes. He still saw glimpses of that spark when she looked at her husband—*thank the Lord for that*—and when she played with her nieces. But even then, he detected pain. He knew God had a purpose in all this . . . He always did. "But please don't wait too long to give them children, Lord," he whispered.

"What'd you say, Grant?"

Audrey's voice startled him. He hadn't realized she was still out here. "Nothing . . ." He reached for her and drew her close. "Just thinking out loud."

He planted a kiss on the top of her head. "We've had a pretty good life, haven't we?"

She pulled back to study him. "We have. But, um, it's not over yet, dear."

"No, but it could be. It could all be over in the blink of an eye. A kumquat could fall off the shelf at the grocery store, and bingo, I'm history."

She cracked up, which, of course, had been his goal. He did so love making her laugh.

She gave him a dismissive kiss and wriggled out of his arms. "You go ahead and stand there with that smug grin on your face. I'm going in to load the dishwasher."

"I'll be there in a few minutes." He squatted to pull Huckleberry close. If he couldn't hug his wife, there was always the dog. Despite making Audrey laugh, he felt the melancholy creep over him again. Huck seemed to sense it and leaned heavily against him.

Eyeing the dark sky, the ache of sadness—one that autumn always seemed to bring—grew heavier. It would pass. It always did. But something about the death of everything in nature, and the long winter to come, caused his heart to be heavy.

Before heading in to help Audrey with the dishes, he checked the yard one last time for the usual Tuesday night detritus of errant paper plates and the occasional pink sock. Five granddaughters now. That ought to be enough to lighten any man's heart. But still. Danae . . .

He walked slowly toward the house, watching his wife silhouetted through the kitchen windows. As much as Audrey loved these family nights, they were a lot of work for her.

When he opened the back door a few minutes later, she looked up from a sink full of pots and pans. "Everything okay?" The question in her eyes said he must be wearing his worry on his sleeve.

He didn't want to open a can of worms, but he didn't think he was imagining things either. "Did you think Danae seemed a little . . . *off* tonight?"

"How so?"

"I don't know. It just seemed like she was distracted, kind of off in her own world."

"Why? What happened?"

"I don't know that anything happened . . . she just seemed a little down. And she was short with Corinne. That's not like her."

Audrey winced. "I think it's hard for her to be around the babies. Especially the twins. But I hope she's not taking it out on her sisters. They can't help it that they have kids." The way she said it made him wonder if she knew more than she was saying.

"I know, but it's got to be hard seeing them both having babies left and right when she wants one so badly. I just hope she's the next one to get pregnant."

Audrey stilled. Then sighed. "Too late for that."

"What? What are you talking about?"

She turned and leaned back against the sink, pressing her palms on the counter ledge behind her. "Corinne's pregnant again."

"What?" He put his dishtowel on the counter. "How did I miss that announcement?"

"Oh, there hasn't been an announcement yet. At least not that I know of."

"When did she tell you?"

"She didn't. A mother knows these things."

He cocked his head. "That's a pretty serious . . . accusation, Audrey."

"*Prediction.* A mother knows," she repeated.

"You think a sister knows, too?"

Audrey shook her head. "I don't think so. But Corinne is probably waiting as long as possible, knowing it will be hard news for Danae to hear. Especially in public."

"Well, that might explain the tension between them. But why wouldn't she tell *us*?" Grant frowned. "Has Danae said anything about how they're doing on that front?"

"The baby front?" Audrey shrugged. "I haven't asked in a while. Lately it seems like she'd rather not talk about it." She took the damp dish towel from his hand and replaced it with a fresh one.

He had to admit to being disappointed. A person would have thought there's-a-baby-on-the-way news would have been celebrated in this family, but if Corinne and Jesse's news was rife with tension, it would mean that exactly half of the new grandbaby announcements in their family had come with trepidation. It just wasn't right.

About the Author

Deborah Raney dreamed of writing a book since the summer she read all of Laura Ingalls Wilder's Little House books and discovered that a little Kansas farm girl could, indeed, grow up to be a writer. After a happy twenty-year detour as a stay-at-home wife and mom, Deb began her writing career. Her first novel, *A Vow to Cherish*, was awarded a Silver Angel from Excellence in Media and inspired the acclaimed World Wide Pictures film of the same title. Since then, her books have won the RITA Award, the HOLT Medallion, the National Readers' Choice Award, as well as being a two-time Christy Award finalist. Deb enjoys speaking and teaching at writers' conferences across the country. She and her husband, artist Ken Raney, make their home in their native Kansas and, until a recent move to the city, enjoyed the small-town life that is the setting for many of Deb's novels. The Raneys enjoy gardening, antiquing, art museums, movies, and traveling to visit four grown children and a growing brood of grandchildren, all of whom live much too far away.

Deborah loves hearing from her readers. To e-mail her or to learn more about her books, please visit www.deborahraney.com.

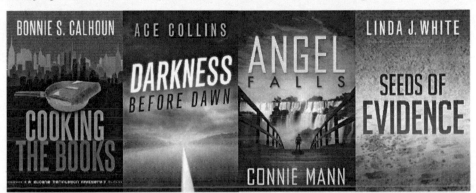

CPSIA information can be obtained at www.ICGtesting.com
Printed in the USA
LVOW08*1145250515

439485LV00001B/2/P